You're About to Become a *Privileged Woman*.

INTRODUCING
PAGES & PRIVILEGES™.

It's our way of thanking you for buying
our books at your favorite retail store.

GET ALL THIS FREE
WITH JUST ONE PROOF OF PURCHASE:

◆ **Hotel Discounts** up
to 60% at home and
abroad ◆ **Travel Service**
- Guaranteed lowest
published airfares
plus 5% cash back
on tickets ◆ **$25 Travel Voucher**

$50 VALUE

◆ **Sensuous Petite Parfumerie** collection

◆ **Insider Tips Letter**
with sneak previews
of upcoming books

You'll get a FREE personal card, too.
It's your passport to all these benefits— and to
even more great gifts & benefits to come!

There's no club to join. No purchase commitment. No obligation.

Enrollment Form

☐ *Yes!* I WANT TO BE A *Privileged Woman.*

Enclosed is one *PAGES & PRIVILEGES*™ Proof of Purchase
from any Harlequin or Silhouette book currently for
sale in stores (Proofs of Purchase are found on
the back pages of books) and the store cash
register receipt. Please enroll me in *PAGES
& PRIVILEGES*™. Send my Welcome
Kit and FREE Gifts -- and activate my
FREE benefits -- immediately.

*More great gifts and benefits to come like these
luxurious Truly Lace and L'Effleur gift baskets.*

▲ ▼ DETACH HERE AND MAIL TODAY!

NAME (please print)

ADDRESS   APT. NO

CITY   STATE   ZIP/POSTAL CODE

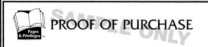

PROOF OF PURCHASE SAMPLE ONLY

**NO CLUB!
NO COMMITMENT!**
*Just one purchase brings
you great Free Gifts
and Benefits!*

Please allow 6-8 weeks for delivery. Quantities are
limited. We reserve the right to substitute items.
Enroll before October 31, 1995 and receive
one full year of benefits.

(More details in back of this book.)

Name of store where this book was purchased_____

Date of purchase_____

Type of store:

☐ Bookstore   ☐ Supermarket   ☐ Drugstore

☐ Dept. or discount store (e.g. K-Mart or Walmart)

☐ Other (specify)_____

Pages
& Privileges ™

Which Harlequin or Silhouette series do you usually read?

_____

Complete and mail with one Proof of Purchase and store receipt to:

U.S.: *PAGES & PRIVILEGES*™, P.O. Box 1960, Danbury, CT 06813-1960

Canada: *PAGES & PRIVILEGES*™, 49-6A The Donway West, P.O. 813,
North York, ON M3C 2E8   **PRINTED IN U.S.A**

Graywolf spotted the sheer lingerie spilling from a drawer of the nightstand, and the thin, lacy nightgown on the bed.

An image flashed into his mind—one that had nothing to do with extrasensory powers or second sight. He saw Mallory on the bed in the thin, translucent gown—her tall, slender body showing golden through a sea of white lace.

He clenched his hands into fists and quickly looked away. What was the matter with him? He didn't want this woman—he didn't even particularly like her. She was from a world that had no understanding of his.

The small room had suddenly become stifling, suffocating. He needed air. He needed space. And he needed to be as far away from Mallory Wakefield as he could get.

Dear Reader,

Welcome to another month of wonderful reading here at Silhouette Intimate Moments. We start right off with a bang with our Heartbreakers title, penned by popular Linda Turner. *Who's The Boss?* will immediately catch you up in the battle raging between Riley Whitaker and Becca Prescott. They're both running for sheriff, but there's a lot more than just a job at stake for these two!

Next up is Sharon Sala's *The Miracle Man,* our Romantic Traditions title. This one features the classic "stranded" hero—and the heroine who rescues him, body and soul. *The Return of Eden McCall,* by Judith Duncan, wraps up the tales of the McCall family, featured in her Wide Open Spaces miniseries. But you'll be pleased to know that Judith has more stories in mind about the people of Bolton, Alberta, so expect to be returning there with her in the future. Another trilogy ends this month, too: Beverly Bird's Wounded Warriors. *A Man Without a Wife* is an emotional tale featuring a mother's search for the child she'd given up. You won't want to miss it. Then get Spellbound by Doreen Roberts' *So Little Time,* an enthralling tale about two lovers who never should have met—but who are absolutely right for each other. Finally, in *Tears of the Shaman,* let Rebecca Daniels introduce you to the first of the twin sisters featured in her new duo, It Takes Two. You'll love Mallory's story, and Marissa's will be coming your way before long.

Enjoy them all—six great books, only from Silhouette Intimate Moments.

Yours,

Leslie Wainger
Senior Editor and Editorial Coordinator

Please address questions and book requests to:
Silhouette Reader Service
U.S.: 3010 Walden Ave., P.O. Box 1325, Buffalo, NY 14269
Canadian: P.O. Box 609, Fort Erie, Ont. L2A 5X3

TEARS OF THE SHAMAN

REBECCA DANIELS

Published by Silhouette Books

America's Publisher of Contemporary Romance

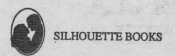

SILHOUETTE BOOKS

ISBN 0-373-07654-1

TEARS OF THE SHAMAN

Copyright © 1995 by Ann Marie Fattarsi

Books by Rebecca Daniels

Silhouette Intimate Moments

L.A. Heat #369
L.A. Midnight #431
Fog City #467
Lawyers, Guns and Money #563
*Tears of the Shaman #654

*It Takes Two

Silhouette Romance

Loving the Enemy #987

REBECCA DANIELS

will never forget the first time she read a Silhouette novel. "I was at my sister's house, sitting by the pool and trying without much success to get interested in the book I'd brought from home. Everything seemed to distract me—the kids splashing around, the sea gulls squawking, the dog barking. Finally, my sister plucked the book from my hands, told me she was going to give me something I wouldn't be able to put down and handed me my first Silhouette novel. Guess what? She was right! For that lazy afternoon by her pool, I will forever be grateful." That was a few years ago, and Rebecca has been writing romance novels ever since.

Born in the Midwest but raised in Southern California, she now resides in Northern California's San Joaquin Valley with her husband and two sons. She is a lifelong poet and song lyricist who enjoys early-morning walks, an occasional round of golf, scouring California's Mother Lode region for antiques and traveling.

TYVMFE!—
For the Pleasant Peasant Girls.
Long may ye reign.

Chapter 1

Mallory Wakefield reluctantly pulled the car to a stop, letting the motor idle restlessly. It was hot, and beads of perspiration drizzled down the small of her back. Squinting against the afternoon sun, she peered dubiously over the steering wheel of the economy rental car to the small cluster of crumbling adobe cubicles.

Huddled together against the barren landscape, the small lodges looked forlorn and abandoned, as forlorn and abandoned as Mallory felt after the long hours of driving. In the yard, a torn, sagging sofa sat in the dust, pushed against the front wall of the nearest structure and collecting what little shade there was from the blistering sun. Pieces of scrap metal, wire and rubble littered the ground everywhere, and in the distance two deserted, tireless pickup trucks rested, propped up on blocks and rusting beside a small, dry growth of brush.

Surely this couldn't be the place, Mallory thought as she glanced down at the directions she'd scribbled from the sergeant at the Navajo Tribal Police Station back in Tuba City. But she'd followed his instructions to the letter. This had to be the place. This had to be the home of Benjamin Graywolf—shaman, medicine man, tracker.

Warily, Mallory reached for the ignition key and turned the motor off. The abrupt silence was almost startling, causing the anxiety in her stomach to feel very much like fear. As with most people, years of urban living had made her cautious, and she glanced around uneasily. But there was no one around, no sign of life, no sound—nothing except the wind. It gusted about, buffeting the sides of the small car and sending dust swirling in all directions.

As she had so many times in the last four days, Mallory felt frustrated with the remoteness of the region and with the enormity of the western Navajo reservation. It was like another world to her, another planet, where customs and conventions were rigid and strange, lacking even the most basic of conveniences. If only there had been a telephone—a simple telephone—she could have called Benjamin Graywolf and saved all this time.

Time. The knot in her stomach twisted tighter, and again she had the feeling that time was running out. If only she could get the police to listen, if only she could get them to understand. Marissa was in trouble—Mallory knew it, she could *feel* it—and she had to do something before it was too late.

Emotion gripped her chest, and an overwhelming feeling of dread settled around her. But she did her best to push the feelings aside. She wasn't going to think about that now— she couldn't. She knew what she had to do. She had to get out of the car and march up to that door. She had to take matters into her own hands. One way or another she was going to find Marissa, and if that meant she'd personally have to look under every rock, every stone, in the Four Corners area, then that's what she'd do.

In one swift, determined motion, Mallory opened the door and stepped from the car. The hot, acrid wind stung her face, drying her sweat-soaked back almost instantly. She lifted her long, honey golden hair from her neck, letting the wind touch her overheated skin. As she started to walk, her cramped, tired muscles reminded her just how long she'd been driving.

She stepped carefully through the littered yard, dodging debris and stepping around tumbleweeds, making her way toward the worn, weather-beaten door of the small adobe structure. Clenching her hand into a tight fist, she rapped loudly.

"Hello?" she called after a long moment. She waited, then knocked again—harder this time, causing pain to shoot through her knuckles. "Is anyone home?" She listened again, every muscle in her body alert for any sound. She had no idea what to expect. What did a Navajo shaman look like? She leaned forward, hoping to hear something inside. "Is anyone in there? Hello? Is anyone home?"

Nothing. No sign of anyone, no sound of anything except her own breath as it entered and exited her lungs, and the incessant wind as it gusted around her. Mallory's entire body sagged as she released a weary sigh. Now what did she do? Return to Tuba City? Camp out at the state police station in Flagstaff? Go back to Marissa's tiny apartment in Sedona and quietly go crazy?

"Damn," she muttered, taking her fist to the door and pounding it hard. She jumped a little, surprised when the latch suddenly gave way from the force of her blow. "Yoo-hoo," she called, gently pushing the door open and peering into the darkness inside. "Is someone there?"

"Entering someone's hogan uninvited is considered rude even in the *biligaana*'s world."

Mallory bolted around violently, jarred by the sound of the voice behind her. "I—I'm sorry. I—I didn't—"

Her trembling voice failed in a strangled gasp at the sight of the man standing behind her. A mixture of fear and excitement rendered her mute.

He glared down at her, his eyes narrow, and he made no effort to hide his suspicion. "What do you want here?"

"I—I want—" Mallory cleared her voice loudly, taking a deep breath. He towered over her, and she was suddenly very aware that she was alone with this man, hundreds of miles away from anyone who could help her. He wore no shirt, but his legs were covered by some kind of buckskin leggings. His long black hair fell loose across his powerful chest, his skin was baked bronze and dark. The strength in his arms and chest was obvious, but it was the cold in his eyes that sent a frigid chill running through her despite the sweltering heat of the sun. "I'm . . . looking for Benjamin Graywolf. I was told this was his house."

"What do you want with Graywolf?"

She blinked, staring up at him. Despite the fact that he scared her to death, she bristled at his curt tone. "Could you tell me if this is the Graywolf house or not?"

His gaze slowly traveled the length of her, then he made a low, caustic-sounding laugh in his throat. "This is the *hogan* of Benjamin Graywolf."

"Oh, right, you're right. I'm sorry," she said quickly, grimacing. Of course, how stupid. It was hogan, not house, she knew that. "But this is it? This is his hogan?"

"It is."

"Thank goodness." She sighed, her excitement building and causing her to forget all about being afraid. "Is he here? Could I see him?"

"That depends," he said evasively.

She blinked, becoming annoyed again. "On what?"

His eyes narrowed even more, and he lazily lifted one shoulder in an insolent sort of shrug. "On what you want him for."

All fear and excitement disappeared, leaving her to deal with the frustration. "Look, I'm really not interested in playing games here. I need to talk with Benjamin Graywolf. It's very important. I need his help. Now, is he here or isn't he?"

"You a cop? FBI?"

"What?" Mallory choked, clearly surprised. "No."

"Who are you? What do you do?"

Mallory shook her head, exasperated. "My name is Wakefield— Mallory Wakefield. I'm a reporter with the *Washington Chronicle*, but that's not why—"

"Get out of here," he said abruptly, cutting her off.

"What?" Mallory snapped, surprised.

"I said leave," he repeated. "Get off my property."

"Your property?" Mallory was astounded. "You mean...you? You're him? *You're* Benjamin Graywolf?"

"You're trespassing," he informed her, taking her purposefully by the upper arm and propelling her toward the rental car. "And I've asked you to leave."

"Stop that," Mallory insisted, shrugging to free herself from his hold. "No! Wait, *please!* If you would just let me explain. Please, I need your help."

"I don't help reporters," he stated flatly, freeing her with a small thrust toward her car.

"I'm not here as a reporter," she insisted, scowling at him. What was the matter with this man. Was he crazy? "For God's sake, I'm not here for a story."

"I don't talk to reporters," he told her flatly as he turned and started back toward the hogan. "For any reason."

"But if you would just give me a minute, let me explain," Mallory called after him. "Please. I need your help." But he had already disappeared inside the hogan, slamming the door closed behind him.

Mallory stared at the weathered door, a mixture of fury and total bewilderment churning inside her. Sergeant Begay had been so certain this Graywolf could help her. She'd driven all this way, had endured long hours in a miserable little car with no air-conditioning, had tolerated unbearable heat and washed-out roads, and used precious time—for what? To be tossed aside? To be evicted from the property because *he* didn't care for reporters?

Mallory slid behind the wheel of her car and twisted the key in the ignition. Benjamin Graywolf might not like talking to reporters, but he damn well was going to talk to her.

The turquoise chip slipped into the small silver cavity that had been carved for it, creating a tiny eye on the face of the crescent moon. Graywolf straightened up, his muscles protesting the long hours spent hunched over the workbench. Rubbing a hand over his tired, strained eyes, he reached up and switched off the light above his head.

He glanced down at the meticulously crafted piece of jewelry he'd just completed. A crescent moon. The crescent shape, along with a distinctive arced cluster of stars, had become familiar figures in his work the last few weeks. What did they mean? Why were those designs filling his head? Why was he plagued by the images?

Graywolf thought of the woman. The sight of her had shaken him. He had immediately thought of the crescent moon and the cluster of stars. For it had been those shapes, along with the image of a *biligaana* that had filled his visions for weeks now. But not just any *biligaana*—a *biligaana* woman, a white man's woman—a perfect white woman with hair the color of the sun and eyes as blue as the sea.

Benjamin Graywolf had learned not to ignore his visions. There was a time when he'd scoffed at the traditions and rituals of the shamans, when he'd scorned his legacy and reasoned away his talents. He'd insisted that his succession from a great line of shamans had nothing to do with the occasional flashes of "insight" he would have. His father and grandfather had tried to nurture his visions, to teach him the ways of the shamans, to help him understand and accept his gift, but Graywolf had wanted no part of it. He had called the ways of his fathers superstitious, had thought of them as little more than myths and legends, and had refused to listen.

Instead, he had left for the white man's schools, to learn the secrets of the white man's world. He had wanted to learn how to educate his own people, to free them of the myths and the legends, and of the superstition and fear that he believed perpetuated the endless cycle of poverty and suffering on the reservation.

But he had been young and foolish back then, and he was older and wiser now. It had been a painful lesson, but Graywolf had learned to accept his visions, to trust them. But trusting a white woman was something he'd never do again. Susan had taught him that.

Susan. Beautiful Susan. So sweet, so curious, so full of love—or so he'd thought.

Graywolf closed his eyes, knowing the lesson in betrayal he'd learned from her was one he'd never forget. He had given Susan his heart. He had told her his secrets, shared with her his dreams, and yet she had betrayed him, selling his secrets to the newspapers and making him look like a fool.

Graywolf thought again of the woman he'd found at his door, and felt the muscles in his stomach tighten. She had been the *biligaana* from his visions. He glanced back down at the silver crescent he'd just completed. Picking it up slowly with a soft denim cloth, he placed it beside the dozen or so other pieces of silver jewelry he'd created that bore the same moon-shaped design. He was obsessed with the image and it reflected in his work. What did this woman—this *reporter*—have to do with the crescent, and what were they both doing in his dreams?

Graywolf still remembered the tabloid headlines—Shaman's Magic Finds Missing Child and Medicine Man Thwarts Kidnappers. He remembered the reporters, their questions and the flash of cameras. He'd learned the hard way about how reporters could distort your words and color the message. They had made him a caricature, painting him as a dime-store Indian, a mystic in a headdress.

Turning suddenly, he grabbed his denim jacket from the rusted hook beside the door and trotted off across the yard toward the Jeep. He didn't want to think about visions now, or crescent moons, or pale-skinned women with haunting blue eyes. With enough firewater, he could block the images in his head. *Todilhil,* the water of darkness, *biligaana*'s whiskey—white man's gift to the Navajo, which like so many gifts from the white man, had become a curse. But Graywolf was grateful for the gift tonight. He didn't want to think about the woman, about the flawlessness of her beauty or the helplessness in her eyes. He didn't want to think about her because he didn't trust white women—or reporters—even when they came to him in his dreams.

The letter *n* flickered on and off, causing the faded red-and-yellow sign to alternately read Barney's, and then Bar ey's. But even without the sign, Mallory wouldn't have had any trouble finding the place. The roadside tavern sat by itself, situated south of Gray Mountain, just off the reservation on Highway 89, and just where the clerk at the general store in Tuba City had told her it would be. The clerk had also told her the dingy tavern was the place where Benjamin Graywolf went almost nightly to meet with his friends.

The sun had just begun to sink beneath the horizon when Mallory had pulled into the gravel parking lot. Then the lot had practically been deserted, but that had been almost two hours ago. Now it was lined with a variety of vehicles—all of which looked as though they'd seen better days. Still, despite her careful examination of each patron who'd entered the noisy tavern, she hadn't yet seen Benjamin Graywolf.

She studied the run-down establishment with its sagging frame and tarpaper roof. It sat alone and neglected, a tiny oasis of light amid the bleak desert terrain. What was she doing here? she wondered as she watched an old man stumble up the stone steps and stagger along the uneven porch to the door. Was it stupid to just sit and wait? Was she wasting her time?

The questions plagued her, but she continued to wait. Something kept her there. Instinct, maybe, or maybe just plain stubbornness. She wasn't sure. She just knew she shouldn't ignore it. *Something* told her if she had any chance of finding Marissa, it lay with Benjamin Graywolf. Sergeant Begay had told her he'd had success in finding missing persons, and despite what the police wanted to believe, she knew Marissa was definitely missing.

Mallory felt her eyes sting with tears. This was supposed to have been such a special time for the two of them. It had been so long since they'd seen each other, and they'd had big plans. But now everything was turning into a nightmare.

As soon as Mallory's editor at the *Washington Chronicle* had given her the assignment to cover this year's annual Native American Tribal Powwow and Convention, she and Marissa had begun making plans. They hadn't seen each other since Marissa had moved from Washington the year before to take a teaching job at a school in Sedona. So getting an assignment that actually required her to go to Arizona had been like a gift from the gods for Mallory, and she'd jumped at it. While covering the powwow on the Navajo National Fairgrounds, where tribes from all the nearby nations gathered for the week-long conference, would be interesting, what had really excited her had been the chance to spend some time with her sister. She'd quickly arranged to take the two weeks before the powwow as vacation, and she and Marissa had looked forward to spending the time together.

But four days ago, when Mallory had arrived at the airport in Flagstaff, Marissa hadn't been there to meet her. Immediately Mallory had sensed something was wrong. She had checked everywhere for her sister—Marissa's house in Sedona, her school, her friends, even the hospitals. It was as if Marissa Wakefield had disappeared without a trace, and Mallory knew her twin was in trouble.

Mallory couldn't remember when it had started—the "intuition," the special radar, that "twins thing" she shared with Marissa. It had just always been there, something they'd both possessed, like blond hair and blue eyes. For as far back as she could remember they'd intuitively known what the other was feeling —joy, sadness, excitement, even love. When they were younger, the pediatrician who had cared for them in their small hometown of Jackson, California, had sent them to Stanford Medical Center where they had been tested and evaluated. Special communication between identical twins was not unusual, but rarely was it as strong as it was between the Wakefield twins. It didn't seem to matter where they were, or how far away, the link between them remained.

When Marissa had failed to show up at the airport and there had been no trace of her at her small house in Sedona, Mallory had known something was wrong. She'd contacted the principal of the school where Marissa taught, and to her alarm she learned that Marissa had failed to show up for school on Monday morning, as well. The principal, sounding worried over the phone, had told Mallory that she had thought Marissa had planned to spend her weekend tutoring students at a Navajo school on the reservation. But after checking, Mallory learned that even though the people at the reservation school had expected Marissa, she had never shown up.

With her fears growing, Mallory had contacted every law enforcement agency in the state, but no trace of Marissa could be found. And her feelings of foreboding had grown worse.

The police provided little assistance. They filed a missing person's report, searched Marissa's house, ran her name through their computers and put an APB out on her car. But since there was no sign of foul play, no leads, and nothing other than Mallory's "feeling" that something was wrong, there was little else they could—or would—do to help. It was Sergeant Sam Begay at Navajo Tribal Police Station in Tuba City who had suggested Benjamin Graywolf. Mallory was determined to find Marissa, and if that meant sitting in front of this dingy bar in the middle of nowhere all night waiting for Graywolf to show up, that's what she'd do.

Just then a flash of headlights glared bright, lighting up the interior of her rental car and temporarily blocking her vision with a curtain of white. Mallory squeezed shut her eyes, but it was too late. Large, brilliant white circles filled her view, blinding her to everything else. She blinked in a frantic effort to regain her sight, but it took several minutes for the ghostly circles embedded on her eyeballs to fade into the darkness. They just cleared in time for her to see Benjamin Graywolf's towering frame disappear behind Barney's sagging, paint-chipped front door.

"That's him," she gasped aloud in the empty car, jumping with such surprise that she knocked her knee painfully against the gearshift knob. She reached for her purse and slid toward the door, but when her hand reached the handle, she stopped abruptly. She sat there, with one hand on the door handle and the other absently rubbing the spot on her knee where it had made contact with the gearshift.

She thought of Benjamin Graywolf, and a sudden chill had her shivering involuntarily. Something about the man bothered her, gave her an uneasy feeling in the pit of her stomach. Just thinking about those cold eyes of his, and their menacing stare, made her want to start the car and get out of there—put as much distance as she could between them. She remembered the fury she had seen in them—fury, and anger, and rage. They were strangers. He'd never set eyes on her before, and yet he'd glowered at her as though he'd hated her. What was he so angry about? What had she ever done to him?

She glanced at her hand on the doorknob. Was she sure she wanted to do this? Was she sure she wanted to risk that fury and that rage again?

But her thoughts turned to Marissa, and she felt her sister's fear in her heart. A feeling of urgency clutched at her, and she shoved the door open and stepped onto the gravel lot. Marissa needed her help, and for that reason and that reason alone, she would risk the anger of Benjamin Graywolf once again.

Mallory's first impulse when she'd stepped into Barney's dreary interior was to rush right back out, but she knew she couldn't do that. Smoke filled the stuffy, dark room, hanging just below the ceiling like an ominous, murky cloud. Somewhere in a far corner a jukebox played—Tammy, or Dolly, or Reba singing a sad but clear lament. A row of patrons lined the bar, quietly downing one drink after another, but a noisy group had gathered at a table nearby, laughing and hooting in a loud game of cards.

Unfortunately, Mallory's entrance had not gone unnoticed. Like a silent alarm that had spread through the din, laughing stopped, drinks paused and heads turned. Mallory realized with no small degree of discomfort that not only was she the only white in the place, she was also the only woman.

She wished now she'd taken the time to slip her linen blazer over the sleeveless shell she wore. The cotton blouse and linen walking shorts were hardly revealing, but that didn't stop her from feeling very vulnerable and exposed at the moment. Gratefully, however, she spotted the imposing form of Benjamin Graywolf sitting with several others at a table in the rear of the bar. Feeling terribly conspicuous, as though every eye in the place was on her, she slowly started across the cluttered floor, squeezing between tables and stepping over moccasined feet.

She was aware that he watched her as she approached, and her fists clenched tight with anger. He knew she was there to see him, and yet he made no effort to meet her halfway. Instead, he simply sat there—chair tilted back, leg propped against the table, and shot glass poised at his lips.

"I've come to talk to you," she said, making a conscious effort to keep her voice from quivering.

"I told you before, I don't talk to reporters," he said, tossing the amber liquid down.

"But I'm not here as a reporter. I don't want to interview you. I need your help." She was aware of the two other men at the table who sat grinning up at her and listening to their exchange. "Perhaps you'd let me buy you a drink," she said uneasily, pointing behind her. "At the bar? I could explain?"

Graywolf closed his eyes and let the whiskey burn his throat, then cracked his lids to look up at her. "You can say what you need to in front of my friends. We have no secrets." Pushing his chair upright, he raised his glass to the others. "And we're all thirsty."

"Right, that's right." The other two nodded and laughed.

Graywolf reached for the bottle on the table and poured them all another drink. "And the white man knows how loose an Indian's tongue becomes when he drinks the dark water," he said, raising the glass to her. "So buy away."

"I see," Mallory murmured, wiping her sweaty palms against her shorts. "Uh—okay. It's my sister. She's—she's...missing, and I'd like to hire you to help me find her."

Graywolf shook his head, tossing his glass down onto the table. "Sorry white lady," he said as he rose to his feet. He reached into his pocket and threw some money onto the table. "I've retired from that business." He and the others made their way across the room toward the door.

"Wait, please," Mallory pleaded, running after him. "You don't understand. I have money, I can pay you." When he continued on, she grew more desperate. "I'll—I'll give you anything you want."

"Anything?" Graywolf repeated, stopping and turning to look down at her. He stared into her wide, blue eyes, feeling the alcohol coursing through his system—hot and potent. He moved forward, backing her against the bar, trapping her with his body. "Anything, lady? Are you sure?'' Stepping close, he pressed lewdly against her, grinding his hard body against the softness of hers. "Did you hear that, brothers? The *biligaana* woman says she'll give me *anything*.''

A crowd seemed to have gathered out of nowhere. Everywhere she looked, there were faces—leering, jeering, laughing and goading Graywolf on. She was no longer in the safe, sane world she understood. She'd been transported to some foreign soil, some place wild and untamed—a world so different from her own she'd been rendered defenseless. Fear rose up in her throat, overwhelming her and tasting bitter and black on her tongue. How could this be happening? She'd come here looking for help, but who would help her among these rough people?

"Please," she whimpered, looking up into the cold eyes of Benjamin Graywolf. "Please don't.''

Graywolf had wanted to be crude, he'd wanted to be savage, he'd wanted to humiliate and frighten her away this time so she'd never come back. She was white, she was a reporter, and as far as he was concerned, that made her nothing at all.

But when he looked into her pale, perfect face, heard the pain in her voice, and saw the plea in her eyes, he not only saw her terror, he *felt* it. She wasn't just some faceless, unfeeling creature from a world he wanted to forget. She was the vision—his vision—crying and reaching out for help.

Revulsion had him stepping back. His vulgar, thoughtless actions left him feeling sick with self-disgust. He turned his face away from hers.

"Enough!" he shouted angrily at the others when they called for more. What was the matter with all of them? They were acting like the worst kind of savages. "Get back. Get away.''

Grabbing the terrified woman by the arm, he pulled her through the crowd and out the door of the tavern.

The fresh air revived Mallory, bringing feeling back into her paralyzed body. It took her a moment to realize that the danger had passed, that she was outside and that Graywolf held her by the arm.

"Let go of me," she snapped, yanking free of his grasp. She stepped away from him, rubbing at the spot on her arm where his fingers had left their mark. "How dare you?" she accused, heading down the crooked, uneven steps to the gravel lot. "Is that how you and your friends entertain yourselves?"

"Look, I'm sor—" Graywolf started, moving toward her.

"Don't you come near me," she warned, cutting him off. As angry as she was, it wasn't enough to make her forget that awful fear. She turned and ran toward her car.

"I'm sorry, I really am," Graywolf repeated, following her. "I—we...we were just fooling around. No one meant any harm, not really."

Mallory fumbled for the car key. Finding it, she shoved it into the lock and yanked open the door. "Look," she said, putting her hand up to halt Graywolf. "Either you stop right there, or I'm going to report you and your friends to Sergeant Begay."

Graywolf came slowly to a stop on the opposite side of the car and studied her from across the roof. A full moon made her blond hair glow like white satin, and he suddenly remembered how it had felt to press against her body. "You know Sam?"

With the safety of the car between them, Mallory felt better. "For some ridiculous reason he thought you'd be willing to help me."

Graywolf took a deep breath, pushing his long hair out of his face. "Look, I'm sorry. I didn't mean to scare you. I thought you were here for a story."

"Sergeant Begay said you are good at tracking missing persons."

"I don't do that anymore."

"I'd be willing to pay you," Mallory said quickly, the need for help finding Marissa taking precedence over her anger and fear.

"Who's missing?"

"My sister."

"Have you talked to the police?"

"They're no help. They won't even admit she's actually missing."

"What makes you so sure?"

Mallory thought for a moment. Did she tell him the truth? Did she try to explain her...feelings? She'd finally managed to get Benjamin Graywolf's attention. The last thing she wanted was to come off sounding like a crackpot. What she did tell him was about the plans they had made, about Marissa's failure to meet her at the airport, about Marissa not showing up at work or for her tutoring appointment on the reservation. But Mallory elected not to mention anything about their "twin-telepathy" just yet.

"I know something's happened to her, Mr. Graywolf. I've just got to find her."

"Maybe she had a change of plans," Graywolf suggested halfheartedly. "Just couldn't reach you?"

"You don't understand, Mr. Graywolf. Our time together is...special. My sister and I are very close and we've been apart a long time. We were both looking forward to being together. She wouldn't just go off without letting me know where she is."

Graywolf thought for a moment, remembering his visions. Was this the reason for them? "Do you have a picture of your sister?" he asked finally, knowing that sometimes looking at a face would trigger a sign.

"There's no need," Mallory said excitedly, rushing around the front of the car. She forgot all about her precautions and safeguards. For the first time since this nightmare began, she felt a stirring of hope.

As she rushed toward him, Graywolf was distracted by the delicate necklace that slipped out from beneath her cotton shell as she ran. The light from the neon sign caught the gold charm dangling down from the chain, reflecting colorfully from the small crescent moon.

"You don't need a picture," she said, coming to a stop in front of him.

"I don't?" he questioned, experiencing an odd rushing feeling propelling him forward.

"She looks exactly like me."

Chapter 2

"We're identical," Mallory explained. "Twins!"

"Twins," Graywolf repeated with a murmur. He pointed to the gold crescent around her neck. "What about that?"

"What? This?" Mallory asked, surprised. Her hand reached for the charm and she looked up at him quizzically. "My necklace?"

"It's a crescent moon."

"Yes," she said carefully, growing cautious.

"Where did you get it?"

"Why?" she asked, her suspicions returning.

He glared down at her. "Just tell me."

"My father," she said warily. "He always said he'd give us the moon and the stars, so when Marissa and I graduated from college he gave us these. Mine is the moon and Marissa's is—"

"The stars," Graywolf said, finishing for her.

"That's right," Mallory whispered, trying to read something in his coal black eyes.

Graywolf looked away. He should have known there was a reason for the visions—there always was, one way or another. "Tell me again why you're so sure your sister's in trouble."

Mallory took a deep breath. "My sister and I," she began, then paused. "We've always been close, and there's always been this...*feeling* between us. The doctors have told us it's not uncommon for twins—especially identical ones—to have a sort of sixth sense about each other. I don't know." She shook her head. "Marissa and I have just always had this...*thing* between us. I don't know what it is—ESP, mind reading—you can call it whatever you want. We're able to tell when each other is happy, or sad, or afraid, or...in danger. I know it sounds crazy, I know it's something most people can't understand—that's why I didn't say anything about it to the police." She shook her head again and looked up at him helplessly. "I *know* my sister's in trouble. I can *feel* it."

Graywolf felt oddly winded, as though he'd finished a long run across the desert. He gazed down into her clear eyes, seeing the fear and uncertainty in them.

She was afraid he would think she was crazy—no doubt that was what the police would have told her had she gone to them with her story. But she didn't sound crazy to him. He understood all too well about special "feelings" and sensations of foreboding. Too many times he'd seen the doubting looks and questioning stares when he'd tried to explain to others about his visions. He'd learned the hard way to keep his foresight to himself, to trust no one with his secret and to deal with the pain alone.

"I think you'd better come with me," he said suddenly, reaching for her arm.

"Where?" Mallory asked as he led her around the car and opened the driver's side door.

"Follow me," he said, practically pushing her behind the wheel. He nodded to the Jeep parked nearby.

"But where are we going?" Mallory asked again, but it was too late. He had slammed her car door and was off across the gravel lot.

She watched as he climbed into the Jeep and coaxed the motor to life. She didn't understand Benjamin Graywolf, or anything about him. He hadn't exactly said he was going to help her, and yet he'd seemed interested in what she had to say. Still, standing in the dimly lit parking lot in front of Barney's tavern hardly seemed an appropriate place to conduct business.

But then, she thought as she started her car's engine and pulled out of the lot behind him, none of this was going as she'd expected. What was he so suspicious of? He'd acted as though he'd hated her at first. What had happened to change that? How was it he could look at her with such contempt one minute, and then with such intensity the next that it left her feeling dazed and uncomfortable?

Maybe it would be wiser to forget about all of that and not look a gift horse in the mouth. At least he hadn't looked at her as though she were some kind of nut, at least he hadn't called her crazy and sent her packing. She'd told him about her "feelings" and the special method of communication she shared with her sister, and he'd still been willing to listen. Maybe he really would be able to help her. Maybe he was just the man for the job. But driving down the lonely Arizona highway with only the glow of the Jeep's red taillights to serve as a guide, she had to admit she had her doubts.

"I don't understand," Mallory said, her hand absently going to the pendant hanging from her neck. She stared down at the neat rows of silver crescents and star clusters that lined the cluttered workbench and felt a chill travel down the length of her spine. "They look just like..."

"Your pendants," Graywolf said. "I know."

"But how?" she asked, looking up at him. The room was dark, lit only by the small light above the workbench. In the white glow of the bulb, Graywolf's dark skin looked strangely pale, causing the hard, precise features of his face to seem dreamlike and unreal. Mallory thought of the ancient masks she'd seen on display at the Smithsonian last year while she covered an exhibit of Native American artifacts for the paper. Their wild, timeless expressions looked no more primitive, no more feral, than Graywolf's did now.

"How do you know what your sister feels?" he asked simply. He lifted his gaze, looking at her from across the workbench. "It's just there, right?"

Mallory drew in a deep breath, straightening up. "You've lost me."

"Feelings," Graywolf said. It wasn't necessary that the *biligaana* woman know everything about him. She didn't need to know about his visions and dreams, his hunches and intuitions. The visions may have made him feel compelled to help her, but they didn't make him trust her.

"You have them, too?" she asked. That would explain why he hadn't laughed in her face. "You get...feelings about people?"

Graywolf shrugged, reached for a wooden match from a ceramic pot on the workbench and struck it against the edge of the table. "Something like that."

Which is what made him good at finding missing persons, she concluded silently to herself. It made sense. "And you'll help me find my sister?"

Graywolf lifted the chimney of an oil lamp hanging from a hook on the wall and lit the wick. "I can try."

Mallory looked at the array of silver jewelry again. The crescents and stars were various sizes and designs, but they all bore an eerie likeness to the ones she and Marissa wore around their necks. "This is very strange."

"Maybe." Graywolf shrugged, blowing out the match and reaching up to switch off the light. "But then so is reading your sister's mind."

Mallory had to smile. "You have a point. Has this ever happened to you before?" she asked, gesturing to the silver on the table. "I mean with the jewelry and everything?"

With the electric light off, the small room was filled with the soft yellow glow of the oil lamp. Graywolf regarded her carefully from across the workbench, wondering absently if her white skin would feel as silky and as soft as it looked. "Not really."

It was obvious that he didn't want to talk to her about the significance between the silver pieces he'd made and their necklaces, but she could understand that. Telling people about her "feelings" was something she wasn't very comfortable with, either. "This is what you do then, for a living?" she asked, changing the subject. "You're a silversmith?"

"Sometimes."

"And the rest of the time?"

He walked slowly toward her. In the lamplight, her skin looked flawless, and her long blond hair appeared as fluid and rich as pure, thick honey. Again he thought of the incident in the bar, of his crude actions and unreasonable anger. He'd been bent on frightening her then, determined to humiliate her so that she'd never bother him again. They were from different worlds, different planets. But he was still a man, and despite his anger, the man in him hadn't been able to ignore her softness, hadn't been able to deny the perfect feel of her body against his.

"The rest of the time," he said, coming to a stop just inches from her, "I'm just a savage."

Mallory stared into his dark, cryptic eyes and felt her heart lurch in her chest. She remembered how he'd looked in the gloom of the tavern—wild, unpredictable, dangerous. She was suddenly aware of the darkness, of the desolation, and of the isolated location. What had ever possessed her to follow him? She was alone, helpless, with a man she knew nothing about. He was a stranger, and a self-proclaimed savage. For all she knew, he could be a madman.

"I should pay you," she said, her voice sounding small and faraway to her own ears.

"Yes, you should," he said nonchalantly. Her discomfort was so obvious, there was no need for second sight. He could see it in her eyes, could spot it in her every move. How typical of the *biligaana* to still fear the red man, to quiver and cower at the thought of a savage.

"Would you take a credit card?" she asked, fumbling for her purse as the sound of her heart pounded in her head.

He threw his head back and laughed. "What does this look like, lady? A fancy boutique?"

"No, you're right, of course," she mumbled, her nervousness leaving her brain momentarily impaired. "Would traveler's cheques be all right?"

"Cash would be better," he said, gazing down at the tablet of American Express drafts in her hand. "But traveler's cheques will do."

"What is your usual retainer?"

"Two thousand," he said, purposely making the amount hefty and noticing she didn't even blink an eye. It never ceased to amaze him how the white man took his wealth for granted.

"Okay, so how do we do this?" she asked, fishing out a pen from the bottom of her bag. "Half now, and the rest when you find my sister?"

"Two thousand," Graywolf repeated solemnly. "Up front."

"The whole thing?"

"The whole thing."

"But what if you just take the money and..."

"And what? Take off?" He didn't wait for her to answer. "That's just a chance you'll have to take."

Mallory's eyes narrowed. "Is there something about me you don't like? Or are you always a bastard?"

"Two thousand up front, lady," he repeated, wondering why it pleased him so to irritate her. He wasn't the kind of man who normally got a charge out of giving women a hard time. This one just seemed to make it so easy. "Take it or leave it."

Mallory whipped open the tablet of checks and began signing furiously. When she'd finished, she tossed the cheques onto the workbench in front of him. "Two thousand, up front. When can you start?"

"First thing in the morning," he said, picking up the tablet and fanning through it. "Leave me a number where I can reach you. I'll be in touch."

"What do you mean, you'll be in touch?"

He looked up from the traveler's cheques and shrugged. "I mean, I'll let you know what I find out."

"Oh, no," Mallory said, shaking her head. "I'm not going to just sit around and wait for you. I'm in on this thing, too."

"Uh-uh," Graywolf said, shaking his head now. "I work alone, lady."

"You work for *me*," she pointed out.

He glared down at her. Her blue eyes looked green in the amber glow of the lamp. There was no trace of fear in them any longer, no apprehension or uneasiness. They were filled only with anger—anger and stubborn determination. He could push her, it seemed, but only so far.

"I have a friend on the force in Flagstaff. I'll be heading there in the morning to talk with him."

Mallory yanked the zipper of her purse closed, satisfied that was as close to an agreement as she was going to get from him. With their business concluded, she stalked across the small room toward the door. But before she could reach for the handle, it turned and the door swung wide. Startled, Mallory jumped back.

"*Yaa' eh t'eeh,*" said the old man standing in the doorway. He moved slowly across the threshold, his bent, withered frame making him look unbelievably delicate. But when he looked up at Mallory, his dark eyes grew bright, and a wide smile broke across his weathered face. "Do I know the beautiful yellow hair?"

"Hello, Grandfather," Graywolf said respectfully, slipping the tablet of traveler's cheques into the pocket of his jacket. "This is . . ."

He looked at her as his voice trailed off.

"Mallory Wakefield," she quickly added, extending her hand. From the corner of her eye, she saw Graywolf's dark scowl, and wondered what tribal custom she'd broken with the gesture.

"This is Hosteen Johnny." Graywolf dispensed with the Navajo tradition of making introductions by maternal clans. The courtesy would only be wasted on the white woman. "My grandfather."

"It's very nice meeting you Mr.—er . . . sir," Mallory stammered, feeling heat fill her cheeks.

"Remind me, since my memory is old and not so good anymore, but we've never met before, have we?" Hosteen Johnny Bistie asked, holding her hand gently in his. "I'm sure I would have remembered Hair of Sunshine."

Mallory smiled, suspecting that despite what he said, there wasn't much that escaped those bright eyes that danced lively behind the careworn face. In the dim light of the lamp, he studied her carefully. "No, we've never met before."

"She's hired me," Graywolf said, stepping across the room. "To find her sister."

Hosteen Johnny's smile faded slowly. "You must need help badly to come so far a distance."

"Yes," Mallory murmured, getting the uneasy impression that the old man saw more than he let on. "Yes, I do."

Hosteen Johnny gestured to his grandson with a nod of his head. "You've made a wise choice. Ben—he's a good tracker. He'll find your sister."

"That's what I'm hoping," Mallory said sincerely.

"Miss Wakefield was just leaving," Graywolf announced curtly, not caring if he sounded rude or not. The situation made him uncomfortable. He didn't want the white woman patronizing his grandfather, didn't want her smiling and winning an old man's heart.

"You've seen the beautiful silver jewelry," Hosteen Johnny said, ignoring his grandson's rudeness and leading Mallory by the hand back into the room.

"Yes," Mallory said, aware how Graywolf watched her with such angry eyes. "It's beautiful."

"For many generations my clan has worked with the earth." He looked down at the array of moons and stars displayed across the workbench, making a sweeping gesture over them with his hand. "It is a gift to create such beauty. It is the work of my father, and my father's father." He stopped and looked at his grandson. "But Ben, he has a special talent."

"Miss Wakefield has a long drive ahead of her," Graywolf insisted, reaching for the handle and holding the door open. "We shouldn't keep her, Grandfather."

"He didn't want to follow the road of his fathers. He ran away. He went to the city of the white man." Hosteen Johnny shook his head, making a sound of disgust. "Washington, D.C. His work was not special there."

Mallory's eyes grew wide with surprise. Benjamin Graywolf in Washington? What had he been doing there? She looked at him, standing beside the open doorway. In the dim light his face was shadowed, and his stern, rigid features gave nothing away.

"But he is home now," Hosteen Johnny continued. "Where he belongs. Doing the work of his fathers as a shaman, keeping the People in harmony with the universe." Hosteen Johnny led Mallory back across the room to the door, patting her hand with his. "He will find your sister."

Mallory felt her eyes sting with tears. The old man's words sounded so reassuring, so promising, and she wanted so much to believe him. She prayed he was right, prayed that Benjamin Graywolf would find Marissa—safe and alive— and bring her back.

Driving home after she'd mumbled a courteous goodbye and had arranged a time to meet Graywolf at the Flagstaff police department, she thought of Hosteen Johnny. Staring into the small circle of light created in the blackness by her headlights, she thought of the things he'd said. She'd gotten the strange feeling he was telling her more than just the words he had said. Did the "special talents" of his grandson have anything to do with the crescent moon and clusters of stars? And the part about D.C. had surprised her. What had taken Graywolf there?

Mallory moved one hand from the steering wheel to the chain around her neck. Feeling the delicate gold pendant against her fingers, she wondered about Marissa's cluster of stars and where it was at this moment.

An almost overwhelming feeling of sadness and uneasiness filled her, and she pressed her foot down harder on the accelerator. Benjamin Graywolf had to find Marissa—and he had to find her soon.

"You hired him?"

Mallory nodded, staring down at the message sliding across the face of the fax machine. It wasn't the one she'd been waiting for and she looked up, frustrated. "To find my sister."

"Hmm," Wayne Clair mused, tapping an absent finger against his lips. "I'm surprised Graywolf is doing that again."

"Doing what?" Mallory asked, forgetting about the fax machine for a moment.

Wayne leaned back in his chair, the glass panels behind him showing a spectacular view of Flagstaff's skyline. "The reports Glen is faxing should tell you everything. It's been a few years, probably before your time at the *Chronicle*. Happened when he was living back in D.C."

Despite the long hours on the road and the late hour she'd arrived back at Marissa's house, Mallory had awakened before dawn and called her editor at the *Chronicle*. Wanting to help, and sensing there might be a story in all of this, Glen Harvey had promised to fax any information he could gather on Benjamin Graywolf to his old college buddy Wayne, who was managing editor of the *Flagstaff Register*. He knew Wayne would make sure the information got to her.

"Was he in trouble?" Mallory asked, speculating. "Arrested or something?"

"No, no," Wayne said, shaking his head. "Nothing like that. He'd assisted on a kidnapping. Helped rescue some diplomat's kid."

"You're kidding."

Wayne shook his head. "No, really. He's got ESP or something, I don't know. But the press was all over him for a while."

Mallory digested this for a moment. That certainly explained his hostility when she told him she was a reporter. But ESP? Was that what Hosteen Johnny had been referring to when he talked about Graywolf's "talent"?

"You mean he's like . . . a psychic?"

"I don't know. It was all pretty hush-hush for a while," Wayne admitted. "No one really wanted to report much about that."

"Nobody?" Mallory asked skeptically, having been in the newspaper business long enough to know a story that was ripe for reporting.

"Well." Wayne shrugged. "Until the tabloids got a hold of it—blew it up all out of proportion. Made him out to be some kind of sorcerer or something—really played up the Indian angle. Called him a medicine man, a shaman with mystic powers—crap like that." He sat up, resting his elbows on the desk. "The poor guy was pursued by every crackpot in the country. It got so bad he left D.C. and came back to the res. Has pretty much kept a low profile ever since." Wayne shook his head. "Too bad, too. The work he'd been doing had really been getting some things done on the reservation."

Mallory gave him a quizzical look. "You mean the jewelry-making?"

Wayne blinked. "Jewelry? What are you talking about?"

"Isn't that what he does? Makes silver jewelry?"

"I don't know about that. I know he's a lawyer—Georgetown, I think. He'd been working for a coalition in Washington that lobbied lawmakers—Native American issues, stuff like that." The fax machine began humming again, receiving another message. "I guess he felt the publicity didn't do much for their cause. Here he'd been working to change the image the country had of the Native American, and he became this almost cartoon character of one. Tough break."

Mallory's head was spinning. She tried to picture Benjamin Graywolf in her mind—lawyer, psychic or savage? She glanced at the paper slowly crawling out of the machine. The cover sheet indicated it was from Glen, and she pulled each sheet free as it passed out.

The copies were downsized and not very clear, but Glen had faxed enough articles and information to fill in Wayne's brief outline. Mallory read through everything, from the *Chronicle*'s straightforward reporting of the kidnapping, to each lurid tabloid account, trying to picture the man described in print as the one she'd met only the day before. But it was impossible—she could no more picture Graywolf as a Washington lobbyist than she could as a sideshow medicine man.

Yet as amazed as she was to learn of Graywolf's background, she couldn't deny it all made an odd kind of sense. From the moment she'd met him there had been something about him—something different, something she couldn't quite explain. For some reason she knew she could trust him—with the job of finding her sister, and with two thousand of her hard-earned dollars. Maybe it was the anguish she'd seen in his eyes after he'd attempted to humiliate her in front of his friends in the bar, or maybe it was the careful detail he'd shown in his work with the silver. She wasn't sure. She just knew there had been something more to him than the tough-talking, cold-hearted barbarian he tried so hard to be.

She tossed the last of the articles on the stack in front of her. And now she knew.

"Thanks, Wayne," she said finally, gathering up the papers from his desk and stuffing them into her purse. She reached across and offered him her hand. "You've been a lot of help."

Wayne stood and took her hand. "Good luck with your sister."

"Thanks." She turned and started for the door, but before she had a chance to open it, he stopped her.

"Oh, and Mallory?"

"Yes?"

"If there happens to be a story in all of this," he said carefully, "keep me in mind."

Chapter 3

Mallory checked her watch. Ten after one. She was late. She'd told Graywolf she would be at the Flagstaff police headquarters at one o'clock to meet him, and she doubted he would be pleased with her tardiness. That is, if he bothered to notice at all. In her mind she imagined his face, the dark eyes and the deep frown lines showing his dissatisfaction better than the curt comment he would no doubt make.

Stepping down hard on the gas pedal, she sped through the intersection just as the signal changed from amber to red. Glancing quickly over her shoulder, she changed lanes and sailed past a slow-moving transit bus. By the time she'd made a sharp left turn into the parking lot of police headquarters, she had her explanation for him planned and rehearsed in her head.

She thought again of the newspaper reports she'd read, and what she learned about Benjamin Graywolf in the last few hours. She'd been trying all morning to digest it, but it hadn't been easy. Still, it had explained a lot—the hostility, the suspicion, the anger and even the "feelings." And it had helped her justify the trust she'd put in him. It made her feel better to know that he seemed to be a responsible person who'd had some experience in finding missing persons, rather than just a con man with an attitude who would abscond with her two thousand dollars and do nothing to find Marissa.

Marissa. Thinking of her sister, Mallory struggled to suppress a hopeless feeling of panic. She slipped the car into the first available stall, then leapt out and started across the parking lot on a run. In the final tally, she thought as she took the stairs to the lobby two at a time, what Benjamin Graywolf's background was or wasn't didn't really matter. All she needed was for him to find her sister. She didn't care if he used bloodhounds, deductive reasoning or second sight. She just wanted Marissa back as soon as possible.

"There really isn't much else we can do," Lieutenant George Robins said, lifting his feet up and resting them on the end of his desk. Leaning back, he adjusted his horn-rimmed glasses across his nose and cradled his head in his hands, watching Graywolf across the desk through slitted lids. "You know as well as I do that if an adult wants to drop out of sight for a while, there's no law against it. And since there's no evidence to suggest this is anything other than that—no sign of a crime or foul play—our hands are tied."

Graywolf glanced up from the copy of the police report made by Mallory Wakefield the day earlier and gave the officer a deliberate look. "You mean until the body is found." Graywolf was glad for the chance to talk frankly with George before Mallory arrived.

George Robins smiled, sighing deeply and adjusting his glasses again. "I love it when you decide to play the jaded, embittered Indian. You do it so well, so noble. It's been too long, Graywolf."

Graywolf rolled his eyes and peered at the report. Having roomed with Robins for four years at Arizona State, Graywolf had gotten used to his candid humor and wry wit long ago. "Come on, George. This woman didn't just decide to drive off into the sunset and you know it."

"Do I? Lord, Ben, I can't even figure out whose jurisdiction it is. She lived in Sedona, worked at a school outside Flagstaff, tutors on the reservation, and it's anybody's guess where she was when she disappeared." He shook his head. "My head's spinning."

"The fact that she's gone should be enough. She's a teacher. She has a job, responsibilities. She was planning a vacation with her sister. Now she's missing." Graywolf tossed the report down onto the desk. "Someone like that doesn't just take off without a word to anyone."

George gestured to the file cabinet behind him. "I hate to tell you this, but it happens all the time."

Graywolf shook his head. "Bull."

"Tell me, Ben," George said, dropping his feet to the floor and sitting up. "Why are you so interested in all of this? Is it your mystical shaman's intuition, or does it have more to do with a blonde with killer blue eyes and a nice set of casabas? Tom Layton, the Sedona cop who took her report, told me she was drop-dead gorgeous."

"You're a sick bastard, Robins," Graywolf said, disgusted. He pushed himself out of the chair and walked to the window. "You know that, don't you?"

"Well of course I am," George agreed amicably. "I'm a cop."

Just then a young woman opened the door and stuck her head in. "George, there's a woman here to see you? A Miss Wakefield?"

"Well, well, well," he said, shooting a wicked glance at Graywolf. "Speak of the devil. Show her in, Diane."

Graywolf watched in sullen silence as Mallory Wakefield walked into George's small office and introduced herself to him. She hadn't been there to meet him when he'd arrived, and he'd begun to hope she'd changed her mind and decided not to come.

Wrong again, he thought darkly as George ushered her to a chair and rushed to get her a cup of coffee. The sight of her made the muscles in his stomach tighten uneasily. She was the antithesis of him, with her flowing blond hair and pale complexion—stark contrasts to his heavy, dark mane and sun-baked skin. She was the kind of white woman an Indian could look at, but never touch.

In the harsh glare of the overhead light fixture, her long hair looked whiter, and even more pristine—like pure, unsullied snow dusting the desert. He'd watched the lights of her car disappear into the darkness last night, wondering if he'd made a mistake in agreeing to help her. Her two thousand dollars would buy a lot of paint for the beleaguered legal clinic he and a few loyal friends had been working on. But even without the money, he'd been duty bound.

He thought of his vision again—the vision of a woman who looked like her, surrounded by a shining white brilliance, that faded into a galaxy scattered with crescent moons and stars. Duty bound, or just curious, it really didn't matter. He'd been compelled by the vision to help her, and that had been enough. Still, it didn't mean he had to like it. He was leery of her. He didn't trust white women, and he didn't trust reporters, and this woman was both. It would be wise to tread carefully around her.

He watched as she talked with George—her clear eyes alert and attentive, her voice soft and intense. Was she aware of the things she did, or were they really just her nature—the tilt of her head, the slight parting of her lips, the ardent, earnest way she followed your every movement with those blue-green eyes of hers? Even George, who prided himself on being such a seasoned, hard-nosed cop, was mesmerized by her—it really was pathetic.

Graywolf shifted his weight uneasily, rubbing at the tension building in his gut. The shade of her eyes changed like the color of the ocean—brilliant blue one moment, dark murky green the next. The woman made him uneasy, even though that ever-changing gaze of hers had given him only the briefest of glances since she'd walked into the room.

"But like I've told Mr. Graywolf here," George said magnanimously, gesturing broadly with his hand. "We'll do everything we can to aid him in his search for your sister."

Mallory shot a gaze in Graywolf's direction, then back to the ruggedly pleasant face of Lieutenant George Robins. "I appreciate that," she said quietly.

The telephone rang loudly, and George picked it up before it had a chance to ring again. After listening for a moment, he hung up and stood. "They've just brought in a suspect I need to talk to." He glanced at Mallory, and then turned to Graywolf. "I'll be back in just a few minutes, if you have any other questions."

Graywolf shook his head. "I think I've got all I need." He extended his hand to George and the two men shook. "Thanks."

"My pleasure, pal." George smiled, slapping Graywolf on the arm. He nodded to Mallory. "And let me know if there's anything I can do to help."

Graywolf nodded, and after a brief goodbye to Mallory, George left. Graywolf made no attempt to speak, made no effort to disturb the silence that followed George's exit. Standing with his back to the window, he stared across the small office at George's cluttered wall with its crooked pictures and faded reports pinned to it.

But he saw none of that. He was too busy turning the situation over in his mind—outlining a plan of action, designing a course of attack. When Mallory spoke, he jumped. He'd almost forgotten she was there.

"I was late," she announced, as though he might not have noticed.

"Were you?" he said, sliding his gaze down slowly to where she sat. He'd never quite understood the white man's discomfort with silence, and their penchant for small talk.

"Was your friend any help?"

Graywolf walked to the desk and handed her the copy of the police report she'd made at the Sedona Police Department. "Not really. But George might come in handy later on." He turned and started for the door.

"You're leaving?" she asked, rising quickly to her feet. She stood so quickly that her purse tumbled off her lap and to the floor.

He turned back to her. "There's really nothing more I can do here."

She reached down, retrieving the purse. "Where are we going now?"

"We?"

She pushed an errant strand of hair out of her face. "I told you I wanted to be a part of this."

He studied her for a long moment, noting the determined expression and the stubborn set to her shoulders. "Yeah, right, you did," he conceded. He opened the door, stepping gallantly aside to allow her to pass through before him. "After you."

Mallory slipped her purse strap over her shoulder, and walked out. "Where are we going?" she asked again when they'd reached the bank of elevators that would take them to the ground floor.

"Your sister's house."

She looked up at him. She wasn't sure exactly what she'd expected him to be wearing—denim, maybe, like he had on last night. But he'd managed to surprise her again. He looked so different now, with his long hair neatly tied back and wearing a crisp, pale blue chambray shirt, khaki slacks and moccasin-style loafers.

She thought again of the articles Glen had sent, and the things she'd learned from them. Somehow, seeing him now, she found them a lot easier to believe. This morning he looked much more like a lawyer and a lot less like a silversmith. Still, the casual attire was a far cry from the three-piece suit a Washington lobbyist might wear.

"My sister's house?"

"Yeah," he said, looking down at her. "You have a problem with that?"

"No, no, of course not," she said, shaking her head. The elevator arrived and they stepped inside. "But I've already looked through her things. What are you looking for?"

He shrugged, punching the button for the lobby. "I'll let you know when I find it."

"What's this?"

Mallory glanced up from the bureau drawer she was looking through to the small, domed trunk Graywolf had dragged from the closet. "That's Marissa's treasure chest."

Graywolf made a face. "Treasure chest?"

Mallory laughed. "Aunt Bernice sent us each one when we turned ten." She crossed the bedroom and knelt down beside him in front of the chest. "They're really old, and I suppose quite valuable. Aunt Bea said they were to be our hope chests." Mallory laughed again, running a hand over

the tooled leather that covered the sturdy wood frame, remembering. "But to Marissa and me they looked like
something from a pirate ship. We called them our treasure
chests."

Graywolf looked quickly away, running an uneasy hand
along his stomach. He had a muscle spasm again, and he
slowly rose to his feet. He'd watched her as she spoke, seeing how the tension had left her face as she remembered the
childhood memory. Maybe it was foolish, but watching her
had moved him. Suddenly she'd become a real person—not
just a reporter, and not just a white woman. He knew she
had a sister, but he hadn't really thought of her as having a
life—with a family, and a past. In that brief moment, she'd
become more than just a vision to him, and he wasn't sure
he liked the change.

"It's locked," he announced, watching her hands as they
slid over the chest. "Do you know where the key is?"

"As I recall," she said as she bunched her hand into a fist,
"we shouldn't need one." She gave the chest a formidable
rap on its side, and the shiny black hasp snapped open.
Looking up at Graywolf, she slowly raised the lid and
smiled. "See?"

Graywolf ignored the smile, telling himself the uncomfortable feeling in his stomach was merely a lack of food and
had nothing at all to do with her clear blue eyes. He slowly
knelt down beside her and peered into the chest, half expecting to find a pirate's treasure inside.

But there was no cache, no jewels or doubloons, just a
small stack of loose papers, an orderly collection of files,
and a neat row of photo albums. He reached down and
picked up a paper from the stack. It was a child's drawing—a crayoned creation picturing two people with oversize heads and huge eyes, smiling and riding inside a car with

a sagging roof and four undersize wheels. The name Josh was scrawled in the corner in black, uneven block letters.

"One of her students?" he asked, tilting the picture so Mallory could look.

Mallory glanced down at the child's picture, and the smile slowly left her face. "No," she said, shaking her head. "Josh is our brother Caleb's son."

Graywolf fingered through the rest of the stack. "Looks like she has quite a collection."

Mallory followed his gaze to the mound of pictures. "Yeah. Josh and Marissa used to be really close."

Graywolf looked at her. The tension had returned to her face. "Used to be?"

Mallory shrugged, reaching for one of the photo albums. "We lost Caleb a couple of years ago—an auto accident. Josh had just turned thirteen, and it hit him pretty hard. Then his mom—my sister-in-law Penny, died a few months ago. Of course, my parents were there to help. They took Josh in, but it's been pretty rough on everyone. I don't think Josh has felt close to anyone for a long time."

Graywolf returned the picture to the chest, reaching for one of the files. While Mallory sat leaning against the door and gazing at the photos, he leafed through files of tax receipts, old letters and the random papers Marissa Wakefield had found worthy to save. There was nothing useful in any of them, nothing that gave him a "feeling" for the woman.

From one of the files, a loose photograph fell. Picking it up, Graywolf stared down at the two identical faces. Mallory and her sister looked to be about ten in the photo, sitting together on a huge, iron-framed bed with a dainty pink comforter and frilly, ruffled pillows. They smiled into the camera, their pale curls tousled and disheveled, and their blue eyes sparkling and full of mischief.

He thought about the two of them—growing up a matched set, two perfect little dolls. He suspected they could have melted the hardest heart. Was it any wonder their father had wanted to give them the moon and the stars? What parent wouldn't want to pamper such flawless little beauties?

He looked at the room with its frills, and bows, and bright colors. So different, he thought. So different from the narrow mattress tossed on the floor and the drab brown cardboard that lined the walls of the small room he'd shared with his brother. He'd bet the Wakefield twins had been indulged, spoiled and catered to all their lives. They came from a different world, a different existence.

Mallory Wakefield and her sister wouldn't understand about going to bed with an empty stomach, or walking miles in the harsh, winter wind in shoes too small and a coat too worn to offer any protection from the cold. They wouldn't know about a father forced to labor too many hours for too little money, or a mother so weary of struggling against the hopelessness of life that she lost the will to live. But he knew.

Graywolf thought of his own family—his parents and younger brother Billy. Life on the reservation wasn't easy, but he remembered the good times. His father had never been too tired to toss a ball with Billy and him, and his mother would sit for hours, holding them in her lap and telling them beautiful stories of the Navajo—the People— and their journey from the underworld. His parents had been good, hard-working people who had deserved a better life, and as a kid Graywolf had vowed to give them one. But the years of constant struggle and crushing poverty had taken their toll. When Graywolf was twelve, his father had died of a massive heart attack, and his mother had literally died of grief a year later.

Hosteen Johnny had taken them in then, giving them a roof over their heads and teaching them the way of the shaman. But Billy had no patience for study. As soon as he could, he left the reservation and joined the Army, making it a career. They still kept in touch, but the military had bred most of the Navajo from him. He was a white man now, hidden beneath a red skin.

Graywolf slipped the photo into the pocket of his shirt, telling himself he'd keep it as a reminder, something he could take out and look at just to help him remember how different he and Mallory really were.

He reached down into the chest for the last file. When he opened it up, a large manila envelope slipped out onto the floor. He reached down to pick it up, but when his hand touched the faded, golden paper, he suddenly was struck with an unexpected, helpless feeling of sadness.

Graywolf immediately became alert. Feelings like this usually meant something, and he'd long ago learned to pay attention to them. Slowly, he opened the envelope, and looked inside.

"Certificate of birth," he read, slowly unfolding the official-looking document to full length.

Mallory looked up, letting the photo album she'd been browsing through slide down her lap to her feet. "What?"

"It's a birth certificate."

"Marissa's?"

Graywolf shook his head.

Mallory lifted herself up to her knees. "Let me see that."

Graywolf handed her the document. "Why would your sister have a birth certificate for your nephew?"

Suddenly angry, Mallory folded the paper closed and slipped it back inside the envelope. "Is all this really necessary? These are my sister's private papers, her personal business. They're not going to tell us where she is."

"But they might tell us why your sister is listed as Josh's mother."

Mallory sank back to the floor, leaning her head back against the door frame. She squeezed her eyes tightly shut, using sheer willpower to stop the sting of tears. "I already know why."

"Then, why don't you tell me."

She opened her eyes and looked at him. "Because it's none of your business. Because it's nothing that's going to help you find her."

"Let me decide that."

Her eyes narrowed. He was purposely being hard. He seemed to take a perverse pleasure in being a bastard to her. She pushed herself away from the wall and rose to her feet. "I don't know how this could help. You've probably figured it out already." She walked to the bedroom window and gazed out at the red mountains in the distance. "Marissa had a baby when she was in high school. Caleb and his wife Penny couldn't have children so they adopted the little boy." She turned back around and gave him a deliberate look. "That's it. Are you satisfied?"

Graywolf was hardly satisfied. He suspected there was much more to it than that, but he decided not to push. He thought of the picture in his pocket, of the two perfect little faces smiling up into the camera. Maybe even in a perfect life, things weren't always so perfect. "Why the birth certificate?"

Mallory felt chilled, and she crossed her arms over her chest. How many times in the last fifteen years had she held Marissa in her arms and cried with her? "It nearly killed my sister to give up her baby, Mr. Graywolf. She loves her son very much, and she did what she thought was best for him— just like now. She hopes to file for custody of him, now that Caleb and Penny are both gone. Josh knows he's adopted, but he has no idea Marissa is his birth mother. She told me she'd kept it—the original birth certificate, I mean—to remind herself that Josh really had belonged to her once."

Graywolf watched Mallory's face as she spoke. She'd been right, of course. There was nothing in all of this that would help him find Marissa Wakefield. But it had done one thing. It had helped him understand a little better, helped him appreciate that special communication Mallory had tried to explain. Graywolf had felt the pain of a young woman who'd been forced to give up her son, and he'd seen that pain on the face of her sister.

Graywolf scanned the remaining contents in the folder rapidly, and finding nothing else of interest, tossed it back into the chest. He gazed around the room, trying to imagine Marissa Wakefield living there.

"This is how you found the room?" he asked Mallory suddenly, spotting the thin, lacy nightie on the bed and the sheer lingerie spilling out from a drawer of the nightstand. "Just how your sister left it?"

"Well, no," Mallory said uneasily, following his line of vision. Marissa was as neat as a pin. Mallory was the one who left her things scattered everywhere. She rushed across the room and quickly began to tidy up, stuffing the clothing into the drawer and shutting it tight. "Actually, I've been staying here at the house." She purposely kept her eyes diverted from his, feeling her cheeks fill with heat. "I've slept in here."

An image flashed instantly in Graywolf's mind—one that had nothing to do with extrasensory powers or second sight. He saw Mallory on the bed, in the thin, translucent gown—her tall, slender body showing golden through a sea of white lace.

His hands clutched into fists, and he quickly looked away. What was the matter with him? He didn't want this woman—he didn't even particularly like her. She was from a world that had no understanding of his, a culture that viewed the Indian as less than human.

"There's nothing more I can do here," he said in a flat, unemotional voice. The small room had suddenly become stifling, suffocating. He needed air. He needed space. And he needed to be as far away from Mallory Wakefield as he could get.

"So where do we go from here?" Mallory asked, following him out of the bedroom, through the living room and into the small foyer.

"*We* don't go anywhere," he told her, not bothering to disguise the sarcasm in his voice. "*I'm* going to try and retrace your sister's steps."

"But how can you trace her steps when we don't know where she went?"

At the door he stopped and turned to her. "We know she left work Friday afternoon, and she planned to go to the reservation Saturday morning to tutor. You found schoolbooks on the table from her classroom, so let's assume she made it home from work. Her car is gone, so I'd be willing to bet she left for the reservation."

"So that's where we'll look? The reservation?"

"And the route there."

Mallory thought for a moment. "That seems so easy."

"There's a lot of highway between here and there," he pointed out.

"I'm going, too."

"I told you, not this time. I'll keep you informed."

"Not good enough," Mallory said, her hands resting defiantly at her hips. "I want to be there—with you. I want to help."

"I don't need your help."

Mallory glared up at him, biting back her frustration. Did he honestly think she could just sit back and do nothing? "I have to come with you."

"Where I'm going, you can't come," he insisted, reaching for the door.

"But I have to."

He took a deep breath and regarded her for a moment. "Why don't you just let me do the job you paid me for?"

"I hired you to *help* me find my sister," she pointed out. "Not to leave me behind."

"You'll just get in the way."

Mallory grabbed his arm. "I don't care. I'm going with you."

He saw the determination in her face, and the stubbornness and the fear. "Look," he said, trying his best to be reasonable. "I don't know exactly where I'm going, or what I'm going to find. I could be gone for a couple of hours, or days—sleeping on the ground, camping out. It wouldn't be very pleasant."

"It doesn't matter," Mallory insisted. "I want to come with you."

"I work better alone," he said, turning to leave.

"Graywolf," she whispered. *"Please."*

She didn't touch him. She didn't grab at him and try to force the issue. She didn't rant or rave, or even stamp her foot. She simply looked up at him, her soft blue eyes filled with tears, her velvety voice barely above a murmur.

Benjamin Graywolf hated himself just then, hated the fact that he reacted to her, hated the fact that she could get to him. He was Navajo, and he liked to think of himself as immune to the white man's woman, especially after the way Susan had treated him. He'd convinced himself since leaving D.C. that he'd been inoculated against ever falling victim to the wiles of a white woman again.

He glared down at Mallory. This woman was the epitome of what he didn't want. And in that one, precise instant he knew he was in trouble—the worst kind of trouble he'd ever been in in his life.

Chapter 4

"What is it?" Mallory felt the Jeep begin to slow abruptly and she sat up in her seat.

"There," Graywolf said absently, pointing to a small stand of bent and withered cottonwoods off the road at the bottom of a small ravine.

"Where?" Mallory said, her eyes frantically searching the brush. "I don't see anything."

Graywolf pulled off the highway, bringing the Jeep to a stop. He wasn't sure what he'd seen himself—a hint of color through the trees, a flash of light...a feeling. He opened the car door.

"Stay here," he ordered, stepping out onto the dry, hard ground.

"But I want to go with you," Mallory protested, but it was too late. Graywolf was already gone, carefully making his way toward the trees.

He stopped suddenly, kneeling down to stare at the ground. It was hard and flat, but the carpet of dry dust that lay atop it was a mass of footprints and tire tracks. They were too tangled and too fragmented to be of any good, but it was obvious there had been some activity in the area recently.

Rising slowly, he continued down the dusty ravine. As he drew closer to the trees, he saw patches of gray and faded blue through the brush. Clearing the undergrowth, he saw a worn and battered pickup, sitting deserted and alone—its doors open wide, and its hood up.

Graywolf knelt again, surveying the lay of the land. Footprints were everywhere here, too, and a maze of tire tracks had left their intricate patterns in the dirt. It had rained in the area only three days before—just a drizzle, but enough to have left its mark in the dust.

Graywolf studied the prints again. Most of them had been made since the rain, well after Marissa Wakefield had disappeared.

"It's a truck."

"I thought I'd told you to wait in the Jeep," Graywolf said, annoyed. He stopped her from going any closer with a hand on her arm.

"But how in the world did you ever see this from the highway?"

Graywolf didn't answer, just dropped his hold on her arm and walked slowly to the truck. He peered inside. Colorful wires dangled from beneath the dashboard, and an ugly, gaping hole was left where a radio had once been. Walking around the front end, Graywolf surveyed the engine compartment. It hadn't fared much better. The battery was missing, the carburetor had been removed, and it looked as though the radiator had been used for target practice.

"Do you think it was just abandoned here?" Mallory asked, peering over Graywolf's shoulder into the pilfered engine compartment.

"Or stolen," Graywolf said, stepping away from her. Despite the fact that she was dressed in jeans and rugged hiking boots, he couldn't seem to escape the smell of her perfume. He walked to the fuel tank, removed the cap and sniffed the rim. "Empty."

"What does that mean?"

He shrugged. "Not much."

Mallory watched as he walked past the trees. He knelt down and studied the ground again, then climbed to the top of a huge boulder and stared out across the desert. She tried to follow his line of vision, scanning what she could see of the panorama, but saw nothing of any particular interest. What was he staring at? What did he see?

She shifted her weight from one foot to the other, restless. He looked lost in thought, preoccupied, and she was reluctant to disturb him. Yet she was curious. What was there about this old junk heap that had him so interested? Was there something here that could help them find Marissa, or was he just being a weirdo and acting strange?

She watched him as he stood, his rugged profile showing dark and classic against the brilliance of the clear morning sky. He looked nothing like a lawyer now. He was pure Indian, a modern picture of the noble savage with his long hair flowing and wearing a weathered denim jacket and jeans.

Yesterday, when he'd finally agreed to let her help with the search, she'd had no idea what she'd gotten herself into. He'd shown up at Marissa's house this morning at dawn, his Jeep laden with bedrolls and supplies. He'd warned her that she would have to keep up, that he wasn't going to allow her to slow him down or interfere in any way, and he'd lectured her long and hard that she was to do what he told her, and not argue.

She'd climbed into his Jeep, feeling a little like a kid who'd been allowed to go with the adults for the first time, and they'd been driving in sullen silence ever since. He'd stopped at a number of small outposts since they'd left civilization and entered the vast expanse of desert—gas stations, modest café's, small general stores—chatting with the owners, asking about Marissa, about her car and if they'd seen it. Mallory had dutifully waited in the Jeep at each stop, as he'd ordered, sitting on pins and needles until he'd returned. She would ask him excitedly if there was any news of her sister, but he would merely shake his head no. Saying that he'd spotted the abandoned truck was literally the first thing he'd said to her that wasn't a terse, one-word order since leaving Sedona.

She fidgeted with her hair, wishing he'd quit staring out into space and tell her what he was thinking. But he didn't, he just stood and stared, and her impatience grew. Finally, when she couldn't stand the waiting any longer, she started up the boulder after him.

"So, what do you think?" she asked, trying again to see what it was he found so interesting out in the desert.

He turned around and looked at her, trying not to notice how blue her eyes looked in the morning sun. He could see no trace of green in them now. "I think someone ran out of gas up there on the highway and left the truck."

Mallory glanced back at the pickup, trying to suppress her annoyance. Was that what he'd been thinking about all this time, that damn truck? "But if you'd just run out of gas, why would you walk away and leave it?" She turned around and looked up at him again. "Wouldn't you want to come back for it?"

"Of course you would. But not if somebody pushed it back here behind the trees and helped themselves to what they wanted."

"You think that's what happened?"

Graywolf turned back and gazed out across the desert. "Come here."

Mallory felt the hairs on the back of her neck prickle as she climbed up to where he stood. "What?"

"See that?" he asked, pointing in the distance.

Mallory squinted in the direction he indicated. "I don't see anything, except a dirt path of some kind."

"That's what I'm talking about."

She looked up at him. "I don't understand."

He turned back around and pointed to the ground near the pickup. "See where the tracks end, how different the ground looks." Mallory nodded her head. "It rained three nights ago— nothing much, just a sprinkle. All those tracks by the truck have been made since the rain. But those." He pointed again. "Those are tire tracks, made before the rain." He turned his head to look at her. "I think they're from your sister's car."

Mallory felt a chill travel the length of her spine. "B-but how," she stammered, astounded as to how he could have concluded such a thing. "Why? Why would Marissa leave the highway?"

"I don't know," he mumbled, shaking his head. He pointed to the tracks, his finger following the two shallow ruts barely visible along the desert floor until they disappeared in the distance. "But we go that way."

She looked up at him, wondering at that moment if he were a mystic, or a madman. "How do you know? I mean, how could you possibly know?"

He gazed down at her, skepticism clouding the blue of her eyes. "It just feels right."

Mallory stared out the window at the endless horizon. She'd read about the vastness of the Southwest, seen pictures and watched movies. But none of those things came close to preparing her for the reality of it. The desert seemed to go on forever, mile after endless mile.

They'd been driving for hours, and yet little had changed in the landscape. The mountains seemed permanently painted on the horizon, looming up out of the earth like jagged shadows against the sky. To her, the road had all but disappeared, but that didn't seem to bother Graywolf. He was intent on its course. She began to wonder if their path was only visible to those gifted with a special sight to see it at all.

The silence wore on her, drained her of her strength just as surely as if she'd been running the interminable miles through the desert. Add to that her overwhelming feelings of restlessness and uneasiness, and it did not make for a pleasant ride.

There had been nothing to break the monotonous drone of the engine, nothing to interfere with the unchanging scenery and ever-constant sun. The slant of her shadow against the dashboard was the only testament she had to its fiery movement across the sky. Otherwise, the tedium might have convinced her she had happened upon a window in the cosmos, a place where time stood still and the moments stretched on into eternity.

Graywolf seemed to have forgotten she was there at all. He sat almost perfectly still, making only those small movements that were needed to keep the Jeep on its route. His dark eyes stared out across the vastness of the desert, slightly squinted and seeming to concentrate on something that eluded her.

Mallory stared at his profile, seeing an entire history in its classic facade. She thought again of the newspaper articles and tabloid accounts she'd read about him. The glaring headlines and tabloid sensationalism had fed on his Native American heritage and his "special" talents. They'd played up the fact that he was Navajo, blown out of proportion the fact that he was descended from a long tradition of shamans. The whole thing had been unfortunate, not only because they had fueled old stereotypes, but because it had taken attention from the real truth. Benjamin Graywolf had saved the life of a child. He had led police to the kidnappers and had found where they had buried their young hostage alive. He had been a true hero, and all the lurid headlines and crazy distortions had only served to overshadow his heroic actions.

She studied him, trying to imagine what it was that went on in his head. What was behind those dark eyes and that angry scowl? What did he see when he looked at her? What kind of "feelings" did he have? Were they anything like the "vibes" she shared with Marissa, or could he see much more than that?

She twisted uneasily in her seat, thinking of the rows of silver moons and stars in his workshop. It had never occurred to her before, but just what did he pick up from her? Were her thoughts her own, or could he tap into them, as well?

"Didn't your mother teach you it wasn't polite to stare?"

Mallory jumped violently, knocking her knee against the console. "I—I'm sorry," she mumbled, rubbing at the painful spot. "I didn't realize."

He looked at her. "Bored?"

Her gaze collided with his. How had he known that? What else did he know? In a panic, she tried to remember what she'd been thinking. "How did you know?"

He smiled, glancing back to the road. "We've been at this awhile. It wasn't difficult to figure out."

"I haven't complained, have I?" she asked, unable to hide the defensiveness in her voice.

"No, you haven't," he admitted. He turned and looked at her again, a satisfied expression on his face.

Mallory quickly looked away. His dark eyes made her uncomfortable, made her feel oddly exposed.

"You know, you don't have to worry," he said, her uneasiness making him smile.

She gave him a puzzled look. "What are you talking about?"

"I don't read minds."

She squinted skeptically. "Then how did you know what I was thinking?"

He laughed out loud. "Lucky guess?"

Mallory saw nothing amusing, and her eyes narrowed. "This is all pretty funny to you, isn't it?" she said in a chilly voice, settling back in her seat and crossing her arms over her chest. "Just one big joke."

The smile faded slowly from his lips. "Is that what you think?"

"You're the mind reader," she said caustically. "You tell me."

He gave her a cool look. If she thought she could bait him, she had another think coming. "I'm no mind reader."

"No? Then what is it with you?" she asked, glaring up at him. She was angry, but the fiery emotion felt good after so many long hours of unrelenting silence. "I mean, what are we doing out here? We're in the middle of nowhere. What makes you think Marissa even came this way?"

"I don't know," Graywolf admitted honestly, but purposely he kept a glib tone. He controlled his anger, held it inside. He refused to give in to it, refused to give her the satisfaction of knowing she could rankle him. Getting angry was only admitting that the woman mattered, and she didn't—he wasn't going to let her. He *didn't* care about her, so what did he care what she thought? Let her believe he was a mind reader, a sideshow freak. What difference did it make to him? "A hunch?"

Mallory closed her eyes, pulling in a shaky breath. What was she doing? She wanted to hate him for his flippancy, wanted to rage at him for not taking her seriously, but instead she let her anger fade. The fact was he did take her seriously—he was the only one who had. She wasn't angry, she was frightened—frightened that they might not find Marissa, and frightened of what they might find if they did. She was scared and exhausted, and it felt as though they'd been driving forever.

"I'm..." She shook her head, and looked up at him. "I'm sorry. I don't know why..." Her voice faded, and she shook her head again.

Graywolf looked away, turning his gaze back to the faint trail in the sand. He didn't want to look at her, didn't want to see the fear and frustration in her eyes. He knew she was frightened for her sister, knew she was tired and uncomfortable from the long drive, and yet he'd been particularly hard on her today. He'd been angry at her for forcing the issue, angry at her for insisting on coming with him. But mostly he'd been angry at himself for giving in, for allowing her to come. He'd purposely pushed on, purposely kept on driving despite the fact that his muscles ached and his eyes burned with fatigue. He'd wanted to punish her, wanted to make sure it was unpleasant.

"Don't worry about it," he said, feeling awkward and contrite. He slowly eased his foot off the gas pedal.

"Why are we stopping?" Mallory asked, sitting up suddenly. She glanced up at Graywolf. "Do you see something?"

Graywolf shook his head. "I could use a break," he said, turning to her. "How about you?"

Mallory sighed, feeling almost giddy. "Yes," she said, nodding with a small smile. "Oh, yes."

Graywolf brought the Jeep to a stop in the meek shadow of a small cluster of dry, twisted brush. When he turned the key, the engine sputtered, then fell silent. He slowly opened the door, the creak of metal against metal sounding loud and intrusive in the sudden quiet of the desert. A flutter of wind rose up, sending a small cloud of dust flying, but the afternoon sun felt pleasant and warm.

Graywolf stepped out onto the dry, hard ground, and every muscle seemed to protest the move. After a few stiff steps, he turned to Mallory. "Little girl's room is over there."

He pointed to a small gully just beyond the road as he trotted off in the opposite direction. Mallory watched as he disappeared behind the brush, then stepped gingerly out of the Jeep.

She groaned as her sore muscles stretched and elongated, but it was such a sweet agony. Standing up, she was suddenly aware of just how heavily the cup of coffee she'd had hours earlier rested against her bladder, and she hobbled off in the direction he had indicated.

By the time she'd seen to her most immediate needs, the muscles in her legs felt almost normal again. She traversed the short distance back to the Jeep with a little jog. She slowed to a walk, however, when she spotted Graywolf, squatting in front of the Jeep and studying the rutted road before them.

"See anything?" she asked, walking up behind him.

He shook his head and rose to his feet. "Not really."

She tried to read him, tried to decipher those dark eyes and that stern expression, but it was impossible. "Do...do you still think this is right? I mean, do you still think Marissa came this way?"

He turned and started back for the Jeep. "I think so."

Mallory stared out across the endless expanse of desert and mountains. What would Marissa be doing out here? What would have caused her to come so far off the highway and into such a desolate wilderness—or whom?

A cold chill traveled down her spine, and she shivered violently. That awful panic threatened to seize her again, the terrible gut-wrenching fear that told her that her sister was in trouble and needed help. She struggled to bank it down, struggled to keep the lid on her fear.

She turned and glanced back at Graywolf, who was busy digging around in the supplies stored in the back of the Jeep. She hoped he was right about all this, hoped that this desolate trail to nowhere would eventually lead them to Marissa. But it all still seemed so crazy to her, it seemed to make no sense. Yet there was something about Benjamin Graywolf, something in his manner, something in his infuriating silence and guarded answers, that gave her assurance, that made her believe, and that made her trust him.

"What are you doing?" she asked as she watched him pull bedrolls and lanterns from the back of the truck.

"Setting up camp," he said simply.

She blinked, surprised. "We're staying *here* tonight?"

He tossed the bedrolls down. "I warned you we'd be roughing it."

"Oh, I know, I know," she said.

"Then what's the problem?"

"No, n-nothing, no problem," Mallory stammered. "It just seemed so...early."

"Is it?" He glanced up at the sky. "It's after four, and we're going to lose the light soon."

Mallory's eyes widened and followed the line of his vision to the yellow sun hanging heavy in the sky. "That's amazing. You can tell that just by looking at the sun?"

Graywolf looked back at her and smiled. "I can tell that from looking at my watch."

Mallory's shoulders dropped, and she gave him an apologetic look. "I guess that was pretty stupid. I'm sorry."

"Don't worry about it," he said, lifting a duffel bag from the back of the Jeep.

"Do you get a lot of that?" she asked, thinking of the powwow and some of the issues she'd researched for the assignment. She picked up the bedrolls and began to slowly untie them. "Just because you're an Indian, people expect you to have some kind of special kinship with the wilderness—attuned to nature, and all that stuff?"

"You get used to it," he told her, lifting a small tent from the duffel bag and carefully unfolding it. "Unfortunately, most people's image of us still comes from the old television stereotypes—war paint, feathers—stuff like that. You'd be surprised how many people ask if I wear a loincloth."

She thought for a moment, thinking about the leather leggings he'd worn that first day they'd met. "Do you?"

He gave her a deliberate look, seeing in her face the impish smile of that ten-year-old in the picture that he'd taken from her room. "One correction, though. I'm Navajo."

"What?"

"You called me an Indian. I'm Navajo."

Mallory grimaced a little. "Indian is a mistake?"

He laughed, reaching for the tent poles and snapping them together. "Let's just say it's no longer politically correct."

"I thought the politically correct term was Native American?"

"That's acceptable," he conceded. "But that covers a lot of territory—Hopi, Zuni, Cree, Apache, Comanche, Cherokee."

"And you're Navajo."

Threading the poles through the loops on the tent, he smiled. "Now you're getting it."

"You know," she mused, nosing through the box of canned goods he'd set out. "I've often wondered. If Columbus had thought he'd found ... oh, I don't know, say ... China instead of a new route to India, would we have been calling you Chinese all this time?"

He laughed out loud. "Interesting concept. I guess I should be glad he didn't think he'd stumbled across Turkey."

She smiled. His joking, and the sound of his laughter, surprised her. He seemed so sober, almost too serious to find much of anything amusing, but obviously that wasn't the case. She'd heard him laugh only once before, during that humiliating episode at Barney's. But there had been nothing pleasant or humorous about the sound of his laughter then. It had just been a kind of mocking, sneering sound. This was entirely different. This sounded genuine, and real, and ... warm.

"SpaghettiOs," she shrieked, spotting the familiar colored can in the box and lifting it out. "I love these."

"You're kidding," Graywolf said, glancing up from the tent and wishing now he'd paid more attention to what Hosteen Johnny had packed for supplies. He stared at her standing there, hair falling loose and free around her face and her eyes as dark as the sea. Again he saw traces of the child Mallory Wakefield had once been—animated and full of life. "What else is in there?"

"You don't know?"

He shook his head. "I was in a hurry last night. My grandfather packed the supplies."

"Well, let's see," she said, searching through the carton again. "We have two cans of baked beans, three cans of fruit cocktail and . . . one, two, three, four, five corned beef hash.''

"And one SpaghettiOs," he added dryly.

"Dibs!" Mallory said, shooting him a quick smile.

"Be my guest," he murmured, feeling strangely winded. A sudden, unpleasant tightness in his chest made it difficult to breathe, and he quickly looked away. He finished assembling the small tent and began searching the area for firewood.

The wind had come up, and despite the afternoon sun, there was a definite chill in the air. Mallory walked back to the Jeep and reached for a sweater. It was Marissa's sweater—just like the jeans and the boots she wore. The early spring weather was mild and pleasant, but Graywolf had cautioned that the temperatures in the desert could fall rapidly at night and had insisted that she bring along warm clothes.

Slipping into the bulky, shawl-collared sweater and pulling it snugly around her, Mallory was glad now that she had. She turned around, staring at the small tent and wondering exactly what the sleeping arrangements were going to be. When she'd been safe in her sister's house in Sedona, the idea of "roughing it" in the desert hadn't sounded so bad. But standing here, with the shadows growing long and the cold wind buffeting her, it felt lonely and desolate.

She turned and watched as Graywolf arranged wood for a camp fire, a feeling of apprehension building in her stomach. Did he expect the two of them to sleep together in that tiny tent? It hardly seemed appropriate, and yet this wasn't exactly the time or the place to be worried about propriety or appearance. She'd gone into this thing with her eyes open and, if the truth be known, if it meant saving her sister's life, she was willing to deal with the devil.

Mallory studied Graywolf's face, the setting sun throwing him into shadow and making him look ominous, almost sinister. Was he a devil—diabolic and dangerous? They were alone out here in the middle of nowhere, and whether she liked it or not she was at his mercy. If he decided to behave less than . . . honorably, she'd have her hands full trying to talk him out of it.

And yet he wouldn't. She watched as he coaxed the camp fire to life, wondering again what it was that made her trust him. She was no closer to an answer now than she was that night at Barney's, but it no longer mattered. She trusted Graywolf—with her chastity as well as her sister's life.

She glanced back again to the small tent near the fire circle, and felt her apprehension increase. Still the thought of sharing the small enclosure with him made her uncomfortable. It seemed such an indelicate intimacy for two strangers.

Graywolf watched the tension stiffen her expression as she stared across their small encampment to the pup tent behind him. He knew very little about her—almost nothing outside her relationship with her sister. He knew she was a reporter, and that she was from D.C., but other than that, she'd said very little about herself.

Looking at the small tent with the bedroll inside, was she fighting some of her own stereotypes now? Was she wondering just how much "savage" was left in him? A part of him wanted to shock her, wanted to shake her up and disturb her the way she disturbed him, but that only made him think about that stupid stunt of his at Barney's. He remembered the fear in her eyes then, and the vulnerability.

"You might want to get a jacket," he said, arranging a large piece of manzanita in the flames. "The temperature's dropping pretty quick."

Mallory nodded with a shiver, walking back again to the Jeep and finding Marissa's heavy down jacket. She slipped it on over the sweater, immediately feeling its protection from the cold gusts of wind. The sun was disappearing quickly, and the sky was streaked dark with burgundy and purple. She walked back to the fire, thinking of Marissa, and wondered if she were cold right now. Mallory hugged the jacket to her, wishing her sister had the jacket with her—wherever she might be.

"You're thinking of your sister," Graywolf said quietly, recognizing the strain on her face.

She looked up at him suspiciously. "How...did you know?"

He smiled. "Relax. I told you, I don't read minds." He poked at the fire. "Lucky guess, that's all."

"Well, I almost wish you could," she said with a heavy sigh, lowering herself to the ground and sitting before the fire, Indian-style. "Then you could tell me where she is, tell me what she's thinking and why she can't come back." She brushed a hand along her warm down jacket. "This is hers. I was thinking that if she is out there somewhere..." She stopped and gestured to the darkening horizon, blinking back tears. "Is she cold? Is she hungry?"

Graywolf didn't have to feel her pain, he could see it in every move that she made. "You and your sister have something special between you. It's easy to see." She looked up, gazing at him from across the camp fire. "Relax for a minute," he said. "Close your eyes and concentrate. Think about Marissa. Focus all your thoughts on her. What do you feel?"

Something in his quiet tone touched her, made her think he understood. She felt awkward and self-conscious, but she took a breath and closed her eyes. She tried to block out the wind, block out the desert and all the questions and fears she had. She thought of Marissa—of her smiling face, of the places they'd gone together, of the things they'd done as kids.

She didn't know how long she sat there, lost in her thoughts. She forgot about the tears that stung her eyes, about the darkness that surrounded their small camp. She'd been completely absorbed in thoughts of her sister, and of the two of them together. But the touch of Graywolf's hand on her shoulder sent her thoughts scattering, and reality came rushing back.

"You okay?" Graywolf asked, kneeling down beside her.

She blinked, shaking off a moment of confusion. "I—I'm fine." She looked into his dark eyes, seeing the light of the fire reflected in them. "It's unbelievable. I feel . . . I feel as though she's afraid." In her excitement, she reached out and touched his arm. "But I think she's okay. Mostly there's a lot of tension, a lot of frustration and anxiety. She needs help. I know it, I can feel it, but I don't think she's badly hurt."

Graywolf looked at her, watching some of the tension and worry slip from her beautiful face. He shook his head slowly, a slow smile stretching across his face. "Amazing."

Mallory's mind reeled with the experience. She glanced down, seeing her hand on his arm, and felt a pressure building in her chest. He was so close, and it was so dark and quiet in the desert. He didn't look nearly so threatening now, his black eyes not nearly so cold and unfeeling. In the firelight, his dark skin glowed, and the pressure grew in her chest when she thought of his skin touching hers.

"Is that how it is for you?" she murmured, awkwardly moving her hand away.

She looked soft, almost guileless in the faint light, and he felt himself grow uneasy. It had been amazing to watch her, to watch the play of emotions cross her face as she "tuned in" to her sister. He'd felt like a voyeur, like he was watching something very private, very personal—pure love in action.

It was so different with him—his visions and intuitions came in disjointed, unconnected bursts. For so much of his life he'd tried to ignore what it was he felt, to disregard and overlook his hunches and feelings. For a time, when he'd believed his life was with Susan and as far from the reservation as he could get, he'd thought he might actually be able to bury all those feelings and instincts for good. But then, that had been before that awful night in D.C., and the suffocating feeling of being buried alive.

"Not really," he said, slowly coming to his feet and reaching for another piece of wood for the fire. He stood and stared down into the flames. "It's more like premonitions, forewarnings." He shrugged carelessly, tossing a twig into the fire. "I don't know. I don't think about it much."

She watched his eyes in the firelight, watched them shadow and grow wary. "Is that the way it happened with the boy?"

Chapter 5

His entire body went cold, despite the warmth of the fire. "You know about that?"

"I read something about it," she lied, thinking of the stack of papers Glen had faxed to her only the morning before.

"That's right, you're a reporter," he said, making it sound more like an accusation than a simple fact. "I forgot. Tell me, which angle did you take—the mysterious medicine man, or the savage soothsayer?"

"I never reported on the story," she said quietly. "I wasn't even in D.C. when it happened."

"But it's what brought you looking for me," he said, wondering which of the sensationalized headlines had gotten to her.

"I came looking for you because Sam Begay was the only person who was willing to listen, and he told me you might be able to help."

"Well don't expect any magic," he told her caustically. "I don't have a crystal ball."

Mallory just sat and looked up at him. His face was rigid with anger. It was hard to imagine this was the same man who only moments ago had looked at her with such compassion, such emotion. "All I asked for was help."

Graywolf closed his eyes, knowing he was overreacting, knowing he was taking out his anger on her. He'd never talked about whatever it was that gave him his insights and visions. It was a very private thing, something not everyone understood, or accepted. He'd preferred to keep it to himself, especially after what had happened in D.C. Except for the police, he'd never talked to anyone about what had happened then—no one except Susan. He'd confided in her because he'd trusted her, because he thought she loved him, and would understand how personal it was for him. Alone in their bed when he'd confessed to her in the darkness the truth about his visions, he'd never expected to see his own words spread out across the tabloid press two days later.

He could almost have forgiven Susan her vanity and poor judgment, for getting caught up in the moment and succumbing to the temptation and attention of the media. She hadn't taken any of what he'd told her seriously. Talking to the press had been little more than a lark, a hoot, a joke. But what he hadn't been able to forgive was the betrayal. He'd trusted her with his deepest secrets, and she'd let him down.

"Look," he said, drawing in a deep breath. "I'm sorry if I came on a little strong. You can probably guess this isn't my favorite thing to talk about."

"I understand," Mallory said, picking up a handful of pebbles by her feet and tossing them aimlessly toward the fire pit. "This thing with Marissa and me . . . it's not something everyone understands, either." She tossed a pebble toward the fire. It skipped off the rock and landed next to his boot. "People tend to look at me a little crazy when I try to explain. It's just that I get these feelings." She looked up at him. "Like the feeling I get about you."

"Me?"

She nodded, smiling a little. "Believe it or not, I'm normally a pretty cautious person. I'm not usually in the habit of gallivanting off through the wilderness with someone I don't know anything about." She hesitated for a moment, feeling a little awkward. "But for some reason I...feel I can trust you. I feel you can help me find my sister." She breathed out a small, embarrassed laugh. "Sounds pretty crazy, huh?"

He studied her in the firelight, a little surprised by her honesty. "No more crazy than a vision filled with the moon and the stars."

"A vision," she mused, tossing another pebble into the fire. "Is that why you agreed to help me? Because you'd had a vision, because it almost seemed that you were *meant* to help me?"

He shrugged. "Partly."

"What's the other part?"

He looked up at her and smiled. "Two thousand bucks."

She laughed too, but after a moment the smile left her face. "Was it a vision that had you helping the kidnapped boy?"

"No," he said, the smile fading from his lips too. "It had never happened to me like that before," he said, watching as the pebbles she tossed bounced against the ashen wood and fell into the embers. "The kidnapping had been all over the papers for days. I'd read about it, but hadn't gotten any particular...*feelings* about it or anything. Then one night I woke up and couldn't breathe. I knew right then the boy was buried."

"And you went to the police."

He turned and stared out into the blackness, uneasy with having said so much. "I couldn't have just ignored it. The kid would have died."

"Do you think Marissa might die?"

He turned back. "You should know that better than I. Go with your instincts."

"Is that what you do?"

He smiled a little, thinking it was instinct that had brought him into the desert with her. "I try."

"And that's what makes you think Marissa came this way, right?"

"Something like that," he said. A gust of wind sent dust and ashes fluttering up around them. "I don't know what happened back there on the highway. I can try and put two and two together, make an educated guess. But the road—there's something that just feels right about it, something that makes me think we should follow it."

For some reason, Mallory felt enormously better. She still felt an urgency to find Marissa, still felt uneasy and nervous for her sister's safety, but at least she didn't feel so afraid any more. He'd told her to go with her instincts, and her instincts were telling her Marissa was still alive and still safe, just like they were telling her that she could trust Benjamin Graywolf.

The yawn seemed to come out of nowhere, catching her by surprise and making her gasp for air. The fatigue of the long day settled around her like a dense cloud, causing her lids to grow heavy.

"You look beat," Graywolf said, seeing how her eyes had turned the color of the night sky. "Why don't you turn in."

"I know what you're trying to do," she said, shaking off the wave of sleepiness.

"What are you talking about?" Graywolf asked, puzzled. "What am I trying to do?"

She turned and dove for the carton of cans. "You just want the SpaghettiOs for yourself."

Mallory heard the rumble of thunder from off in the distance, and felt the cold blast of wind gust against the nylon walls of the tent. The small shelter billowed with the draft, groaning meekly and swaying back and forth. She snuggled into the bedroll, trying not to think of the cold seeping up through the floor of the tent and into her tired, aching body.

After having finished her meal of canned pasta, she'd crawled into the small tent and fallen asleep almost immediately. The day had been long and emotional, and it had left her exhausted. But she was wide awake now, staring into the darkness and listening to the sounds of a thunderstorm as it made its way across the desert sky.

She had no idea what time it was, or how long she'd been asleep—and with the paralyzing cold and bitter wind, she wasn't about to wrestle open her jacket and bedroll just to get a look at her watch. From the way her body ached and her muscles protested the solid mattress of the desert floor, she had a feeling a number of hours had passed.

It was still awfully dark, and the white nylon that covered the small tent's domed top glowed eerily in the blackness. The thought of lying there, cold and uncomfortable, through the long hours to dawn made her restless, but options were limited at the moment. She shifted her weight, twisting in the sleeping bag in an effort to take the pressure off the painful spot on her hip where it dug into the hard ground. Her stiff muscles made her clumsy, and she collided with the sides of the tent, sending it swaying and swinging even more. Thank God she was alone in the small enclosure, or she'd never be able to move at all.

She thought of Graywolf, asleep outside on the ground beside the fire ring. She had to admit to being relieved when she realized the tent had been assembled for her benefit—relieved, and a little surprised at his thoughtfulness. He'd made such a point of telling her how rough and primitive the conditions would be.

She shifted again, moving her weight off what felt like a boulder in the middle of her back. And he hadn't lied about that—these were definitely primitive conditions. Still, she'd already made up her mind she wasn't going to complain—no matter what kind of sleeping arrangements he'd had in mind. She was just glad they'd worked out the way they had.

She thought of him—of his coal black eyes with their thick lashes and dark brows. She remembered how the sun had streaked across his face, accentuating the high cheekbones and rugged chin, how it had shone brilliantly against the black strands of hair, gleaming dark and rich. She thought of his hands, strong and smooth on the steering wheel. She thought of what it would be like to have them touch her—to feel their strength and power, to have them move over her—searching, probing.

She thought again of that first day, that day at his hogan when he'd surprised her from behind. She hadn't known what to expect, hadn't been prepared for what she'd found.

A small shiver traveled through her as she thought of how he'd looked—tall, strong, powerful. He'd looked every bit the savage—his black hair falling loose, his shoulders broad and straight, his chest bare and hard. What would it be like to feel that kind of strength, to touch those hard muscles and have them touch her?

She remembered the bar, remembered how he'd ground his hard body against hers. She'd been too frightened then to think at the time, too overwhelmed by the crowd and the circumstance, but she wasn't frightened now. She remembered with crystal clarity how it felt and how it made her feel.

She imagined them together, his dark skin against her pale complexion, his black hair falling, mingling with her long, platinum strands, the weight of him against her, the feel...

She shuddered again, violently this time, and sprang up in the bedroll. Sitting up, she covered her face with her hands. What was she doing? Had she lost her mind?

She forgot about the cold, about the gusting wind and the stony ground. Suddenly it was too warm in the tent, it was too small and too uncomfortable. She felt closed in, breathless and claustrophobic.

She blinked her eyes furiously, struggling to see despite the thick darkness. What could she have been thinking of? How could she be fantasizing at a time like this, at a time when she should be concentrating only on finding her sister? And how could she be fantasizing about Benjamin Graywolf? He was a stranger, from a different world, a different culture. He had nothing but contempt for her world, he could barely be civil to her. To think of the two of them together... it was ridiculous, lunacy, insanity.

She sank back into the bedroll, wishing she could just fall asleep, start all over and forget about her foolish fantasies. Thunder rumbled again, sounding closer and more ominous. She thought of Graywolf, unprotected beneath the stars. She knew the tired old stereotypes about Indians weren't true, but there was something about him—something feral and untamed. As a reporter she could understand why the press had gone after him with such relish—he had a mystery about him, a presence. He would have been a dream come true to a journalist hungry for a story, an easy prey—ripe for exploitation.

There was another rumble of thunder, low and foreboding, and it took her a moment to realize the tapping sounds against the tent were actually raindrops falling. She sat up again, unzipping the tent flap and peering through the darkness at Graywolf's shadowy form lying a few feet away. He seemed oblivious to the thunder, and the drops that splashed against the dry ground. She considered getting up, climbing out of the tent and awakening him, inviting him into the protection of her small shelter. But remembering her fantasies, and how uncomfortable they had made her, she decided against it.

She closed the flap, lying back against the hard ground, thinking. The fantasies really shouldn't upset her. At least they were a healthy sign—a sign that she was still living, still alive. There was a time there when she wasn't so sure, when she thought that part of her life was over—put to rest forever.

Growing up in rustic Jackson, in the heart of California's gold country, had been just about perfect. The Wakefield family had been part of the mother lode since the rush of 1849, and everyone in town had known the Wakefield twins. Marissa had been the quiet, studious one—captain of the debating team, president of the honor society and class president. Mallory had been the popular one—cheerleader, prom queen and the student voted most likely to become a millionaire.

Millionaire, she thought darkly, twisting in the sleeping bag and shifting her weight heavily to one side. How foolish it was to think money could make up for anything. The Wellingtons had been millionaires all right—many times over, but their son Randy had been one of the neediest people she'd ever met.

Mallory had known from the moment they'd met at freshman orientation at the University of Maryland that Randy was troubled, but his uncertainties and defenselessness were what had drawn her to him in the first place.

Maybe things had always come too easy for her—school-work, friends, relationships, opportunities—or maybe she hadn't understood how deeply rooted Randy's problems really were. She'd liked being needed by him, liked having him depend on her. And she'd honestly thought she could help him sort through his troubled relationship with his family, help him conquer his struggle against alcohol and drugs as easily as she'd conquered everything else in her life.

But she'd been living in a dreamworld. Randy hadn't needed a cheerleader, hadn't needed someone to champion his cause and root him on. He'd needed someone to help him face his problems head on, not through violent out-bursts or drunken hazes, and it was there where she'd failed him miserably. She hadn't realized until it was too late that Randy first had to admit he needed help before anything was ever going to change.

Mallory didn't suppose a broken marriage was ever easy, but for her it had been devastating—not just because she'd loved Randy and hadn't been able to help him, but because she'd screwed up. She'd failed, and it had been a rude awakening. The most popular girl in school, the perfect cheerleader with the perfect twin sister and the perfect life had finally received her comeuppance.

She listened to the droplets of rain as they hit the top of the tent. They made a sad, bleak sound as they splashed against the thin nylon—like tears spilling down from the sky. She thought of how foolish she had been, how naive. It had been three years since the divorce, and yet she still felt its effects. Randy was doing great now, and she was happy about that. Their failed relationship had done nothing to dampen his spirit to want to try again. He'd married some-one he'd met in rehab, and they had two sons now.

She, on the other hand, still felt as though something were dead inside her. She'd shied away from involvements, preferring instead to let time heal the wounds. There had been no one special in her life, but that had been the way she'd wanted it. And even though she'd convinced herself her reluctance to begin a new relationship wasn't because she was afraid to try again, she had to admit there were doubts that hadn't been there before.

She thought again of Graywolf—of his dark eyes and broad shoulders, and of the scenes she'd fantasized in her head. A warm, weak feeling spread through her arms and legs, making her twist uncomfortably in the sleeping bag. It was as though life had finally returned to her body in one glorious burst. Perhaps her healing had been completed, perhaps it was time for her to get on with her life.

But with Benjamin Graywolf? What was it about him that had gotten to her? What was it about this strange, brooding man that had reached out to her, and had her emotions roaring back to life?

She thought of the way he had looked at her, thought of his dark, probing eyes, and the way they seemed to see and know more than she was comfortable with. He said he was no mind reader, and she hoped that was the truth. How embarrassed she would be if he knew what she was thinking when she looked at him.

He reached for her, but her hand was just out of reach. And yet she beckoned to him—please come, please come. Her eyes pleaded with him—implored, entreated. She needed him...needed him. Her arms begged, outstretched.

He reached out again, wanting nothing more than to catch her up into his arms, to hurl her across the chasm and press her to him. Her blue eyes were clear and radiant, the color of the sea in the morning. Her long hair looked almost white, like streaks of moonlight through the clouds.

He wanted her, more than he'd ever wanted a woman in his life. She belonged to him, and he wanted to reach out and claim what was his.

But something was happening, something had gone wrong. She was crying, her huge blue eyes spilling over with tears. They were falling down on him, tasting wet and salty. She was slipping away, falling back—just out of touch, just out of reach. He grasped for her again, struggling desperately, but something was holding him back, something confined and restricted his movements. He watched helplessly as she slipped away, struggling, struggling....

It was only when his shoulder made painful contact with one of the hard rocks of the fire ring did Graywolf realize he was dreaming. Confused and disoriented, he struggled to sit up, trying to blink away the darkness. Perspiration poured from him, and his heart thundered in his chest. His lungs gasped for air, and drew it in huge, deep breaths.

He'd thrashed around in his sleep, tossing and turning, and succeeded in tangling himself in the bedroll. With the dream still skirting the edges of his consciousness, he tried his best to clear his mind and concentrate on disengaging himself from the confines of the sleeping bag.

He turned, glancing back at the small pup tent behind him. Apparently he hadn't disturbed the *biligaana* woman. The small enclosure was still and silent, little more than a black shadow in the darkness.

With the bedroll straight, he lay back down. A sudden splash of water against his face made him jump, making him aware it was drizzling. Only then did he realize his face was wet, and the sleeping bag damp. Still, he made no move to dry himself or take cover. It was barely more than a mist, and the coolness of the rain felt good against his heated skin. The droplets had a soothing, rhythmic feel against his face.

He lay there, staring into the darkness, forcing himself to concentrate on what stars were visible, forcing himself to think about the rain and the desert, and not about the dream, or the woman in it. But it was impossible. It would seep into his thoughts, permeate his consciousness and bring her into the forefront of his mind. He could see her, how she had looked in the dream—her lips red and full, her eyes dark and pleading, her arms reaching and inviting. With each drop of rain that pelted his face, he thought of her, and of the tears she had shed.

He had dreamed about her. Mallory Wakefield—a woman whose prim, proper name was as much a part of the white man's world as her long, golden hair. She had invaded his subconscious, his private sanctum, a place she'd had no right being. She had called out to him, had beckoned to him. She had held out her arms to him and invited him in. How dare she?

Thinking about it made him angry—furious, in fact. It was an unforgivable, inexcusable, egregious sin she had committed. He blamed her for creeping into his brain, for disturbing his peace. He blamed her for having the kind of beauty that haunted a man, and made her impossible to forget.

But the worst part—the *very worst* part of it all—was remembering how desperate he'd been to get to her, how urgently he had struggled to gain the comfort of her embrace. He couldn't blame that on her. That was something he had to take full responsibility for, and he hated himself for it.

His visions of the moon and the stars, of the woman with hair of sunshine and eyes the color of the sea, had become familiar during the last few weeks. But this had been no vision, no calling out from that cryptic, secret enigmatic voice crying from somewhere beyond the boundaries of his mind. This had been a dream—a real honest-to-God, *ordinary* dream—something born of his own desires, rooted in his own longing. And that was what made it so unforgivable.

He didn't want her, he couldn't. She wasn't Navajo, wasn't a part of his world, and never could be. There was a time when he thought the gap between their two worlds could be bridged, but he knew better now.

He rolled onto his side, turning his back to a cold gust of wind. He thought of Susan, with her bright red hair and pale green eyes. Her smooth, white skin had been flecked with color—freckles that darkened whenever she walked in the sun. He'd been so captivated by her, so dazzled. She'd been so different, so unlike anyone he'd ever met before. He'd liked her finishing school manners, her independence and sophistication. She had a way of making things seem so easy, so affable—like nothing bad could ever really happen. He remembered telling her about the reservation, about growing up poor—of the hardships and suffering his people had endured, of the prejudice and injustices.

But he doubted now if Susan had ever truly believed him. For her life was easy and uncomplicated, and the struggles and anguish of a people whose customs were strange and unfamiliar to her seemed distant and unimportant.

Graywolf twisted restlessly in his sleeping bag, turning around and shifting his weight to the opposite hip. Maybe that's what bothered him the most. Maybe being with Susan had been his way of forgetting, too—forgetting the years of crippling poverty, of growing despair, and of just getting by. Maybe it had been his way of turning his back on the customs of the shamans, the *yataalii*, and of Hosteen Johnny. He'd left the reservation to find himself, and for a while, he'd done that in Susan's arms.

But he'd learned the hard way that life in the white man's world was as volatile and unstable as the love of the white man's woman. He'd made a mistake leaving the reservation, trusting Susan. The truth had been a bitter pill. He now knew that what demons he had to face, he had to face here—on the reservation—among his people and his past.

As he stared at the tent, it shifted and swayed to one side. She was moving around inside. He imagined her in D.C.—pictured her there and her life as a reporter. She didn't belong here. This was his world, and there was no room in it for Mallory Wakefield—no room in his life, in his head, or in his dreams.

Chapter 6

Mallory reached for a fresh tissue. The one in her hand was little more than a handful of shriveled fibers. She tossed the wadded mess onto her lap, adding to the considerable stack that she'd accumulated over the course of the last few hours, and wiped her wet brow with the fresh one.

It was blistering hot. Beads of perspiration covered her, and her shirt was wet and stained. She would have given anything for a pair of Bermuda shorts at the moment. Her denim jeans felt like woolen leggings against her skin. It was hard to believe just a little over twelve short hours ago she'd been bundled in Marissa's bulky down jacket, and thought she would freeze to death.

She glanced at Graywolf, whose dark eyes were focused on the road in front of them. He'd shed his denim jacket and flannel shirt long ago, leaving only a white T-shirt that clung to him. He'd pulled his long hair back, working it into a braid, and his skin gleamed dark with moisture. He didn't appear to be nearly as uncomfortable as she was, but still she felt better knowing he wasn't as impervious to the heat as he apparently had been to the cold.

It had been another miserable day of endless driving, and the temperature had climbed as the hours wore on. It was nearly five now, and the glare of the sun through the open window of the Jeep felt like burning embers against her skin.

She had no idea where they were, or what direction they were traveling, and her eyes were tired from having spent hours scanning the countryside looking for a sign that might indicate they were on the right track. She took heart that the mountains had grown closer, but as far as she was concerned, the road they'd been following had all but disappeared. Yet Graywolf seemed set on his course and she was reluctant to disturb it. Still, his silence bothered her. If only he would say something to her once in a while, something more than just a grunt, or a nod, or a shrug.

Even though the long hours of driving had seemed endless, Mallory had been grateful for the few brief stops they'd made since they'd started out this morning. One stop had been at a lone hogan they'd come upon early in the morning where Graywolf had made an inquiry, and another had been a moment to study the road when it forked into opposite directions. But later, as they followed the right fork of the road to the east, they'd come upon a dilapidated cluster of buildings and rusted-out vehicles huddled together that seemed to appear out of nowhere.

To Mallory's amazement, the deserted-looking outpost was actually inhabited, consisting of a general store with a faded neon sign proclaiming Smokes Inside through the dingy window, a lone gas pump, a shack and an outhouse.

The chipped and weathered placard above the general store read Hank's Place in faded red-and-black letters, but when Graywolf walked inside, he greeted the man standing behind the counter as Rawley. A heavyset, flushed-faced white man, who sported one yellowed tooth in the center of his mouth, Rawley had welcomed them inside. He was alone in the small, sparsely stocked store, except for an ancient-looking Navajo woman whose face was worn with wrinkles, who sat in a rocking chair near the front window. A beautifully woven Navajo blanket of bright colors lay draped across her bent shoulders despite the stifling temperature, and she sat staring out across the desert, mumbling to herself and oblivious to everything else.

After the usual pleasantries had been exchanged, Graywolf had inquired about Marissa. Rawley had seemed interested, and told him that two hunters, a group of archaeologists from Flagstaff, and a young pregnant Navajo woman had drifted through their place in the last week, but regretfully added that no *biligaana* woman had passed their way.

As strange as she found the tiny, isolated oasis to be, Mallory relished the opportunity to stretch her weary muscles, buy a few warm colas and potato chips, and take advantage of the primitive "facilities." She'd remembered hearing her grandmother talk about growing up with a "two-seater," and after her visit to Rawley's outhouse, she had a much clearer understanding of the term. By the time she'd finished, Graywolf had filled the Jeep and its auxiliary tanks with gasoline and was sitting in the idling truck waiting for her.

He had driven back to the spot where the trail had divided, surprising her by actually explaining to her his feeling that they should explore the other fork, as well. As hot and as miserable as she was, Mallory had given him no argument. For reasons she didn't really understand, she trusted the voice that seemed to lead him, and she knew she had to follow.

She'd been surprised to smell coffee brewing when she'd awakened at dawn. She'd stepped out of the tent to find Graywolf sitting before a fire, sipping coffee from a tin cup and munching on a strip of beef jerky. All signs of the rain that had pelted her tent in the night had disappeared. The ground had been bone dry, and the sky a clear blue.

Graywolf had allowed her little time for breakfast, pouring her a cup of bitter coffee and offering her some of the jerky. She'd taken the coffee, but refused the jerky, and within thirty minutes they'd broken camp, repacked the Jeep and been on their way.

Mallory lifted her hair up, dabbing at the moisture at the base of her neck, and staring out across the windswept landscape. It was rugged country—harsh and brutal. It wasn't a land that treated its inhabitants kindly, but it had a vastness and a breathtaking beauty like no other place on earth. It amazed her that people could actually survive in such a ruthless environment, and yet Rawley's small outpost and the occasional house—*hogan*—they'd passed were testaments that they did.

Mallory thought of her cramped D.C. apartment, of the noisy rush hour traffic, and her neighbors whose teenage son liked to turn the stereo up to blasting. That urban world seemed like a million light years away from all of this—from the quiet and the solitude, and the unlimited, empty space.

The Jeep hit a pothole, causing it to lurch violently and sending her painfully against the door. She banged her head, and the collection of crumpled tissues in her lap went scattering.

"You okay?" Graywolf asked, slowing the Jeep to a crawl.

"Fine," Mallory mumbled, rubbing the tender spot on her forehead. Actually, she was hot and uncomfortable, but she wasn't about to confess that to him. If he could take it, she could take it.

"You might want to hang on," he cautioned, his gaze returning to the road. "It's pretty rough through here."

Mallory peered out the windshield at the rocky canyon they'd entered, and shook her head. "It just seems impossible that Marissa could be out here. Look at this place, it's full of rocks and boulders. It's awful. What could she be doing wandering around out here?"

"Maybe she got lost," Graywolf suggested, shifting in the seat in an effort to ease the stiffness in his back. "Maybe she gave someone a ride."

Mallory shook her head. "It just doesn't make any sense. I mean, I've thought of all those things, and it still doesn't make sense. She's been gone for seven days. *Seven days.* Where is she? What would have made her come all the way out here?" She shook her head again, groaning in frustration. "The not knowing drives me crazy."

Graywolf knew her questions were figurative, that they came from her frustration and fears, and that she wasn't really asking him for answers. "Maybe it's just as well that you don't."

Despite the perspiration streaming down her body, Mallory felt a sudden chill. "What does that mean?"

Graywolf turned the wheel sharply, swerving just in time to avoid another large pothole. "Nothing, forget it."

"I won't forget it," she said insistently. "Explain what you meant."

He gave her a cool look. "It doesn't take a genius to figure out in all likelihood someone *brought* your sister out here."

Mallory sat up in her seat, straining against the seat belt. A sickening, cold feeling spread through her body. She remembered the child in Washington, about Graywolf's sense of suffocation and knowing the child had been buried alive. "Do you know something? Have you had a . . . a feeling or something about Marissa? Are you keeping something from me?"

Graywolf cursed to himself. He heard the accusation in her voice, but it was pure fear in her eyes. It had been a stupid thing to say, bringing up the possibility of foul play—stupid and insensitive—and he felt like a heel. She was a smart woman. She'd no doubt already figured out for herself that the possibility that her sister had fallen victim to something unseemly was a very real consideration. But blurting it out like that had been cruel. She'd been trying very hard to cling to the hope that her sister was still alive, still safe, and he'd ravaged that effort with one malicious remark.

"No," he said meekly, feeling contrite and small. "Nothing like that."

"Are you sure?" she demanded. "Are you telling me the truth?"

His head snapped up at the notion she might think he was lying to her. Yet he knew he deserved her rancor. "Look," he said in a quiet voice. "Let's make a deal. You tell me any *feelings* you might have about your sister, and I'll tell you mine. Deal?"

Mallory stared into his dark eyes, hating him at that moment. The way she felt right now she wasn't inclined to tell him anything ever again. All she'd wanted from him was a little conversation, something to divert her attention away from the heat and the discomfort, but he'd been sullen and uncommunicative all day. Now she just wished he'd never talk to her again.

Graywolf watched as she turned her cold, blue gaze away from him to the rugged scenery outside. What was the matter with him? Why was he acting like such a coldhearted bastard? Maybe he was restless and annoyed, maybe he was even a little angry, but that gave him no right to be cruel. Yet he'd struck out at her in the meanest way possible, for no reason at all.

Well . . . that wasn't entirely true. There was a reason—it was a small, petty one, but it was a reason. The fact was he was angry about the dream—that stupid, meaningless dream that he couldn't seem to stop thinking about. He was irritated to think she had managed to creep into his thoughts, that she'd interfered with his rest, and that she could make him wonder what it would be like to hold her in his arms.

It didn't seem to matter that the woman was innocent, that she virtually had no control over what filled his dreams or what thoughts bounced around his subconscious. He'd realized his anger was unreasonable, that it was illogical and made no sense. He knew he was being completely unfair to her, knew how ridiculous and absurd the whole thing was, but it hadn't changed the way he felt. He blamed her for the dream. He blamed her for the fact that he was curious about how her skin would feel, that he wondered how her soft body would fit against his own, and how her smooth, soft lips would taste—he blamed her for all of that.

The mountains loomed around them, and the afternoon sun sent long shadows falling across the canyon floor. Graywolf pulled the Jeep to a stop near a shaded clearing, sheltered from the sun by a twisted stand of cottonwoods and overgrowth.

"What is it? Why are you stopping?" Mallory demanded, sitting up in her seat again.

"We're losing the light," Graywolf said, twisting the ignition key off and setting the parking brake. "We'd better make camp before it gets dark."

Mallory stepped out of the Jeep, stretching her cramped muscles and rubbing at a stiff spot on her neck. It was still miserably hot, and even the wind against her face felt dry and burning. She turned and watched as Graywolf opened the back of the Jeep and began to unload their gear for the night.

What was it with him? He acted as though the very sight of her annoyed him, as though she made him angry. In fact, he'd been acting that way all day—impatient and snappy. What had she done to make him dislike her so much?

She thought back over the day—of the places they'd stopped and the things they had done. She'd tried to do everything he'd asked her to—everything he'd *ordered* her to do. She'd endured the long hours in the Jeep, she'd endured the rough terrain, the heat and the discomfort without so much as a hint of complaint, so what could she have done to have made him so angry? Had she inadvertently broken some sacred Navajo tradition? Had she spoken when she wasn't supposed to, walked where she shouldn't have?

But then, this wasn't Jackson High School, and she'd stopped being everybody's favorite cheerleader a long time ago. Maybe she should accept the fact that Benjamin Graywolf didn't like her very much.

And that was just fine with her, she decided as she walked to the back of the Jeep and began to help him set up camp—he didn't have to like her. The arrangement between them was strictly business. Services had been rendered, fees had been paid. It wasn't necessary that he like her, it wasn't even necessary that he be nice to her. All she wanted from him was to find Marissa—the sooner, the better.

* * *

Graywolf watched as she hammered the stakes of the pup tent into the hard ground, and felt the tension building at the back of his neck. It had surprised him when she'd carried the tent from the Jeep and began assembling it. She hadn't exactly struck him as the "camp out" type, and yet she seemed to know what she was doing.

He glanced away, lifting the lantern and coffeepot from the back of the Jeep and carrying them to the fire pit he'd formed from a pile of rocks. He tried not to think about the way the sun streaked her hair, or the way the wind had sent it fluttering around her face.

It wasn't as though she refused to speak to him—she had. It was just that there was nothing friendly in her words, nothing congenial in her tone. And judging from the looks she'd been giving him, there was a good chance there never would be again.

But that would suit him just fine. He didn't want her friendliness, or her humor or good nature. He didn't want to talk to her, didn't want to think about her. He just wanted to get this whole thing over with—find her sister and get her out of his life once and for all.

He walked back to the Jeep, reaching for the bedrolls. She was threading the poles through the tent now, slipping them into place at the corners and popping the dome into shape. She'd done this before, he thought as she adjusted the hoops and pulled the nylon tight. Somehow he wouldn't have thought that. In his mind he'd pictured her as strictly an urban creature, a woman out of place in the wilderness, a woman whose idea of roughing it was staying in a hotel with no room service, a woman like... Susan. He'd thought after two days in the desert she would be begging him to take her back, itching to return to civilization where she belonged.

He watched as she unzipped the tent flap, rolling it up and securing it with the Velcro ties. Unfortunately it looked like it wasn't going to work out that way. The last two days had been rough; their pace had been grueling and the conditions had been harsh. He hadn't spared her a thing. And yet watching her as she pitched her tent and secured its moorings, she didn't look anywhere near to cracking, anywhere near to throwing in the towel.

She straightened up and marched over to where he stood holding the bedrolls. In the shadow of the canyon walls, her eyes had turned a dark green, and they glared up at him like cool emerald gems.

"I can take that," she said, reaching a hand out for one of the bedrolls.

He relinquished one of the sleeping bags, telling himself he didn't care that she hated him. But watching as she crawled into the tent and prepared her bedroll for the night, he thought of that awful look of dread that had filled her eyes after he'd made that thoughtless crack about her sister meeting with foul play. He'd struck out at her, blamed her for creeping into his thoughts, for crawling under his skin and staying there when all along he should have been blaming himself.

He didn't want to want her. So why couldn't he stop thinking of her? He was Navajo, a singer, a shaman, *yataalii*. He could make powerful medicine, walk with the spirits, and see through time. There was no place in his life for the *biligaana*, no place in his heart for her.

"What's that sound?"

Graywolf stopped for a moment, letting the small pile of kindling rest, and listened. "I don't hear anything."

Mallory swiped at a bead of perspiration that rolled down her forehead. "That," she said again. "That rushing sound. Like . . . like . . ." She let her words drift.

"Like water running?"

She turned to him. "Yes, that's it. Water."

Graywolf continued stacking the kindling, getting the fire ready to light. "There's a creek just over that bluff."

Mallory stood up, the hot wind making her sweat-soaked shirt feel clammy and uncomfortable. "A creek?"

Graywolf searched through their supplies until he found the matches. "Yeah, it comes down from the high ground," he said, motioning with his chin to the jagged canyon wall that soared up at the horizon. "Runs along the canyon just over there. They can get pretty swollen this time of year."

Mallory squinted in the direction he'd indicated, noting the richness of the vegetation. "Is it close enough... I mean, could I walk over?"

Graywolf struck the match head against the sandpaper strip along the box. "What for? We've got plenty of water."

"I know," she said, glancing down at him. "I just thought maybe I could, you know." She shrugged, gesturing at her sweat-stained shirt. "Wash up a little."

The dry grass and kindling caught, and the campfire slowly began to come to life. "You know, the temperature's going to start dropping as soon as the sun goes down," he said.

She glared at him and swiped at the perspiration on her forehead. "But it's hot *now.*"

He looked up. The annoyance in her voice was obvious. It had been a long day, and a blistering one, and for some reason he just couldn't seem to stop acting like a bastard. "Yeah, it is, isn't it," he conceded, feeling just a little contrite. He watched as she turned and started toward the bluff.

"Why don't you grab that canteen? Might as well fill it up while you're at it."

Mallory dutifully retrieved the round, insulated canteen from the back of the Jeep and slung it over her shoulder. She had taken only a few steps when he stopped her again.

"It gets dark faster here in the canyons," he pointed out, tossing a larger piece of wood onto the fire. "Better not be gone long."

"I won't," she said, starting out again. "Just a few minutes."

"Watch your footing," he warned. "It's rough along there."

She rolled her eyes and kept on walking. "I will."

"And don't get lost."

She sighed heavily. "I won't."

"And keep an eye open for snakes."

She stopped dead in her tracks. "Snakes?"

He almost laughed at the look on her face. "Yeah, snakes."

"There are snakes around here?"

He saw the doubtful expression. "There are snakes everywhere around here. Just be careful, okay?"

"Okay," she said, eyeing the ground suspiciously.

She followed the sound of the water, over the bluff, and across the canyon floor. Despite the long shadows and weakening sunlight, the air was stifling and sweat poured down her forehead and into her eyes. To her surprise, the creek turned out to be a fast-moving torrent, which twisted over its rocky bed, churning white and frothy. The water cut a path along the cliff, dropping down from a ridge in a short waterfall.

Mallory hadn't thought she'd seen anything so beautiful in her life. The water looked clear and inviting, and seemed to call out to her hot, tired body. Her intention had been to just dip a hand in, cool off her flushed face and sweaty arms, but all she could think about was the feel of the crisp, clean water against her overheated skin. A bath. She was almost ready to kill for one.

She glanced around quickly, considering the idea. There certainly was no one around to see her—no one but Gray-wolf around for miles, in fact—and the thick, lush green-ery along the bank provided a solid barrier between her and Graywolf back at camp. She had a clean T-shirt back in the Jeep—one of Marissa's—and a spare pair of underwear.

She looked around again. It probably wasn't such a good idea, but the thought of a clean body and fresh clothes was too great a temptation. She squatted to the ground, and be-gan to unlace her boots.

Graywolf paced back to the camp fire. His shadow stretched out long on the ground in front of him, extending over the rocks and the tumbleweeds in a crazy, disjointed form. He stopped, resting his hands on his hips and glanc-ing up to the sky. Streaks of color marked the clouds—pink, rose and burgundy.

"Damn woman," he growled aloud, kicking at the small pile of firewood he'd gathered. Where the hell was she? It was getting late, and she'd been gone too long.

With an exasperated sigh, he checked his watch again. Twenty-seven minutes. It felt more like hours, but it was still longer than he was comfortable with. He'd *told* her it would be getting dark, he'd *told* her to watch her step, and he'd *told* her to come right back. *He'd told her....* But appar-ently she hadn't heard a thing. Where was she?

He turned and stalked back toward the Jeep. It would serve her right if something happened, if she'd gotten lost and couldn't find her way back. He should let her wander around the darkness for a while and see how she liked it. See how anxious she'd be to go out wandering on her own again.

He glanced in the direction of the bluff, hearing the sound of the water and feeling the muscles in his stomach tighten. He'd known small creeks to swell rapidly in the spring, and their swift currents could be treacherous at times. He'd never thought to ask her if she could swim—he'd just assumed...but he should know better than to assume anything when it came to the whites. Growing up on the reservation kids learned quick to swim and climb and take care of themselves.

He reached into his pocket and pulled out the picture of ten-year-old Mallory and her twin sister. What kind of world had they grown up in? What kinds of games had they played, what kinds of dreams did they dream?

He stared at Mallory's smiling face, and then at her sister's. There was no need for special insight or divining skill to know they had known nothing but the best in life. Never would they have known a day without a full belly and a warm bed. There always would have been clothes on their backs and shoes that fit their feet. There would have been none of the hardships and difficulties, none of the despair and hopelessness, that had marred too many lives of children on the reservation.

Was that what fascinated him so? Is that what he saw in her—all the hopes and dreams that he'd had to put on hold, all the chances and possibilities that had been lost to a world of poverty and neglect?

He slipped the picture back into his pocket, staring out across the bluff again. He didn't want to think about all that now. All he wanted was her back here—now!

He ran a frustrated hand through his hair. Where was she? What was she doing? Had she fallen down? Stumbled over a rock? Twisted her ankle? Had she been frightened by something—a field mouse, a coyote, a . . . snake.

He started for the bluff at a run. He was through waiting. It was getting cooler, and the milder temperatures would bring out the snakes. He was no baby-sitter, but like it or not he had an obligation to keep the woman safe. He was going to find her and bring her back to camp—even if that meant he had to drag her back kicking and screaming.

Chapter 7

He could only stand there and stare. She was more than just a woman, more than a vision, more than beauty. She was perfection.

The breath left his lungs in a long, slow sigh. He hadn't been prepared for this—not the sight of her beneath the pulsating spray of the waterfall. Sprinting down the shallow bluff from their campsite, he'd half expected to find her wandering around—lost and confused. It wouldn't even have surprised him to have found her injured, or hurt. But this . . . in a million years he hadn't expected this.

He knew he should look away, knew he should divert his eyes, turn around, walk away, leave her to the privacy she thought she had. But he couldn't seem to do that. He couldn't move, he could barely breathe. And so he stood there, hidden in the tangled overgrowth, and watched her.

Her skin was the color of honey—rich, golden and flawless. In her clothes she looked tall and slender—without them she was beautifully rounded. Her hair streamed down her back, made dark from the water. It looked like wet silk, slick and glossy. The water coursed over her, leaving droplets in its wake and making him thirsty to drink its dew from her skin.

His body roared to life. It didn't matter that he disliked and distrusted her. It didn't matter than she wasn't Navajo, that she was everything he'd come to loathe, everything he held in contempt. She was a woman, and as a man he couldn't deny that he wanted her.

A gust of wind blew, beating against his hot skin and sending dust circles dancing. Almost in a trance, he watched as she closed her eyes, letting the water flow over her, sending tiny rivulets streaming down her soft, pink breasts, and felt his mouth go dry. He wanted to close the distance between them, wanted to gather her cool, clean body next to his. He wanted to touch her, to taste the honey of her skin, to bury himself in the sweet valley of her breasts and coax their soft, pink centers to harden and turn dark. He wanted her to reach for him as she had in the dream, plead to him to come to her.

But a harsh sound from above broke the spell, bringing reality crashing down around him. A hawk circling high in the sky above the creek shrieked loudly, causing a jackrabbit to dart wildly from a bush on the far side of the stream. Graywolf jumped, wrenched violently from his daydream by the sudden intrusion. Mallory, too, had heard the disturbance. With hands crossed over her breasts, she ran for the bank and reached for her clothes.

Graywolf dropped his gaze, slowly stepping back into the shadows. He was disgusted. What was he doing, standing there watching her like some kind of pervert? What had he been thinking? He had no right being there, no right watching her, no right wanting her.

He turned and soundlessly made his way back to camp. He cursed himself, shame tasting dark and bitter on his tongue. He wasn't sure what disturbed him more—his behavior, or the realization that he wanted the white woman. His behavior was inexcusable, but wanting her was out of the question.

He'd had no right to invade her privacy, to intrude on her solitude. It wasn't as though she'd been careless or bold. She'd chosen an isolated spot, had been justified in believing herself to be safe from observation. And although he was convinced she'd had no idea he'd been there, no clue that he had seen her, he felt guilty and ashamed. It hadn't been like the dream where she'd enticed him to come to her, or lured him into watching. He could have quietly backed away, could have turned away and no one would have been the wiser. And if he had, maybe he would have spared himself a lot of grief.

But the fact is he hadn't. He'd stood there in the bushes and watched, rendered motionless—and nearly witless—by the sight of her. He'd stood there and felt his body's reaction, felt a desire inside him he didn't welcome, and wanted no part of.

The small camp fire had burned low, and Graywolf reached for several pieces of the firewood he'd gathered. The sun was setting, and as he'd predicted, the wind had taken a turn toward cooler. He tossed the wood onto the embers and stoked them until the flames burned bright. She would want the fire's warmth by the time she returned. She would be cold—and wet.

He thought again of her beneath the spray of the falls, of her softly curved body and delicate white skin, and closed his eyes to the surge of emotion that assailed him. Somehow he had to find a way to forget, find a way to ignore the desire pounding inside him. This wasn't the woman for him—no white woman was—and it was up to him to remember that.

"You're right."

Graywolf bolted violently at the sound of her voice. He looked up from the fire, finding her searching through her backpack near the Jeep. "What?"

"I said you were right," she repeated, gathering up a few pieces of fresh clothing and heading for the tent. "It is turning cool."

He just nodded as she disappeared inside the tent. But she was out again in a few minutes, sporting a clean, dry T-shirt.

"Your hair's wet," he said, feeling awkward with the playacting. He knew exactly how it had gotten that way.

Mallory's hand went to her hair, and she smiled sheepishly. "Yeah, it is. I sort of ended up with more of a shower than just washing up," she confessed. "The stream was really quite large, and there was a waterfall. I was so sticky and hot, I just couldn't resist." She rubbed a hand over the opposite arm. "I feel a hundred percent better now."

Graywolf glanced back to the fire, trying not to notice the outline of her breasts against the T-shirt. It was too easy to remember how they had looked beneath the water's spray with their soft fullness and dusky centers.

He shook his head and cleared his throat loudly. "You should probably stay close to the fire now, though," he said, poking at the flames with a stick. "So you won't catch a chill."

"It feels good," she said, sitting across the fire from him and warming her hands. "Have you eaten yet?"

Graywolf shook his head. "No. Would you like something?"

Mallory smiled and nodded. "Actually, I'm starving."

Graywolf turned and reached for the box of canned goods that Hosteen Johnny had packed. "What do you feel like tonight—beans, fruit cocktail, hash or..." He picked up the last can and shrugged. "Or more beans?"

"No more SpaghettiOs?"

He held the smile. "Sorry."

She shrugged, tossing a small twig into the fire. "You decide, then. What can I do to help?"

He handed her a small skillet, then pulled out a can of corned beef hash and a can of fruit cocktail and began opening them with his knife. He handed her the hash, and while she scooped it into the skillet, he found the beef jerky and pulled out several large strips. He offered one of the strips to Mallory, and she hungrily gnawed off a piece.

"This is delicious jerky," she said, savoring the salty-spicy flavor. "This has got to be homemade. Do you make it yourself?"

"You're just hungry." Graywolf took the skillet back from her and set it over the embers. He wasn't in the mood for her schoolgirl manners or her friendly chitchat. He found them condescending and irritating. Why the incessant need to talk? The Navajo liked silence, understood it, were comfortable with it. Why couldn't she just shut up?

"Well, you're right about that," Mallory agreed with a friendly shrug. "But I'm serious, this is great. I haven't had jerky like this in a long time. Where do you get it?"

"They sell little packages of the stuff in every convenience store in the country," he said sarcastically, sure now that she was patronizing him. "Even in D.C."

If Mallory noticed his sarcasm, she ignored it. Instead, she made a face. "Yuck, you call that stuff jerky?"

He looked up at her. "You don't, I take it."

She shook her head. "My Grampa used to make jerky when we were kids. He used to let Marissa and me help. I gotta tell you, I hated having to slice that meat. Grampa would say, 'Thinner, make it thinner,'" she said, mocking his voice and mannerisms. She laughed then, biting off another mouthful of dried meat and gazing into the fire. "He would work for days getting his special marinade just right—all the spices and seasonings. I can still remember the smell." She held up the piece of jerky in her hand. "This is the best I've had since then."

Graywolf took a wooden spoon from his small cache of supplies and stirred the frying hash in the skillet. He didn't want to hear this, didn't want to know about her life and her background. He didn't want her to be any more real to him than she was right now. "My grandfather makes it."

Mallory reached for a plastic spoon from a paper bag and took a scoop of fruit from the can. "See? I knew it. You can't get jerky like this out of a package." She took another bite, her jaws working hard to chew. "Randy hated jerky. I could never understand that."

"Randy?"

"I'm sorry," she said as she finished chewing and swallowed. "Randy, my husband."

Graywolf's heart lurched in his chest. "You're married. I...didn't know."

"No, I'm not," she said, setting the rest of her jerky aside. Suddenly she didn't feel so hungry anymore. "Not any longer."

The wave of pain passed so quickly across her face he would have missed it completely if he hadn't been looking right at her. "You're divorced I take it?"

"Divorced," she mumbled, squeezing her lids closed tight and rubbing them. "Have you ever thought about what an ugly word that is?"

He studied her carefully, remembering how the water had flowed over her rich, honeyed skin. What kind of a man would walk away from beauty like that? "I guess that depends on whether you were the one who wanted it or not."

She opened her eyes and looked up at him. "No it doesn't. It's an ugly word no matter what the circumstances. I mean *divorce.* Can you think of a more sanitary term? Why don't we just call it what—a failure, a screw-up, a *huge* mistake. We're always trying to anaesthetize the end of a marriage, trying to make it sound more palatable. Divorce." She made a quiet, snorting laugh. "It's really just a dressed up way of saying loser."

The anger in her voice surprised him, and he wasn't sure if it was insight or foresight that made him understand she used the harsh, bitter words to cover a very deep hurt. "I take it that it wasn't an amicable split?"

She sat back, surprised. "Oh no, it was amicable. I mean, I think Randy and I both realized it had been a mistake, that we really weren't what the other needed."

He eased the pan of hash away from the flames. "Then what's the problem?"

Her eyes narrowed defensively. "What do you mean?"

"I mean it's obvious you have some regrets," he said flippantly, feeling unreasonably antagonistic. Why did the thought of her married to another man make him so uncomfortable? "If you both agreed it wasn't working, what's the problem?"

"The problem," she said quietly, staring into the flames of the camp fire. "The problem is that I *wanted* it to, and it didn't." She reached down and picked up a handful of dried twigs, tossing them into the fire. "You see, I was the girl everyone wanted to be. I had it made—the perfect sister, the perfect boyfriends, head cheerleader, homecoming queen, lots of friends. Everyone just expected I would take the world by storm." She gave a small, sad smile. "I guess I expected that too." She was quiet for a moment, feeling the heat of the flames along her face. "Do you have any idea how hard it is being perfect? How much pressure that puts on you? I mean things just *had* to turn out perfect for me."

Graywolf had set the frying pan aside, and sat watching her closely. He wasn't sure he wanted to hear any of this, wasn't sure he wanted to *feel* anything else, and yet he was fascinated. The perfect white woman wasn't so perfect after all. "And a less than perfect marriage didn't fit in the picture."

She laughed, but her laughter had a sad, hollow sound. "I took the world by storm all right. Miss Perfect stormed into marriage and screwed up royally." She tossed the rest of the twigs into the fire, watching the flames flare up. "I just wish if I'd had to screw up, I could have done it without hurting anyone else." She gave her head a little shake. What was she doing talking about all this? She'd hired him to find her sister, not listen to her complain. Embarrassed, she took a deep breath and dusted her hands off. "Geez, how did I get rambling about all of that? You must be bored stiff. Is that hash ready yet?"

Graywolf sensed her uneasiness, and understood the reason. Frankly he was a little uneasy himself. She'd revealed a lot just then, obviously more than she'd intended, and maybe they both needed a little time to reflect and absorb. They ate the rest of their meal in silence, mainly because he kept his head down, and his eyes directed on his food. The woman was becoming just a little too real to him, too complex. He'd liked it better when she was just a white woman, just someone he didn't like.

As the night grew late, the temperature continued to drop. Mallory bundled herself up again for the night—adding a shirt to her T-shirt, then a sweater, then the down parka. Graywolf added wood to the fire, coaxing it from a small cook fire to a warm, glowing blaze.

"Do you think it's a bad sign?"

He looked up from the fire to find her studying him. "Is what a bad sign?"

"It's been two days," she said quietly. "We haven't found anything—not even anything that could tell us if we're on the right track." She leaned forward, wrapping her arms around her knees. "Do you think it's a bad sign?"

Graywolf leaned back on his elbow, stretching his legs out in front of him. "Not really."

She picked up a small pebble by her feet and tossed it into the fire. "But it certainly isn't a good sign."

"I don't think it's any *sign* at all," Graywolf said. He made a sweeping gesture with his hand. "They don't call this the Big Res for nothing. There's a lot of territory to cover out here. You can't just do it overnight. And don't forget, your sister has a seven day start on us."

"I guess." Mallory sighed, sounding unconvinced. "I just thought...I don't know. I guess I thought we'd have found something by now."

Graywolf sat up slowly. He really wasn't in the mood to comfort her. "Look," he said, his voice more testy than comforting. "I know it isn't easy, but just try and be patient, okay?"

Mallory nodded her head, but his words had done little to ease her concerns. She stared at Graywolf through the fire, searching for something to get her mind off her fears. "Are you really a shaman, or was that just tabloid trash?"

"I've done some studying," Graywolf said, making light of the long hours of instruction and training he'd done since returning to the reservation.

"Have you ever done a sing?"

He glanced up, clearly surprised she would have any knowledge of the Navajo curing ceremonies. "What do you know about sings?"

"I've done a little reading," Mallory said with a little smile, pleased to know she could throw him a curve now and again. "I thought if I was going to be covering the powwow, it would help to know something about tribal customs and ceremonies."

"Ah, yes, a little reading. Just like a reporter," he said cynically. "And to think people have spent their lives studying our customs. They could take a lesson from you."

Mallory bristled at his sarcasm. "I didn't say I was an expert or anything," she said defensively, wondering why he always put the worst spin on everything she said. "I would think you would welcome an opportunity to educate the public on Navajo practices and rituals."

"Why should we care what the *white* public thinks about us?" he asked, not even trying to keep the bitterness out of his voice. "They don't seem to care what we think about them. Besides, you know what they say about a little knowledge being a dangerous thing."

"I don't believe knowledge is ever dangerous."

He laughed, a sound that had nothing to do with humor. "You have no idea what this powwow means to us. To you it's just some colorful ethnic thing—a souped-up craft fair or festival or something." He shook his head. "Do you have any idea what some of the tribes and lodges have had to do to get here, how long they've had to scrimp and save to make the trip? Some have given up all they have to participate. That's how important it is to them. You think reading some silly article you want to put in a newspaper about Navajo blankets and Hopi pottery will suddenly make people give a damn about what goes on in the reservations?"

"I didn't say that," she said, angry at his cutting description of the work she did. "But surely you can appreciate the fact that a lot of people find your customs and ceremonies interesting."

"Ah, yes, *interesting*," he said caustically. "There are going to be important issues discussed at this powwow—poverty issues, substance-abuse problems on the reservation, health and educational concerns. But will you cover any of that?" He shook his head, not giving her a chance to respond. "You forget, we've been through this before. No. You'll write about the colorful costumes, the funny-looking costumes—feathers, buckskin, loincloths." He laughed again. "By all means make us *interesting* to the American public. Do what you can to promote those old stereotypes." He snapped his fingers. "Hey, I know. Maybe you could help us to become a new, trendy culture—really start something, you know? Replace meditation or New Age philosophies." He held up his hand, envisioning the headlines. "How's this? Invite a Zuni to lunch—or hire a Hopi gardener, try a Cherokee massage. Or maybe study Navajo shamanism as a career enhancer and be the first in your block to ask for good fortune—to have a blessing way."

She studied him for a moment. "Why are you so angry?"

"Angry? You think I'm angry?"

"It certainly sounds that way."

"Does it bother you?" He glared at her from across the fire. "Does it make you a little uneasy to be out in the middle of nowhere with a savage? Are you afraid I'll whip out my war paint? Take your scalp?"

She could not only see the anger in his eyes, she could feel it. "Now who's promoting stereotypes?"

He turned away, staring out into the darkness and wishing she would just leave him alone. It was a stupid conversation they were having. He was arguing just for the sake of arguing, and not because he believed any of the nonsense he was saying. He didn't want her interested in him, or interested in the People. He just wanted her to shut up, he

wanted her to stop talking and leave him alone. He wanted
to forget about her, to get her out of his head and out of his
mind. But he couldn't do that when everywhere he looked,
she was there.

"You never answered my question."

He glanced back in her direction. The fire had burned
low, and the glowing embers made her hair look like liquid
gold. Annoyed, he sighed heavily. "All I've done tonight
lady, is answer your questions."

She knew he was irritated with her, and for some reason
it pleased her. She could rile him, and she would bet Benjamin Graywolf didn't get riled very often. He'd been bait-
ing her ever since they'd met, and it felt good to give the
shaman a bit of his own medicine. "No, you haven't. You
never answered when I asked you if you've ever performed
a sing."

He stared at her, his eyes barely more than dark slits. "A
couple of times."

"Have you cured anybody?" she asked, knowing she was
pushing.

He slowly stood and reached for his bedroll. "It's getting
late. You should get some rest."

Mallory nodded her head, rising to her feet. She started
for the tent, but then stopped. "Graywolf?"

He turned and looked at her. "Yes?"

"I've read where Navajos keep their names secret. Is
yours secret?"

He hesitated as he started to unroll the bag. "How could
it be secret?" he asked sarcastically. "You just said it?"

"No, I mean your *real* name, your war name."

Graywolf cursed silently to himself. She had done *some
reading*. "What about it?"

"Do you have one?"

He straightened the bedroll with a violent shake, purposely avoiding looking at her. "Most Navajo do."

"So, is that a yes or a no?"

"Yes, I have one."

"Is it?"

He stopped and turned to her. "Is it what?"

"Secret?"

He stared at her. In the dim light, her white skin looked soft and inviting, and he felt the muscles in his stomach tighten. He knew what she looked like, knew how beautiful her body was beneath all those clothes, and he hated himself for wanting her. He wanted to close the short distance between them. He just wasn't sure if he wanted to strangle her, or gather her into his arms.

"Go to bed," he said in a tight voice.

"Good night, Graywolf," she said, reaching for the zipper on the flap of her tent. "*If* that really is your name."

"Slow down."

"What is it?"

"I think I saw something."

"What?" Graywolf asked, easing his foot off the accelerator.

"I'm not sure," Mallory said, shoving her sunglasses up to rest on the top of her head. "It was a flash or something, I'm not sure—there!" She leaned forward, pointing at a spot in the distance. "I saw it again."

"There?" Graywolf asked, sensing something in her tone.

"No, there," she said. "Just beyond those trees."

Graywolf squinted, peering through the windshield to the thicket of brush and cottonwoods beyond. Suddenly, he caught a glimpse of light. "I see it."

He gunned the motor, heading for the spot as fast as the rough road would allow. As they approached, he shot a glance in Mallory's direction. She was perched on the edge of her seat, both hands braced against the dash and her eyes intent on the spot where they headed.

He'd awoken this morning with a...*feeling,* and he'd known they were on to something. It happened that way sometimes. He'd get a feeling, an inkling—nothing as clearly defined as a vision, or a forewarning. Just a... feeling.

He turned back to the flash of color in the road in front of them. He wasn't sure yet what it was they'd stumbled on to, but intuition told him it had something to do with her sister. Turning back to Mallory again, he could more than see the hope and excitement in her face, he could feel it. The bond between her and her sister was strong, so strong that it had kept her hope alive for eight long days. But was it strong enough to help her cope with what they might find?

"It's her car," Mallory shrieked, grabbing Graywolf's arm and tugging on it excitedly. "Graywolf. My God, that's it. That's Marissa's car."

It seemed to take an eternity for the Jeep to travel the lengthy distance over the potholed road to where the blue, late model Volvo wagon sat. The Jeep lurched and pitched violently, tossing them around until finally Graywolf brought it to a stop about thirty feet from where the car rested. He'd purposely parked at a distance with the intention of having Mallory wait in the Jeep while he checked things out—just in case. But before he could even reach for the key to turn the motor off, she was out the door and running toward the car.

"Wait," he called, leaving the engine running and taking off after her. "Hey, stop. Come back here."

Mallory heard him calling, but she couldn't stop. It was Marissa's car—right there, right in front of them. Finally, after more than two long days of searching, they had the first tangible piece of evidence to prove they'd been on the right track. At last there was something to show that Marissa hadn't just vanished into thin air.

"Wait," Graywolf said again, catching up with her and grabbing her by the wrist.

Mallory skittered to a stop, held firm by Graywolf's grip. "What's the matter?" she demanded, struggling against his hold. "Why are you stopping me?"

"Mallory," he said, moving his hold from her wrist to her upper arms, and holding her firm. He'd forgotten about the tension there was between them, about his anger and impatience with her. All he could think about was the pain in her eyes, and how he wanted to take it away. "Stop. Calm down for just a moment." He held her until she stopped struggling.

With a resigned sigh, she looked up at him. "All right, all right. I'm calm, I'm calm. What's the matter? Why can't I go?"

"I want to check things out first," he said. His voice was quiet and deliberate, but he emphasized the importance of his words by tightening his hold on her arms. "I want you to wait for me—right here. Do you understand?"

"Wait for you?" Mallory protested, shaking her head and struggling again. "No. Why?"

But she knew why, he could see it in her eyes. "I have to check things out first," he told her again, giving her a small shake to calm her down again. "And you have to wait for me here."

Mallory looked toward her sister's car, then closed her eyes. When she looked up at him, tears spilled onto her cheeks. "You think something has happened, don't you. You think we're going to find her...that she's..."

"No," Graywolf said firmly. Without realizing it, he'd pulled her close. "No, I don't think that." The lie had been a small one, but it had been necessary. "I just want to check it out first, and I need you to help me. I need you to wait for me, right here. I'll come right back for you."

Mallory glanced at the car, and then back into his dark eyes again. "Honestly?"

"Honestly."

"And you really don't think she's . . . she's . . ."

"Hey, we had an arrangement," he reminded her in a soft voice, reaching up and wiping at a tear on her cheek with the back of a finger. "Remember? I tell you any *feelings* I have about your sister, and you tell me yours, right? I haven't had any." He looked down at her, thinking how natural and comfortable she felt in his arms. "Now you'll stay?"

Mallory nodded. "Yes."

"Promise?"

"I promise," Mallory whispered.

He led her back to the Jeep. Reaching across the passenger seat, he turned off the running motor and settled her inside. But as he turned and started back toward the abandoned car, he could feel her eyes watching his every move.

When he got nearer, he slowly began to circle the area where the car was parked, instinctively scanning the sandy ground for any sign of tire tracks or footprints. There were no signs of either. It was as if the sky had opened up and dropped the suburban-looking station wagon into its place in the sand.

But Graywolf knew better. The faint, rippled ridges in the sand were clear signs of a flash flood, something that was as natural to the area as was the sun. And it was obvious that recent floodwaters had wiped all signs of tracks from the area.

He walked carefully to the car. The left front tire was flat and buried to the hubcap in mud, which days ago had dried and cracked around it. Even before he'd peered through the windows, he'd known there would be no one inside. Marissa Wakefield had been here, but she was long gone now. Still, she had left something behind that might help them— a box full of school supplies, and a carload of feelings.

Graywolf opened the car door, taking a seat behind the wheel. Closing his eyes, he immediately smelled the rain, heard it pelting against the roof, and felt it cold against his face. Marissa Wakefield had driven her car to this spot, in the darkness, and in the rain.

Graywolf lifted his hands to the steering wheel, placing them on the spots where Marissa's had rested. He could feel her presence in the car, feel her anxiety and her fear. She had lifted a hand to her necklace, the gold cluster of stars, and she had thought of her sister.

Graywolf opened his eyes, feeling the sun again and feeling the connection with Marissa slipping away. She had been there all right, not long ago. But there had been something else, too. She hadn't been alone.

Mallory thought she would go crazy waiting. She watched as Graywolf studied the sand, checked the outlying area and slowly circled the car. His slow, steady deliberations seemed to take forever, and impatience threatened her very sanity. She hadn't realized she was holding her breath until her depleted lungs had her gasping for a fresh supply.

Mallory felt a lump of emotion form in her throat. The comfortable-looking station wagon looked so endearingly familiar. She and Marissa had shopped for it together before Marissa had taken the job in Arizona. But seeing it now—looking so out of place and forgotten against the rugged canyon walls—made her want to cry.

She'd been so excited, so thrilled, when she'd spotted it. For a foolish moment she'd thought this whole nightmare was over, that she would have Marissa back and everything would be okay again—back to normal. But now, watching Graywolf slowly approaching the car, she wasn't so sure. She was almost afraid of what he'd find.

She knew why he'd wanted her to wait, and she knew it had nothing to do with him wanting to "check things out." He hadn't wanted her with him in case he found Marissa's body.

Mallory closed her eyes. She didn't even want to think about that, even though that thought had plagued her since this whole thing started. Still, Graywolf had told her to trust her feelings, and despite her fears and the evidence to the contrary, her feeling was that Marissa was still alive. They were sisters, they had shared so much, they had always been so close. It just seemed impossible that Marissa could be dead without her somehow knowing it.

Mallory opened her eyes, staring at Graywolf as he sat behind the wheel of the car. Marissa wasn't dead—she couldn't be. He wouldn't be sitting there like that if she were. She had to admit there were times when she thought Graywolf had been leading her on a wild-goose chase. The idea of Marissa driving out here to the middle of nowhere seemed so crazy, so senseless, so hard to believe.

She looked again at her sister's dirty, mud-spattered car. And yet, believe she did. She didn't know how he'd done it, nor did she care, but somehow Benjamin Graywolf had led them to Marissa's car, and she didn't doubt that sooner or later he would lead them to Marissa, as well. She just hoped it would be soon. Even though some instinct or feeling told her Marissa was still alive, she knew all too well that no one could survive out in this harsh, unrelenting wilderness alone for long.

Just then Mallory's heart leapt into her throat. Graywolf had gotten out of the car, and was motioning for her to come.

Chapter 8

SUZIE CHARLEY: finished *Charlotte's Web*. Shows continued improvement, but still having difficulty with hard *r* sounds (pronounced as *w*). Speech therapy referral sent to reservation clinic 2/5—second request mailed 3/25. Loves Laura Ingalls Wilder and E. B. White (note—find *The Trumpet of the Swan*).

TOMAS NEZ: still under task. Attention span limited. Behavior problems increasing—home problems. Gets bored easily (note—try comic books, *Ann Can Fly*, videos?). Check eyesight/hearing. P.S. Loves red vines.

Mallory stared down at Marissa's neat, precise handwriting and felt emotion thick in her throat. She quietly closed her sister's journal and slipped it back into the box of school supplies Graywolf had found in the back of the car. Except for the box, and the normal contents of the glove compartment—box of tissues, car registration, candy wrappers and several gasoline receipts—the car had been empty. There had been nothing to give them a clue as to where Marissa was, or why she'd driven to that spot. Feeling hot tears slip down her cheeks, Mallory pushed the box aside. It was more than she could take right now to look through the rest of Marissa's things, not in the desolate canyon with its hot, dry wind and glaring sun.

"Anything interesting in there?"

Mallory glanced up, swiping quickly at the tears on her cheeks. Graywolf stood with a hand braced against the open hatch of the station wagon, peering down at her. "Just her notes. School supplies," she said with a careless gesture of her hand. "I thought you said you'd looked through it?"

He had. She'd just looked so sad sitting there he hadn't known what else to say. "Just a quick glance," he lied.

Mallory reached back inside the box and picked up the journal again. "I just don't understand," she said, looking up at him helplessly. "I mean, look at this. All her stuff is here—books, reports, papers, supplies. But nothing else—no sign of anything, no tracks—nothing. What could have happened to her? Where did she go?" Mallory shook her head again, frustrated. "What did she do, vanish into thin air? People just don't disappear without a trace."

"Oh, there are traces," Graywolf said matter-of-factly, pushing himself back away from the car. He couldn't take any more of that soft, vulnerable look of hers. It made him feel awkward and inept. She was hurting, and in pain, but he wasn't about to be cast in the role of her comforter. It wasn't his job to console her, he wasn't being paid to bring solace.

"What do you mean?"

He gestured to her. "Follow me."

Mallory slid off the tailgate of the car and trailed after him to the driver's side of the car. At the door, he stopped.

"There," he asked, pointing to the roof near the car's luggage rack. "See that?"

Mallory did her best to follow the line of his hand, studying the car's roof, but could see nothing. Bewildered, she turned to him. "See what?"

"Beneath the dust," he said, pointing again. "They're faint, but look."

Mallory examined the area again, this time realizing there was a large smudged area in the center of the roof, buried beneath a dense blanket of dust. Turning, she looked up at him. "What is it?"

"Not it," he corrected. "Them. They're prints. Lots of them."

"Prints?" Mallory murmured, looking back at the car's roof and feeling gooseflesh rise on her arms. "You mean Marissa was up there? She was on the roof?"

Graywolf shrugged, taking a deep breath. "Well, someone was. If you bend down just a little and look over here…" he said, bending close and positioning her just right with a hand on her shoulder. With his other hand, he carefully pointed to an area in the middle of the roof. "You can make out a handprint here. And—" repositioning her, he pointed again "—another over here."

At the angle he had placed her, Mallory could make out a faint outline of first one handprint, and then another, in the dust. "Handprints, I see them." She turned and looked up at Graywolf excitedly. "She left her handprints."

Graywolf saw her excited smile, saw the exhilaration in her misty blue-green eyes that had replaced the sorrow, and felt a warming in his belly. Only then did he realize just how close they were standing, how delicate and small her shoulder felt beneath his touch. A picture flashed in his brain of her standing beneath the waterfall—hair wet and skin glistening—and the warmth in his belly became an inferno. He stepped back, awkwardly lifting his hand from her shoulder. "Well, someone did."

The smile faded from her lips. "You mean you don't think they're hers?"

"One of them could be."

Mallory cocked her head to one side, confused. "I don't understand."

"The prints," he said, pointing to them again. "They're from two different people."

An icy chill hit Mallory's spine, and she shivered. "You can tell that just from looking, or is that something you've... *seen?*"

"Something I've seen?" Graywolf repeated, almost welcoming the anger. It put things back into perspective, made him forget about the troubling images of water, and wet hair, and smooth, silky skin. "You mean when I gazed into my crystal ball?" he snapped.

Mallory stepped back a pace, surprised by his sudden burst of anger. "Look, I'm sorry."

"You know, I do have some experience in tracking," he pointed out. "You don't have to be a shaman or have second sight to draw conclusions or make assumptions."

Mallory squeezed her eyes shut tight. It had been a stupid thing to say. After all, it had been more than psychic perceptions and impressions that had brought them this far, and yet she was treating him like her genie in a bottle. "I really am sorry. I wasn't thinking. It's just..." Her voice faded, and she gave him a helpless look. "I'm sorry."

Graywolf drew in a deep breath. He felt petty and small. What was he doing? What was it about this woman that seemed to bring out the worst in him? This wasn't the time to get touchy and overreact. She was terrified for her sister's safety, not trying to insult him, and he was acting like a jerk concerned about a bruised ego. "No, I'm the one who's sorry."

Mallory risked a small smile. Tensions were strained enough between them; the last thing she wanted was to make them worse. He could be so hard, so cold to her, and yet she trusted him as she never had anyone else in her life.

"You believe someone's with her," she said after a moment, unconsciously taking a step closer to him. "You think someone made her drive out here."

"It's something we need to consider," Graywolf said, even though every instinct he had told him Marissa Wakefield had not driven alone into the desert. "Someone, or something."

Mallory turned and stared at the prints again. "But on the roof? What was she doing on the roof?"

Graywolf motioned her to follow him again. "Come over here." He led her past the car, to a flat, dry spot in the sand. Kneeling down, he pointed to the ground. "See the rippled marks in the dirt along here?"

She knelt down beside him, poking at the dry, crusty clay. "Yeah. It feels like dried mud."

"It is," he said, slowly rising to his feet. "From a flash flood that flowed through here." He kicked at the dirt. "Probably four, five days ago." He nodded his head, gesturing to the car. "That's what she got stuck in—the mud that formed when the water started to flow down here."

"Oh, my God," Mallory gasped, clasping her hands over her mouth. "And she crawled up onto the roof because the car was sinking?"

"It's been known to happen," Graywolf pointed out. "The water can rise pretty fast in those floods, turn everything to mud—it can get scary."

"So you think she . . . *they* climbed out onto the roof and left the car?"

"That would be my bet."

"Yeah," she murmured, turning all this over in her mind. "That makes sense." She rose quickly to her feet. "So you think they're on foot now?"

Graywolf nodded. "Looks that way."

She looked around them, shaking her head. "But where? Where would they go? There's nothing out here—there isn't even a road anymore. I don't see any footprints."

Graywolf scanned the area with squinted eyes. "The flood destroyed what was left of the road, the water obliterated any tracks they might have left."

Mallory turned to him, bewildered and confused. "So what do we do now?"

Graywolf turned to her, the slightest of smiles parting the hard line of his lips. "I guess we bring out the crystal ball."

Mallory's eyes widened. "I was right, then. You have had a vision. You know something about Marissa."

"Slow down, slow down," Graywolf cautioned, reluctant to describe the shadowy images and sensations he'd picked up from the inside of the car as a clearly defined vision. "There was nothing specific. Just an . . . impression, a hunch."

"Tell me," Mallory pleaded, waving off his caveat impatiently. She knew better than to ignore hunches. "What was it? Where do you think they went?"

Graywolf turned and pointed to the mountains rising up out of the canyon floor. "I think they went that way."

Mallory followed the line of his vision, staring up at the rugged towers of earth and stone. They seemed to go on forever, stretching to the very doorstep of heaven. "We're going to climb the mountain?"

"We're not. I am. You're going to take the Jeep back to Rawley's and wait for me there."

"What?" Mallory turned slowly, staring up at him. "What are you talking about?"

"Mallory," he said reasonably, trying to ignore the look of betrayal in her eyes. "This is a whole new ball game here. Driving around the desert is one thing. But these mountains are rough, they can be killers. I can't take you with me."

"No, no, no," Mallory said, shaking her head and refusing to listen. "We had a deal."

"The deal has changed. This is different—"

"No," she said again, cutting him off. She felt betrayed and angry. He knew how important this was to her, he knew how much it meant to her to be a part of the search. How could he think she could sit back and just wait? "This is not negotiable," she said in a low voice. "I'm coming with you."

"It's too dangerous," he insisted.

"We had an arrangement," she argued, her chest rising and falling with huge gasps of emotion.

"And I'm changing it." He stood with his hands on his hips, staring down at her. Why couldn't she be reasonable just this once? Why did everything have to be an argument with her, a power play?

He braced himself for her fiery response, prepared himself to do battle. He expected her to rage at him, expected her to rant and rave and wrestle it out. Only, as she stood there looking up at him, it was as if all the fight had drained from her. She looked small and exposed, and Graywolf cursed violently beneath his breath.

Mallory gazed into his black, unyielding eyes, feeling exhausted and alone. She couldn't fight him, and all her fears as well. He was her only hope, her only chance of finding Marissa. He just had to understand.

She took a few steps forward, reaching out and placing an unsteady hand onto his arm. "I have to go," she said, her voice barely above a whisper. "My sister's out there, she's in trouble and she needs me." The hand on his arm gripped desperately. "You promised me, Graywolf. You promised to take me with you."

Graywolf felt the cool touch of her hand along his arm and cursed again. *Damn her,* he swore beneath his breath. *Damn her to hell.* He'd been prepared to handle her anger and her arrogance, he was all set to deal with her demands and her insolence. But this helplessness, and the defeated, defenseless look in her eyes, was more than he could take. He felt himself caving in, acquiescing to feelings and emotions he'd been fighting from the moment he'd laid eyes on her.

"It'll be a rough climb, and I can't let you slow me down," he warned, turning away. After a few steps, he turned back. "If you can't keep up, you get left behind—got it?"

"Got it," Mallory murmured, watching as he stalked back across the hardened clay toward the Jeep. There were

a lot of things she could have pointed out to him just then—
the fact that she hadn't slowed him down yet, the fact that
he hadn't shown her so much as a whit of consideration
since they'd left Sedona, and like that he had yet to hear a
complaint from her—but she didn't. Arguing would only
alienate him more, and the strain between them was bad
enough already. The important thing was that he was taking her with him, and they were going to find Marissa.

She glanced back up the steep mountain pass as it rose up
from the canyon and twisted through jagged rock and rugged stone. Marissa was somewhere on that mountain—
Mallory wasn't sure just how she knew it, she just did. And
she didn't care how steep the trail was or how harsh the
conditions became, she was going to find her sister—even
if it meant climbing that sucker all the way to the top.

"Ready?"

Mallory shifted her weight, adjusting the pack on her
back to a more comfortable position. Growing up in Jackson, she and Marissa had done their share of hiking through
the California foothills, so the prospect of steep trails and
harsh terrain wasn't exactly a new one for her. Last summer she'd even accompanied friends on several backpack-
ing trips in the mountains of Virginia and Maryland. Of
course, the trails she'd followed then were tame compared
to the rugged Arizona landscape, and the bulky, unwieldy
pack Graywolf had strapped to her back was a far cry from
the expensive, state-of-the-art equipment she had used then,
but she was determined not to complain. Graywolf would
like nothing more than to find an excuse to leave her behind, and she wasn't about to let that happen.

She adjusted the shoulder straps of the pack, jostled the
load into place and smiled up at him sweetly. "Ready."

After leaving Marissa's car, Graywolf had driven the Jeep
as far as he could up the mountain pass. But the narrow
track and steep terrain soon made the route impassable.
They unloaded what supplies they needed and distributed

them between the two packs, then it was time to strike out on foot.

"Stay close, and don't go wandering off," Graywolf instructed, reaching for the buckle on her shoulder strap and giving it a yank. "And for God's sake watch your step," he added irritably as he turned and started up the narrow pass. "The last thing I need is you with a busted ankle."

Mallory waited until his back was to her, then made a face, mimicking his grouchy expression. If he was trying to hide his displeasure, he wasn't doing a very good job. But he could bully her all he wanted, it wasn't going to work. He might think she was nothing more than a weak, delicate white woman unaccustomed to the ways of the West, but he was about to have a rude awakening. Marissa needed her, and there was nothing—not some sorehead Navajo mystic, not some cumbersome backpack, and least of all not some damn Arizona mountain—that was going to keep her from her sister.

The afternoon was already drawing to a close, but Graywolf had told her he'd hoped to get in a couple of hours of hiking before they lost the light. Mallory dutifully kept pace behind him, taking a curious pleasure in placing her boots into his footprints. She liked to see the easy, effortless movement of his body. It had symmetry and balance, with the graceful sway of his shoulders and the athletic motion of his legs. He was a man used to physical activity. The way he made his way up the steep incline was literally like watching poetry in motion.

She smiled. Symmetry and balance. She'd read enough about Native American traditions to know that both were important to the Navajo. They liked balance—harmony, both in life and in nature, and Graywolf seemed to fit that perfectly. He was physically strong, to which his powerful body could attest. But there was a spiritual strength to him as well—a perfect balance.

But she cautioned herself. She might have come to trust him, might even have come to depend on him, but that didn't mean she had to like him. He was too hostile, too angry, and he'd made it very clear just how little he thought of her and what she did. So instead of focusing on his tall frame and muscular physique, she concentrated on keeping pace, on watching her step and on staying out of his way.

Compared to the long, arduous hours of riding in the Jeep, the ascension up the mountain was almost as exhilarating as it was strenuous. Mallory seemed to forget about the bulky backpack and the strain of overworked muscles. The sheer act of physical movement was a rare treat after the days of confinement in the Jeep. Several times she was aware of Graywolf's backward glances—checking on her, seeing if she was falling behind. It was silly, but it pleased her that she could keep pace with him, pleased her to show him he was wrong about her—again!

It wasn't until Graywolf came to an abrupt halt at a gravelly clearing that Mallory realized just how hard she'd been concentrating. She turned, surprised to see just how far up from the canyon floor they had climbed. The sun had begun to sink into the horizon, and the long shadows streaked out across the desert. Far below she could just make out the outline of the Jeep, parked at the base of the mountain. It looked so tiny and insignificant against the vast panorama.

"It's so beautiful," Mallory murmured, gazing out across the landscape.

Graywolf glanced back. The pale, muted hues from the setting sun gave her skin a soft, rosy glow. It was all he could do to stop himself from reaching out, from touching her and pulling her to him.

"Yeah, well," he said, dismissing the breathtaking panorama with a tight voice. "We'll make camp here for the night."

Mallory gave her head a little shake, forcing her attention away from the incredible sight. "What would you like me to do?"

"It'll be cold tonight. We'll need wood for a fire," he said, slipping off his pack and helping her off with hers. "You could look for some."

"Okay," Mallory said good-naturedly, rubbing her shoulders where the straps had pressed. She surveyed the area for a moment, then headed for a spot up the trail where a tree limb had fallen.

"Watch your step," Graywolf said testily.

"I know, I know," she said, turning back and giving him a deliberate look. "The last thing you need..." She let her words drift off as she turned and started back up the trail.

Graywolf watched for a moment, then turned and began unloading the packs. In a million years he would never be able to figure the woman out. She was the very picture of the fragile, frail white woman with her delicate hands and fair skin. He wouldn't have thought she'd last ten minutes climbing up the steep trail with the afternoon sun beating down on them and the heavy pack strapped to her back. He'd purposely kept their pace brisk, purposely pushed hard, expecting any moment that she would capitulate, admit the task was too much for her and return to the Jeep where she belonged.

He gathered up a number of rocks, fashioning them into a circle to form a fire ring. He'd hoped after a few good hours of climbing she would be crying to return to the Jeep and drive back to Rawley's and wait for him there. But instead, there had been no complaint from her, no plea for rest or consideration—not even so much as a hint of protest or dissent. To his never-ending surprise, she'd kept pace, kept quiet and kept out of his way. The woman was an enigma.

"This enough?"

He turned around, surprised to see her standing there with a huge armload of firewood. Her hair fell loose around her shoulders, and the color in her cheeks was rich and alive. She looked as fresh and as energetic as when they'd started up the mountain, and he found himself cursing inwardly again.

"For starters," he grumbled, reaching for one of the packs.

Mallory rolled her eyes, bending down and depositing the wood near the ring he'd formed with the rocks. "I can get some more if you like."

"Later," he muttered, pulling his bedroll from the pack. "You realize there will be no tent tonight. You going to be okay with that?"

She gave him a sidelong glance. "Careful medicine man, or I might start to think you are actually concerned about my comfort."

"I just don't want you panicking in the darkness, that's all." Graywolf shrugged, unrolled the sleeping bag and positioned it near the fire ring. "Women do that sometimes."

"I don't panic in the darkness," she pointed out dryly, wondering just who these women were that he'd had out in the darkness. "Besides, my sister and I used to sleep out under the stars all the time when we were young." She began to stack the wood in the ring, starting with a handful of small, dry twigs and constructing a shelter of larger twigs atop them. "And for your information, I was also a Girl Scout. I camped out a lot as a kid and know how to cook over an open fire." She reached into her pocket and brought out a small book of matches. Striking one, she lit the dry brush and slowly coaxed the fire to start, first adding twigs, and then larger pieces of wood. "So don't be thinking you Indians have the market cornered on wilderness survival."

"Navajo."

She turned, still smiling, and looked up at him. "Excuse me?"

"I'm Navajo."

"Yes, you are, aren't you," she said with a saccharine smile. She knew he was annoyed with her, but that only made her want to smile more. She could get his goat, and she hadn't enjoyed anything so much since she was eleven years old and she and Marissa did battle with their obnoxious cousin Gregory. If Benjamin Graywolf found her irritating, it was small recompense for all the hard times he'd given her.

Just then a cool gust of wind blew down the mountain, stirring up dust and whipping wildly at the flames in the fire ring. Graywolf drew in a deep breath, swallowing his frustration and reminding himself that nothing about this white woman was of any importance to him. He glanced up the mountain ridge to the spot where Mallory had gathered the wood, and then back to where she sat working the fire. If she wanted to play at being the perky Girl Scout, he might as well give her something to sink her teeth into.

"Since we'll probably want to keep a fire burning most of the night, I think I'll go find some more wood to burn," he announced as he turned and started up the trail toward the fallen limb. After a few steps, he stopped and turned back around. "And since you're such a whiz with the wilderness skills, you can stay up tonight and tend it."

The smile slowly disappeared from Mallory's face. She should have known better than to try to have the last word with him. The man was too stubborn, too pigheaded, to let anyone get the better of him—especially her.

The darkness seemed to fall like a blanket, and with it came the cold. Mallory ate her meager dinner ration of beef jerky and crackers, and began to think staying up to tend the burning fire wasn't going to be very difficult, after all. It was obvious that Graywolf hadn't seriously meant for her to remain up the entire night, but the wind was bitter cold, and it seemed as though the mountain had come alive with strange sounds and dark shadows. The way she felt, she was certain she would never be able to fall asleep, anyway.

Mallory didn't remember feeling sleepy, she had no recollection of becoming groggy. Nor could she remember her eyelids growing heavy or her head lolling back against the rock she leaned against. That was why when Graywolf grabbed her by the shoulders and began to shake her violently, she was utterly confused and disoriented.

"W-what?" she stammered, fighting against his hold and blinking her eyes wildly. "What is it? What's happened?"

"A child," Graywolf said quietly, holding her by the shoulders and staring down into her dazed, sleep-heavy eyes. "Tell me about your sister and the child."

Chapter 9

"Child?" Mallory mumbled, struggling to make sense of what he was asking. "What child? You mean Josh?"

"Josh is her child?" Graywolf asked, releasing his hold on her shoulders. "Her baby."

"Yes," she nodded, slipping the sleeping bag down to free her arms. "But Josh isn't a baby. He's a teenager, almost fifteen."

"No," he mumbled, sitting back and staring into the fire. "No, it's not him."

"What's not?" Mallory insisted. "What are you talking about? Graywolf, what's all this about?"

"I dreamed," he murmured, closing his eyes and rubbing at his temples. "Your sister and a child."

"Well..." Mallory paused, absently scratching her head, struggling to push aside the last remnants of sleepiness. "She's...she's a teacher," she pointed out excitedly. "Maybe one of her students?"

Graywolf shook his head. "No, this child is an infant, a newborn." He opened his eyes and turned to her. "This is a child she loves. A Navajo child."

Mallory sank back against the hard rock. "A Navajo child? I don't understand."

Graywolf stared at her for a moment, thinking of the vision, of the small child in the arms of the *biligaana* woman. Its shock of black hair and flat, wide face was unmistakably Navajo, and yet the woman who held it so gently, weeping tears of joy, was the pale-haired *biligaana* he had dreamed about for weeks—like Mallory, and yet not like her at all.

Marissa, her sister. He understood that now. The woman who had filled his visions, the woman he'd been seeing in his head for so long, was Marissa Wakefield. But what did this last vision mean? What were the images and the feelings trying to tell him? They had been so clear—focused and in great detail. Like frames on a reel of film replaying over and over again the same, brief scene. He could see the small tear on Marissa's long-sleeved shirt, the smut of mud on the cuff—dry red clay like the mud her car had sunk into. She stood before a fire, he could see the light of the flames reflecting golden off her hair. The baby cried—the feisty, spirited wail of a newborn shouting its entrance into the world.

Was this the reason she had disappeared? Was it a child that had brought her into the wilderness, that had brought her to a mountaintop through heat, rain and flood?

"Is there a chance your sister..." Graywolf ran a hand through his long black hair, knowing the question was an obvious one. "Could your sister be...pregnant?"

"What?" Mallory gasped, sitting upright. "Pregnant? No, that's crazy. Marissa couldn't be pregnant."

Mallory's utter rejection of the notion had Graywolf's eyes darkening suspiciously. "Why?" he snorted. "Because she's unable to bear a child, or because it's a Navajo child?"

"No," Mallory said deliberately, glaring up at him. The bitterness and hostility in his voice had been like a hot knife in the heart, showing her once again just how little he thought of her, how little trust he had. "Not because of that. Because she's my sister, and because I'd know if she was going to have a baby."

"How would you know?" he demanded. "How can you be so sure? You said yourself you hadn't seen your sister in over a year. A lot could have happened in that time."

Mallory reached for the zipper on the sleeping bag and angrily yanked it open. "Why would Marissa want to keep something like that from me? *Me*—her own sister."

Graywolf shrugged. "Shame. It wouldn't be the first time a woman was ashamed to bear the child of an Indian."

Mallory hated it when he tried purposely to be insolent and rude. She tossed off the bedroll and rose to her feet. Her chest heaved up and down rapidly, betraying the anger and the emotion she felt. "That's just plain stupid," she scoffed. "Marissa and I share everything—I thought you understood that."

"Everything?" he asked skeptically, rising slowly to stand in front of her. "Would your sister have told you if she had an Indian lover? Would she have been eager to tell you that she'd slept with a savage, that the child in her belly was a half-breed?"

Mallory had never been a violent person, had never struck anyone before—not even Randy when he'd lashed out at her during his mindless, drunken rages. So when the palm of her hand made a sudden stinging contact with the hard surface of Graywolf's cheek, she was as shocked and surprised as he.

It was reflex that had Graywolf reaching out, that had him grabbing her wrist roughly and yanking her to him. Her eyes looked like blue ice, glaring up at him, and he felt their bitter cold all the way to his soul. What was he doing? What kind of power did she have over him? He couldn't even think straight when he was around her, couldn't make sense out of anything he felt or said. Slowly, he released his hold on her wrist and dropped his hand to his side.

"How dare you speak to me like that?" Mallory rasped in a hoarse, ragged voice, rubbing at the raw, red streaks his hand had left on her arm. "How dare you make those kinds of judgments?"

He dropped his gaze, not wanting to talk, not even wanting to look at her. "Okay, forget it."

"If you've had a vision of Marissa and a child," she went on, "a *Navajo* child—then it has to mean something else. Don't you think I'd know if my sister was pregnant, or had a child? Don't you think I'd *know?*"

"Okay," he shouted out defensively. He just wanted to drop it—wanted to forget all the anger, forget all the stupid things he'd said, forget how icy and harsh her eyes had been and how stony cold they'd made him feel. "Just...forget it."

She turned, stomping over the discarded bedroll and reaching for a large log from the pile of wood they'd gathered. "You of all people should understand that. You of all peo—"

"Look," he shouted, cutting her off. He drew in a deep breath. "Look," he said again, in a calmer, quieter voice. "It was a stupid thing to say, I admit it. I'm..." He stopped and ran a hand through his hair again. "I'm...sorry."

Mallory dropped the log on the fire, rubbing her palms together to clean off her hands. "I'm sorry, too, about... well, you know, about the slap."

Graywolf touched the spot on his cheek where it still stung. Susan had tried to slap him once, when he'd confronted her about the news story that had broken in the front page of a tabloid. But she'd been too slow, too uncertain, and he'd caught her hand before it had time to make contact.

There had been nothing slow, nothing uncertain, in Mallory Wakefield's response. She'd taken him completely by surprise. She'd struck out viscerally and automatically, in defense of her sister, and he suspected she'd do the same for anyone she loved.

"Forget it," he mumbled, absently rubbing his cheek.

"It's just that if you knew Marissa," she said, her throat feeling tight, "if you knew the kind of person she is, how much kindness there is in her, how much love... It would be impossible for her to feel ashamed or embarrassed about anyone she loved—especially a child, and especially her own child."

"Okay," Graywolf said with a sigh. "If the child is not hers, whose could it be?"

Mallory shook her head. "I have no idea. What else did you see?"

Graywolf sat back down on his bedroll before the fire and told her everything about the vision. He described in detail the scene that had played in his head—of Marissa holding the newborn Navajo infant, of her torn shirt, dirty face, and the swell of love in her heart. They kicked around a few ideas, tossed out a number of possibilities, and tried to figure out just how it could help them in their search.

Of course, what he didn't share with her was the dream— the real, honest-to-God dream, the just-like-everyone-else-gets kind of dream, the dream the vision had interrupted, the dream he'd had about her. In it she had been back at the stream, standing beneath the flow of water, her bare skin wet and smooth. Only this time, he had stood in the water with her, his hands moving over her wet flesh, exploring and seeking. In the dream there had been no taboos or inhibitions, no doubt or suspicion. It had just been the two of them—alone, with only a desperate hunger for each other. He had pulled her to him, had drawn that slender body of hers next to his. She had sighed his name, had whispered sweet, seductive pleas into his ear. His body had grown hard, desire had pounded at him, making him feel hotter than the flames of the fire. He could feel the wet coolness of her skin, could taste the sweetness of the water on her lips, could feel the pressure of her legs as they wrapped around him.

Graywolf closed his eyes, remembering the dream and fighting off an almost overwhelming feeling of longing. He could understand how his ancestors believed in the mystic powers of the white woman. This one had certainly cast a spell on him. There was no escape from her, no place to run and hide. She was everywhere he looked, every place he went. He was forced to endure her presence during the long hot hours of the day, only to be haunted by her image in his dreams at night.

He opened his eyes, giving his head a shake in an effort to dispel the power of the incantation. It was more important than ever that they find her sister as soon as possible. He wanted Mallory Wakefield and her haunting sea blue eyes out of his world, and out of his life forever. He would tell her everything about the vision, anything she would ever want to know, anything that might help lead them to her sister. But the dream . . . the dream belonged to him. He would bear its torture alone.

"These visions," Mallory was asking as she sank back down onto her sleeping bag and pulled it up around her shoulders. "I'm confused. Are they usually images of things that are happening right now—like in the present? Or are they more like premonitions?"

"Is this off the record?"

Mallory gave him a dirty look. "I thought we'd worked all that out a long time ago?"

Graywolf took a deep breath. Normally he didn't like talking about his...abilities, but for some reason it was easy talking to her—maybe a little too easy. It might be because Mallory Wakefield had her own special "talents" that made her less judgmental and more accepting, or because she was a good reporter and asked the right questions and knew how to listen. He knew he just had to be careful around her—it would be too easy to say too much, reveal more than he intended, and then he'd be left to pay the consequences.

"Generally they're more like precognition," he said cautiously. "Just a short time in the future. But then, like when I was in your sister's car, I can sometimes pick up... impressions of things that have happened there—feelings, emotions—things like that."

"And add to that a few hunches and some deductive reasoning..." Mallory added, purposely letting her words drift.

"And if the truth be known, there's really more of that than the hocus-pocus stuff," Graywolf admitted, giving her a deliberate look. "But that doesn't make for as good a copy."

Mallory regarded him carefully over the flames of the fire. "Is the reason you don't trust me because I'm a reporter, because I'm a woman or because I'm white?"

Graywolf's lips parted sightly in a little half smile, and he scooted down comfortably into his bedroll. "Take your pick."

Mallory leaned down, trying to get comfortable on the hard, gravelly ground. "She must have been really something."

Graywolf lifted his head and peered through the flames at her. "Who?"

Mallory snuggled down deep into the sleeping bag. "The woman who broke your heart."

"Who what?" he snorted.

"Who made you so bitter, so suspicious," she elaborated. "You know, broke your heart."

Graywolf laughed out loud. "She didn't break my heart."

Mallory rose up on her elbow, looking down at him. "Oh, no?"

"Hell, no," Graywolf snapped, laying his head back down. "She betrayed me." He closed his eyes and rolled onto his side. "Now, go to sleep. You'll need some rest."

"You mean with another man?"

He opened his eyes and looked across at her. "Does it matter? Betrayal is betrayal."

"Maybe," she conceded. "But I'd still like to know."

"A reporter's curiosity?"

"Damn it, would you leave that alone?"

He smiled, satisfied to have riled her again. "All right, if you must know—no, not with another man."

"Then how?"

He closed his eyes again. He tried to picture Susan's face, but the image was shrouded and blurred in his memory. "She was someone I knew in D.C., someone I was with during..."

"The kidnapping?" she finished for him when his words drifted. "Was she Navajo?"

He opened his eyes and turned to look at her again. "A Navajo woman wouldn't have sold the story to the tabloids."

Mallory slowly lay back down and stared up into the night sky. So that was it, she thought, stretching her arms back to cradle her head, there had been a woman in Benjamin Graywolf's life—a white woman who had betrayed him and left him angry and bitter. Did he distrust all women now? Was that the reason he looked at her so suspiciously? Was that why he was skeptical of everything she did, every word she said?

Betrayal. Mallory turned the word over in her mind. She tried to picture him with this mystery woman, this woman who had left him so jaded.

She hadn't known Graywolf very long, but it was long enough to understand that a man like him would value loyalty above all else. The circumstances would be of little importance, betrayal of any kind, in any fashion, would be the ultimate transgression, the unpardonable sin. He could mend a broken heart, forgive a failing, even overlook weakness. But betrayal...it could very easily wound him forever.

Whatever joy Mallory might have experienced during their short, rigorous climb up the mountain yesterday had all but disappeared now. The afternoon sun seared her skin, and its unrelenting heat had sweat pouring down her face and into her eyes. The pack on her back felt pounds heavier now than when they'd started out this morning, and the straps dug painfully into her shoulders.

She stopped for a moment, running an impatient arm across her forehead, and blotting at the moisture that dotted her upper lip with the back of her hand. She had given up long ago trying to keep pace with Graywolf's long stride.

While walking in his footprints had been a spirited and up-lifting experience yesterday, it was too much now for her strained muscles and tired feet.

Even though the course they followed was no longer at a continuous climb, it was still rough going. Graywolf had abandoned the idea of following the ridge up the mountain, preferring instead to explore the lower foothills, criss-crossing and searching the small valleys and rocky caverns that Marissa might have reached. Mallory watched as he sprinted along the slope in front of her, the bare skin of his back glistening in the sun.

How was it he could be so unaffected by the heat, so oblivious to the physical demands of the terrain? It made her want to scream. The constant hiking had sapped her energy and drained her strength, making his stamina all the more insulting.

She reached for her small canteen, slipping off the cap and letting the tepid water moisten the awful dryness in her mouth. They'd been hiking for hours, and Graywolf had yet to stop for a break.

Mallory made a face at his powerful back. She was damned if she was going to ask him to stop, admit to him that she needed a rest. She was determined to keep going. Besides, if he could take it, she could take it. He'd warned her it would be rough, and the last thing she wanted was to give him any reason to say "I told you so." So with a deep breath, she screwed the cap of the canteen down tight and started up the grade after him.

She plodded along, placing one heavy foot in front of the other. The natural path they followed had narrowed, hug-ging the mountain on one side and dropping to a steep gully on the other.

Mallory stepped as cautiously as she could, staying as close to the side of the mountain as possible. But the ungainly pack made moving awkward, and her overworked muscles had rendered her legs clumsy and uncertain. When she stepped onto a small patch of loose gravel, the unexpected shift had her scrambling. But her reflexes were too slow in coming, too weak to be of much help. With a helpless realization, she felt herself start to slip. The pack shifted, pulling painfully against her shoulder, working like an anchor to pull her down. Helplessly she fell, her arms grabbing wildly at anything that could save her.

Graywolf heard Mallory's strangled cry and turned back just in time to see her slide down off the narrow ridge and disappear from sight. Dropping his pack, he ran for her, but it was as if his legs had grown heavy and the air had turned thick.

"Mallory," he shouted. He couldn't seem to move fast enough. All he could think of was that deep gully below them with its jagged rocks and broken boulders, and Mallory lying torn and broken among them.

"Oh, God. Oh, God," he cried, panting, terrified of what he might see. *"Mallory!"*

Finally, after what seemed like a journey measured in miles instead of just a few feet, he reached the ledge over which she'd fallen. Peering over the ledge, he saw her perched precariously along the cliff, clutching frantically to a dried scrap of manzanita, with the backpack dangling off one shoulder.

"Help me," Mallory whimpered, her face streaked with fear. "Graywolf, please, help."

"Oh, God," Graywolf groaned again. He felt both relieved and horrified. Her eyes were filled with terror, and all the air had emptied from his lungs. "Okay, now, listen to me," he said in a calm voice. "Listen to me and don't move." He dropped to his belly, stretching over the precipice and reaching for her. "You're going to have to help me now, are you listening?"

"Graywolf," she cried, tears streaming down her face. "Please, help me. Graywolf, help me."

"Mallory, I've got you. Can you hear me?" he said in as soothing a voice as his terror would allow. Reaching out, he grabbed her by the wrists. "I have you. Let me pull you up. You have to trust me, let me pull you up. Let go of the bush."

"I—I'm scared," she stammered, frozen with fear. In a panic, she tried to get a toehold with her foot, but the dry earth gave way beneath her boot, sending gravel and dust falling down the face of the cliff.

"I know you're scared," Graywolf said. "But you have to trust me. Let go of the bush."

She looked up at him, seeing the emotion in his dark eyes, and felt some of the fear slip from her like the gravel slipping down the cliff. Trust. Yes, she would trust him—with her life, with anything.

With a small cry, she let go her death grip on the bush and allowed Graywolf to pull her to the top of the ridge.

"Are you all right?" he asked as he pulled her to her feet. "Are you hurt?"

"N-no," Mallory sobbed, shaking her head and pushing back a lock of hair from her face. "No. I—I'm sorry. It—it just happened. I was walking and...I was trying to be careful. I didn't mean—"

"Stop it," he snapped, pulling the pack off her and dropping it to the ground. What did she think he was going to do, scold her? She'd nearly fallen to her death, and she was apologizing to him as though it was somehow her fault.

He glared down at her—hair disheveled, face streaked and dirty, clothes marked and torn, knee bruised and bleeding. She was a mess—sobbing and upset, and yet she'd never looked more beautiful. Had she really thought he was going to be angry at her? Did she really think he'd be upset? She was alive—alive!—and he said a silent prayer for that.

He cursed himself for having pushed, for having continued on even when he knew she was struggling with the pace and was in dire need of a break. The thought that his foolishness had nearly gotten her killed tore at him. The picture of her slipping out of sight over that cliff would haunt him for the rest of his life.

Mallory looked up at him. She knew she was talking crazy, but she couldn't seem to help herself. She was frightened, and he was staring down at her with such a strange expression on his face—strained and intense. She remembered the look in his eyes when he'd reached over the cliff for her, remembered the dark intensity of his eyes, and felt a rush of emotion swell in her heart.

She forgot about the fall, about the close call she'd just survived. It was as if everything else had just faded away, vaporized into thin air. For her the world had narrowed to a stranger with dark, haunting eyes.

"Graywolf," she whispered, unaware she'd even spoken until she heard his name escape her lips. "I...I..."

But she had no idea what it was she wanted to say. Her words drifted off, scattering like the dust on the wind. Graywolf's hands had slid from her shoulders to her hips, and she could think of nothing but his touch, nothing but how much she wanted it.

Graywolf pulled her to him, her slender body fitting next to his like a long-lost piece of a puzzle. It was as if conscious thought no longer existed, as if mundane issues such as consequence or repercussion were no longer of concern. He was responding to something far more basic, something primeval. There had been no vision, no sense of things to come, and yet standing there, staring down into her eyes, he'd never felt closer to the natural balance of things. He was where he should be, where he wanted to be.

"Mallory," he murmured, slipping his arms around her waist and pulling her close. He liked the sound of her name on his lips. It no longer mattered that he was Navajo and she was *biligaana*. All that was important at that moment was that he was a man, and she was the woman he wanted.

Mallory's hands pressed flat against the hard wall of his chest. His skin felt smooth and supple, yet she could feel the strength and the power that lay beneath. Feelings seemed to spring from some primal part of her being—strange, unfamiliar sensations she'd never experienced before. She thought she knew what it was to want a man, but she realized in that instant just how much about herself she had left to learn.

Mallory Wakefield—the twin with the golden touch, everybody's sweetheart, the girl voted most likely to succeed—wanted Benjamin Graywolf. It didn't matter that he hated everything about her, that he had nothing but contempt for who she was and what she did. *She* wanted *him*. She wanted him in a way she hadn't known existed, in a way that made not having him seem cruel and unnatural.

He touched something basic in her, something feral and uncivilized. He made her aware of the rhythm of nature, made her cognizant of the harmony of the earth. He was as strong as the mountain, as wild as the harsh wilderness that surrounded them. He was a savage, primitive and exotic, but it had nothing to do with his Navajo heritage, or his Indian blood. It came from the fierceness in him, from the sensuality that reached out to her soul. He spoke to her on a lustful, carnal level that made her a savage, too.

"Mallory," he growled, bringing her mouth to within a whisper of his. Maybe she was white, maybe she was an outsider, maybe she did represent everything he'd convinced himself he hated, but all that didn't matter now. He'd gone through all the motions to convince himself he didn't care, that she meant nothing, and that he had no desire for her. But the fact remained that she was in his arms, her delicate body pressed against his hungry one, and he knew without a doubt he wanted her more than he'd ever wanted a woman in his life.

His mouth captured hers, the contact causing a violent shudder to pass through him. It was as if the world had suddenly stopped, as if the moment had become frozen in time—crystallized, pristine, pure. She tasted warm and rich, like everything he'd ever wanted, everything he'd ever hoped to have. Dizzily he remembered the dream, of the two of them together in the stream. He'd thought then he'd known what it was to want her, to feel desire, and hunger, and need. But the fantasy paled when compared to the real her. Nothing could have prepared him for this—no dream, no vision, no omen of things to come.

He felt her body tremble, heard a small groan escape her lips, and his body turned hard with desire. She felt delicate, her slender body seemingly fragile and ethereal, and yet the force with which she pulled at him belied her fragility. He wanted her strong, wanted her sure and determined. He was drawn to her strength, just as he was to her pale skin and haunting eyes. He pulled her more tightly to him, deepening the kiss and feeling his world spin out of control.

Mallory couldn't think, she could only react. For the moment there was nothing else in her world, nothing except the man in her arms, and the desire spreading like fire through her veins. She clung to him, holding on as though he were a lifeline, a savior. She'd known him for such a short time, and yet it was as though she'd been waiting her whole life. For her it wasn't a matter of what was right or what was wrong, what was prudent or what was foolish. It was what was meant to be.

Graywolf felt the emotion growing in her, felt it like waves pouring over him. He tore his mouth from hers, burying his face into the sweet blanket of her golden hair, pressing kisses into her neck and shoulder.

"Graywolf," she murmured, his name on her lips sounding raw and full of need.

He wanted her. But there had been something in her voice, something frank and completely exposed, something he felt in his heart and in his brain. Something that had him pulling back, pulling away.

He stared down into her eyes, seeing the need and the hunger in them. What was he doing? What could he be thinking? This wasn't his woman. He had no right to stir those kinds of emotions in her. He didn't want her love, and he could never give her his.

Reality came back to him in one stunning blow, like flash-floodwaters sweeping through a desert wash. He dropped his hands to his side and stepped away.

"What?" Mallory whispered, dazed and confused. "What is it? What's the matter?"

She searched his face, but it was the face of a stranger. There was no trace of warmth, no intensity of emotion, no hint of desire. She stared at him, feeling sick and alone.

"Graywolf?" she murmured again. "What is it? What's—"

"Look," he said abruptly, cutting her off. "I'm . . . I'm sorry. I was...out of line." He turned and took a few steps. "You need some time to rest. We'll head out when you're ready." He reached down and handed her the pack, then walked away.

Mallory stood there for a moment, feeling stunned and confused. A swell of anger surged through her system. What kind of a cold bastard was he? What kind of game was he playing with her?

She watched as he reached for his pack, slipping his arms through the straps and anchoring it into place. He didn't like her, she thought as he started up the path without her, and he didn't think much of what she did. He'd made his feelings crystal clear on that. But he'd made his feelings clear about something else, as well, something she didn't think he was terribly happy about. He may not like it, and he could do anything he wanted to deny it, but the truth was the truth. And the truth was that Benjamin Graywolf wanted her.

Chapter 10

Graywolf stopped suddenly. Turning around, he looked at Mallory. "Did you hear something?"

Mallory ambled slowly to a stop, still nursing her scraped knee, and listened for a minute. "I don't hear anything."

Graywolf muttered to himself with a scowl, and slowly shook his head. He couldn't trust anything anymore—least of all his senses. First he'd made a fool of himself with that kiss, and now he was hearing things. He turned and started out again, shifting the straps of his pack to a more comfortable position. But after only a few steps he abruptly stopped again.

"You don't hear that?" he demanded, frustrated, giving her a curious look.

"Hear what?" Mallory snapped.

"It sounds like," he murmured. "Like..."

"Like what?" she prompted with an impatient motion of her hand.

"Like... singing."

But just as he said it, something drifted past her ear. It was a sound—low, muffled, and very, very faint. But as she stood there, straining to listen, she slowly began to realize that what she heard was indeed the voice of someone—someone singing.

"I hear it now," she whispered, her eyes growing wide.

"Singing, right?" Graywolf asked, looking to her for agreement.

Mallory nodded her head. "Yeah," she said, concentrating hard. "But... different," she said as she looked up at him. "Almost like a..."

"Child's voice," Graywolf interjected.

She looked up at him and nodded her head. "Yes, that's it. A child's voice."

"This way," Graywolf said, suddenly heading up the steep slope on a run. "It's coming from over here."

Mallory didn't dare hope as she stumbled up the grade behind him. She didn't even dare think too hard about what it might mean. She'd gotten her hopes up before, only to have them cruelly shattered. Still, as she reached the dry, dusty plateau at the top of the incline, she couldn't deny the feeling of nervous apprehension.

"There," Graywolf said, pointing across the mesa to an outcrop of rock, jutting out to form an alcove in the mountain.

There, in the distance, below the overhang of rocks and earth, sat a small child feeding sticks into a fire and singing quietly to herself.

"A little girl," Mallory murmured, feeling more breathless by the sight than by the long climb up the embankment. She turned and looked at Graywolf. "It's a little girl." She took a step closer. "Could she be the one? The child in the vision?"

Graywolf watched the child as she sat before the fire, playing quietly and singing an old Navajo lullaby he remembered from his childhood. He had seen the infant clearly in the vision—tiny and wrinkled. The child before the fire was at least three years old. Turning to Mallory, he shook his head. "No, it's not her."

Mallory turned away. It was foolish to feel so disappointed, and yet she couldn't seem to help it. Ever since Graywolf had told her of his vision, about the child, she'd had a . . . *feeling*. Then, hearing the mournful sound of that little voice, she'd thought...but it was useless to think of all that now. She wasn't the one with visions, with second sight. What she'd felt had been little more than wishful thinking.

"How do you suppose she got out here?" she asked in a tight voice. "Could she be lost?"

"Maybe," Graywolf said, shrugging. "Let's go down and find out."

They started down the mesa toward the child when a woman's voice sounded above the singing.

"Sarah, could you help me, please?"

Even before Mallory saw the woman hobble out of the darkness of the shallow cave with a makeshift crutch beneath her arm, she knew who it was, and for a moment she could do nothing but stand and stare. She watched in disbelief as the woman handed the little girl a small plastic container and pointed off into the distance. It wasn't until the little girl had raced off across the mesa that Mallory felt her heart begin to beat again.

"Marissa," she said, emotion choking her vocal cords and making her voice little more than a whisper.

Graywolf knew even before he saw the woman appear out of the darkness that they had found Marissa Wakefield. Not because of any insight he possessed, but because he could feel Mallory's reaction. And while he knew it was prudent

that they proceed with caution, while he knew it made sense
to wait and assess the situation from a distance, make sure
there was no threat of danger, no sign of trouble, he seemed
to have momentarily forgotten it. Her joy had suddenly become his, and they both started down the embankment on
a run.

"Marissa, Marissa, Marissa," Mallory called as she loped
down the hill, her voice growing stronger and louder with
each step. *"Marissa!"*

"M-Mallory?" Marissa stammered, dropping the gnarled
walking stick she held as a crutch. She staggered forward a
few steps. "Oh, God, Mallory?"

The two sisters embraced each other with such force it
nearly toppled them to the ground. Tears flowed loose and
plentiful, and for the moment the questions of how and why
were not important. What was important was the nightmare was over, and the Wakefield twins were together again.

But tears soon erupted into a frenzy of questions, with
both sisters talking at the same time, and neither listening to
what the other said. There was too much to tell, too much
to listen to, for anything to really sink in.

"Thank God. Oh, Mallory, thank God," Marissa wailed
through a waterfall of tears. "I knew you would find me, I
knew you would come. Oh, God, I *prayed* you would."

Mallory batted away the tears that blurred her vision.
"No one would listen to me. No one believed you were
missing."

Marissa pulled back and took Mallory's face in her hands.
"But you believed, and you found me, anyway."

"I believed." Mallory smiled, taking a deep breath. "And
so did..." She stopped and turned to Graywolf, who stood
quietly by, watching and waiting, and felt a tight constric-
tion around her heart. Even through the tears, she didn't
think he'd ever looked more handsome. She remembered

what it had felt to be in his arms, and a new swell of emotion rose in her throat. "Marissa, this is Benjamin Graywolf. He's a tracker, and a shaman, and without him, I never would have found you."

Marissa gave her head a little shake in an attempt to compose herself and wiped her tear-moistened hand on her pant leg. She turned to Graywolf, giving him an embarrassed smile. She stepped forward to extend him her dry hand, but then stopped suddenly, flinching violently.

Mallory grabbed for her sister again. "My God, Marissa, you're hurt," she gasped in horror. "What is it? What's happened?"

"It's just a sprain," Marissa insisted, nodding to her swollen ankle and waving off her sister's concern. With Mallory's help she hobbled forward to offer Graywolf her hand. "Mr. Graywolf, I don't know what to say. Thank you."

Graywolf took Marissa's outstretched hand, and the fading sunlight caught the gold clusters of stars on the pendant around her neck. Immediately he recognized the backdrop of the cave as the scene from his vision, and he thought of the image of the Navajo infant.

Standing side by side, the Wakefield sisters bore an uncanny physical resemblance to each other—but as much as they were the same, Graywolf sensed the differences between them. He found it strange and a little unsettling to look into faces that were virtually mirror images, and yet see the same features look so very different on each sister. While Marissa's face shared the same extraordinary beauty as Mallory's, Graywolf realized uneasily that it was more than the fair hair, more than the blue eyes and pale skin, that had attracted him to Mallory Wakefield.

"We'd better get you off that ankle," Graywolf said, forcing the disturbing thoughts from his mind. He reached out an arm, helping Marissa toward the rocky ledge near the cave. "It looks broken."

"First let me check on Ruth," Marissa insisted, gesturing into the cave.

"Ruth?" Mallory repeated. "Who's Ruth?" In frustration she threw her hands up in a helpless gesture. "Marissa, what's all this about? What are you doing way out here?"

Marissa gave her a tired smile. "It's a long story. Come inside and let me introduce you, then I'll explain everything."

Graywolf all but carried Marissa as she led them into the shallow cave. Inside, asleep on a brightly colored Indian blanket, was a young Navajo woman. She wore a deep blue velvet vest and a bright, multicolored skirt. But the fullness at her waist revealed a womb heavy with child.

"A newborn," Mallory said almost soundlessly, turning to Graywolf.

Graywolf glanced into Mallory's eyes, which were dark and murky blue in the dim of the cave. He wasn't sure if he'd heard her words, or just felt them. Not that it mattered. What was important was that they both knew in that instant they had found the child in the vision.

"Good, she's resting now," Marissa whispered in a low voice. She motioned Graywolf to a level spot on the rocky floor where he settled her gently to her feet. "She started feeling uncomfortable yesterday. I thought it was exhaustion—the climb up here was hard on her. But early this morning she started having contractions. They were weak at first, irregular. She'd told me it was too early for the baby. I'd hoped it was just a false alarm. Unfortunately, the contractions have continued to get stronger and they're coming pretty regularly now. I can't tell you how frightened I've been. We have to get some help for her." She turned to Graywolf. "She needs a doctor."

Just then the young woman stirred, and Marissa knelt at her side. "It's okay, Ruth," Marissa said in a soothing voice, rubbing a comforting hand along the woman's forehead. "I'm right here. It's going to be all right. Just relax, don't fight it."

The contraction was a strong one, and Mallory held herself rigid watching the young woman bravely endure the tremendous strain to her small body. She turned to Graywolf, and leaned close. "Have you ever delivered a baby?" she whispered.

Graywolf gave her a deliberate look. "What do you think? I went to law school, remember?"

"But I thought you were a medicine man. Isn't that something like a doctor?"

He scowled. He knew the ancient ceremonies, could chant the words of his ancestors, he even carried his pouch of crystals around his waist, but those things were a far cry from a doctor's bag. "It's *nothing* like a doctor."

"Ruth," Marissa said once the contraction was over and the young woman revived a bit. "Ruth, listen to me. I have good news. Help has arrived, just like I promised." She turned and motioned for Mallory and Graywolf to come closer. "Ruth, this is my sister Mallory—the one I told you about. And this is her friend Benjamin Graywolf."

Mallory stepped forward and smiled down at the young mother. "Hello, Ruth."

Ruth's eyes widened at the sight of two such identical faces, and muttered something unintelligible under her breath. "Miss Marissa told me you would come. We prayed you would find us," she said to Mallory, a tear slipping down her wide cheek. She turned to Graywolf. *"Yaa eh t'eeh."*

"Yaa eh t'eeh," Graywolf said, returning the traditional Navajo greeting. They shared a brief exchange in their native tongue, introducing themselves through the clans of their mothers. But as they spoke, Ruth's soft, open expression went suddenly stiff as another strong contraction began.

Graywolf dropped to his knees, watching helplessly as Ruth's small body went rigid with pain. He took her hand in his, and she gripped tight as the contraction peaked with agonizing intensity.

Mallory watched Graywolf. He looked bewildered, completely helpless in the face of this ancient rite of women. He was strong and capable, like the Rock of Gibraltar. But to see him so utterly vulnerable now stirred a powerful emotion in her.

The contraction left Ruth exhausted. The little girl Mallory and Graywolf had seen playing at the camp fire returned with a plastic carton full of water. Marissa introduced her as Sarah, Ruth's four-year-old daughter.

While Marissa helped Ruth sip water from the container, Graywolf pulled Mallory aside. "There isn't going to be time to get her to a hospital. That baby is coming too fast."

Mallory swallowed nervously. "I know."

"Do you think you're going to be able to do it?"

Mallory's head reared up. "What do you mean *me?* We're all in this together, friend."

"Oh, no," Graywolf said, holding his hands up and shaking his head. "I don't know anything about delivering a baby."

"You know as much as I do," Mallory insisted, thinking how woefully inadequate the first aid class she'd taken in high school about a million years ago had been.

"But you're a woman. Women know about these things."

"That's an old wives' tale."

Graywolf stared down at her, his gaze inadvertently drifting to her lips and remembering the taste of her. The memory triggered others—of holding her, touching her—and he shifted uneasily. Taking a deep breath, he turned away. "Well, at least your sister has been through it before. That helps."

Mallory followed his gaze to Marissa, who worked to make Ruth comfortable. She remembered the sterile hospital room in the medical center just outside Baltimore where she and Aunt Bea had comforted Marissa during her long hours of labor. But Marissa had all the advantages medical science had to offer to help her through the ordeal. Ruth had nothing—just a little child, and three very scared adults.

She looked up at Graywolf, remembering his vision of a newborn. "But it also helps to know the baby will be all right."

Graywolf gave her a puzzled look. "What makes you say that?"

"The vision, remember?"

Yes, he remembered, but took little solace in it. He had seen the child, alive and in the arms of Marissa Wakefield. But despite his intuition and second sight, he was still only mortal. Beyond that one glimpse of insight, that one peek at what was to come, he was as much in the dark as to what the future held as the rest of them. He had no way of knowing if Ruth would make it through the delivery, or if there would be complications that would prove disastrous.

"Mallory. Graywolf. Come quick," Marissa cried out suddenly. "I think something's wrong."

Mallory felt a chill. She was a veteran reporter and had covered stories that were dramatic and that had put her in some pretty heated situations. But she knew that the next few hours would be the longest and most tense she would ever remember in her life. All the questions she had for

Marissa, all the things she wanted to know about what had happened, and why, would have to wait. They were mere details—particulars that could be filled in at a later date. At the moment a child was fighting its way into the world—and that took precedence over everything else.

They all worked feverishly together—even little Sarah, who filled and refilled the plastic water container many times over. They were a motley crew, with Ruth stoic and strong, Marissa issuing orders, and Mallory and Graywolf scrambling to follow them, but there was a curious sort of harmony to their movements. As awkward and unconventional as they were, they'd become a team, united in a common cause to bring a new life into the world.

Despite the intensity of the situation, and the constant distractions, Mallory found herself watching Graywolf. It was as though their time alone in the desert had left her supersensitive to everything about him. She found his concern for Ruth genuine and touching. He tried hard to be cold and aloof, to hold others at arm's length, but the flashes of sensitivity and caring were impossible to hide. God knows how many times over the course of the last several days she'd seen him surly and rude, irritable and moody. But there was no sign of that now.

Despite his awkwardness with the situation, he attended to Ruth with compassion and tenderness. He held her hand through the long, painful contractions, bathed her forehead with cool, clear water, and whispered quiet, soothing Navajo words in her ear.

Ruth, like many on the reservation, had grown up hearing stories of the revered *yataalii* Hosteen Johnny Bistie. To have the grandson of such a great singer, who himself was a respected shaman, comforting her during the birth of her child brought her great solace.

The sunlight began to fade, and the cave grew dark. Mallory and Sarah hurriedly collected firewood, while Graywolf fashioned a crude torch with strips of material from his discarded shirt and a mixture of wood chips and pitch he'd gathered from the trees. The moon had just started to rise in the sky when, after what seemed like an eternity, the wail of a brand-new voice broke through the silence of the night.

"It's a boy!" Marissa announced in a shaky voice, tears streaming down her face and holding the wet, wiggly little life in her arms.

"A son." Ruth sighed as Marissa placed the baby in her arms.

"A boy," Mallory murmured. She turned to Graywolf. "It's a boy."

Although the mechanics of the human reproduction process were no mystery to him, Graywolf had never actually witnessed the birth of a child before, and the experience had left him shaken and in awe. He turned to Mallory, seeing the emotion in her face and feeling something stir deep inside him, something he'd been trying to ignore for too long.

She was so beautiful, so full of life—someone special, someone out of the ordinary, and it seemed he'd been waiting for her his whole life. Reaching out, he caught her by the waist and swept her up into his arms. When he brought his lips to hers, he found her warm, and sweet, and receptive.

Mallory gave herself to his kiss completely, holding back nothing. What she felt had nothing to do with the euphoria of the moment, with the celebration of new life, and new hope. What she felt had been in her heart almost from the beginning, churning around and flourishing with each moment that had passed. She might not know everything about the man who called himself Benjamin Graywolf, but she knew all she needed. She knew he was the man she loved.

Graywolf forgot about the cave, about Marissa and Ruth, and little Sarah sitting nearby. There was only the woman in his arms, and the miracle of life he'd just witnessed. He wanted Mallory, wanted to plant his seed in her, give her his child so that they could create a miracle of their own. He wanted to watch her body change and grow, feel the swell of his child inside her belly. And he wanted to hold their child in his arms—the ultimate union—half Navajo, half *bili-gaana*.

"Uh, excuse me, you two," Marissa said in a hesitant voice. She laughed when Mallory and Graywolf jumped apart, surprised and startled. "Look, I hate to interrupt, but I could use some help here."

Marissa stood there, the rocky wall of the cave rising up behind her, balancing carefully on her one good ankle and holding the little infant lovingly in her arms. She'd wrapped him in the clean white cloth she'd pulled from his mother's voluminous underslip, and his tiny lungs bellowed clear and strong. Graywolf realized at that moment he was looking at the scene from his vision.

"Can one of you come and take this little guy?" Marissa asked, smiling down into the tiny face. "I think his mommy could use some rest."

Graywolf tossed another log onto the fire. They were all exhausted as they sat around the fire quietly talking. Marissa sat with her foot propped up, her ankle bandaged in the makeshift splint Graywolf had fashioned for her. Little Sarah lay across her lap, her eyelids drooping while Mallory rocked the infant in her arms. Behind them, in the cave, Ruth slept peacefully, her body recovering from its tremendous labor of love.

"It was foolish, I know," Marissa was saying, continuing the story that they'd finally gotten around to. "But Ruth had an idea where the camp was, and I thought I was familiar enough with the area that between us we could find it." She gazed at Sarah who was sleeping soundly on her lap. "The two of them looked so helpless standing there by that broken-down old pickup. I couldn't just leave them stranded there."

"We saw the truck," Mallory said, swaying gently to rock the baby. "Graywolf followed your tracks off the road."

"I feel so stupid now," Marissa confessed, emotion making her voice tight. "But it was as if everything went wrong. We got caught in that terrible thunderstorm, and it got us all turned around. Then it started flooding, and after a while, one arroyo started looking just like all the rest."

"Well, you were headed in the right direction," Graywolf said encouragingly. He stoked the flames until they burned high, then sat back down. "Shadow Canyon is just beyond that ridge over there. Ruth's husband is working in the canyon?"

"Yes," Marissa said, nodding her head. "At the Anasazi ruins. There's an archaeological dig up there, and he's one of the workers. She was on her way up to surprise him when her truck broke down." She paused, stroking Sarah's long dark hair. "After the car got stuck and the floodwaters started rising, I thought we'd better get to high ground. But the climb was just too hard on Ruth and she started having pain. It was obvious she wouldn't be able to go far on foot. I thought I could leave her in the cave while I went for help. We still had food left from the things Ruth had picked up for the weekend, but then I fell and Ruth went into labor." She stopped and shook her head. "It just became a nightmare."

Mallory reached over and squeezed her sister's hand. "But it's over now. Ruth's okay, the baby's okay, and, hopefully, we're going to get out of here tomorrow.'' She turned to Graywolf and gave him a questioning glance.

"I plan to head out at sunup," he assured her. The smile she gave him caused his heart to lurch painfully in his chest.

He watched her with the child. Seeing the tiny baby fight his way into the world had been the most amazing thing he'd ever seen in his life. It had left him reeling—physically and emotionally—and momentarily he'd dropped his guard. Otherwise he never would have done what he had—sweeping Mallory into his arms and kissing her like that.

He'd cautioned himself after the episode on the cliff about touching her. Touching her was too dangerous, and caused him to forget too much—like the cultures that separated them, and the prejudices that would keep them apart. And yet, caught up in the moment of the miracle of birth, he'd swept her up in his arms and kissed her. It had been a stupid, reckless thing to do, and he would have to be careful not to let it ever happen again.

There was no room in his life for an attraction between them, and that was all he was feeling—an attraction, a longing, a desire for what he knew he couldn't have. They were from two different worlds.

He listened to her soft voice as she sang a quiet lullaby to the sleeping infant. He remembered fantasizing about a child the two of them could create together, and was embarrassed. It was an absurd thought, foolish and impractical.

Half-breed. The words infiltrated his consciousness like a deadly virus, turning the blood in his veins to ice. There could be no life between them, no seed to grow or child to share. There would be no place for a child of theirs, no tribe to embrace, no clan to belong to. Besides, a child should be born out of love, and in the barren landscape where a savage was always a savage, and a white woman would forever be forbidden fruit, love had no place to grow.

He felt himself grow sleepy, the fire glowing warm and comfortable against his skin. He remembered hearing the baby crying, and the sounds of shuffling feet and hushed whispers beyond the glow of the fire. But he was too weary to respond, his eyelids too heavy to lift. A slow, peaceful darkness began to surround him, and he felt himself drifting further and further away.

"Thank you."

He heard the sound of Mallory's voice in his ear, felt the cool palm of her hand along his cheek, the delicate smoothness of her lips along his. He mumbled something—an old ancient chant he'd learned from Hosteen Johnny about women, and love, and desires of the heart. There was nothing after that, just a peace he'd never known, and a love he'd never felt, and a giant bird in the sky.

Chapter 11

The bird was so beautiful, and its song so very sweet. A giant egret, gleaming white as a cloud. Graywolf was captivated by its beauty, dazzled by the ease and symmetry of motion as it floated through the air. He watched it move across the sky—smooth, graceful movements that beckoned to him, made him want to take flight. It drew closer and closer, drifting on the currents, turning its tranquil face toward him, bringing with it peace, and calm, and security. But then, as it dipped toward the earth, a terrible transformation took place. The peaceful face became a cold mask of steel, and grace took a turn toward gruesome.

The flapping of the bird's wings grew fierce, stirring the wind and sending dust flying. Graywolf struggled violently, desperate to get away, but the huge thing leaned its swollen, ugly face close and roared at the top of its lungs. It was a terrible sound, one that would surely awaken the sleeping *chindi*— the spirits of the dead.

"No," Graywolf moaned. He reached for Mallory, he had to protect her. The giant bird threatened, it had come to fly her away, to grab her up in its monstrous talons and take her where he'd never be able to find her again. "No!"

The sound grew deafening, and the fear became sickening. He heard his name being called from some faraway place, over and over again. He could barely hear it over the grotesque caw of the bird, but the plea continued—calling to him, calling to him. He tried to call back, tried to summon help, but it was useless. All he could do was lie there, on his back, staring up into the hideous face of the bird.

Only...now the bird wasn't a bird at all, and he could feel the wind and the sun on his face. He slowly sat up, squinting into the harshness of the light, shaking his head and grappling for conscious thought. There was no giant bird suspended in the sky above him, there was a helicopter. And leaning out of the cockpit, waving down at him, was the wide, weather-beaten face of Navajo tribal policeman Sam Begay.

"A helicopter."

Graywolf jumped, shocked to find Mallory curled on the ground beside him. She scrambled to sit up, turning to him with wide, excited eyes.

"Graywolf, my God, it's a helicopter," she shrieked, jumping to her feet. She pulled at his arm, practically dragging him up to a standing position. She pointed up, recognizing the tribal policeman and waving frantically. "Graywolf, Graywolf, it's him, it's him. It's Sergeant Begay. He's found us." Excitedly, she threw her arms around Graywolf's neck and danced him wildly around. "He's found us."

Reality finally managed to settle in. Somehow, someway, Sam Begay had found them. By the end of this day, they would all be back in civilization again, back to their everyday lives.

Graywolf looked down into Mallory's excited eyes. It was over now. No longer would he have to struggle with his feelings, deny the attraction, or take pains to avoid contact. In twenty-four hours, Mallory Wakefield would just be a memory—out of his life, out of sight and out of mind.

But she was in his arms now, and a feeling rose up from inside him that swept through his entire being. He caught her up in his arms, pulling her to his waiting lips. He ground his mouth down on hers with a force that bordered on brutal, and yet she willingly accepted his savage kiss.

His tongue plunged deep, tasting the rich, heady flavor of her. His hands grew restless, and moved over her with an urgent, ardent need, wanting to remember each soft curve, each delicate contour, and imprint them in his memory. For in a few short hours she would be gone, and memories would be all he'd have left.

Mallory pulled her lips away, breathless and a little surprised. She gazed up into his dark eyes, seeing an emotion in them, and feeling it in her heart. He was a curious and complicated man. He had a chip on his shoulder a mile wide, hated where she came from and what she did, what she stood for and who she was. He didn't trust her, didn't believe in her, and didn't even like her all that much. But the fact remained, he wanted her—he couldn't ignore it, nor could he deny it. And as confused and uncertain as his feelings were for her, hers for him were crystal clear.

"I love you," she murmured, even though the roar of the helicopter drowned out all sound. She hadn't really meant to say it, the words had just sort of slipped out. Yet she had no regrets. They were true, she did love Benjamin Graywolf. It didn't matter that they'd known each other only a short time, it didn't matter that the forces of man and nature would conspire to keep them apart. His spirit had touched her spirit and found communion, and so she said again what was in her heart. "I love you."

Graywolf hadn't needed to hear her voice, nor had he needed to see her lips mouth the words. He knew what she said, knew what she felt—maybe he always had.

He carefully slipped her out of his arms, setting her away from him. Slowly, he turned and walked away. He felt dispirited, and oddly shaken. In the world where skin color mattered and cultural taboos dictated what was right and what was wrong, it was an aberration, an abnormality—like two women with one face, and a singer with second sight.

He stopped and looked up at Begay in the helicopter above. Signaling the pilot to a clearing on the mesa just below, Graywolf started down the rocky slope to meet them.

It had been different in the desert, it had just been the two of them—alone and away from a culture and society that would keep them apart. But all that was over now. The giant bird had come, and even the strongest shaman's magic could do nothing to change it.

Mallory secured the seat belt around her waist, trying as best she could to ignore the sick feeling in the pit of her stomach. She could hear Begay talking to Graywolf, telling him the tip he'd gotten from someone called Charlie Black Hat, who'd seen a woman—"White Hair"—alongside the highway with a woman he thought was Ruth Endocheeny. And how later, when he'd learned Ruth's husband, who worked up at the dig in Shadow Canyon, was worried that his wife and daughter were missing, how he had begun to put two and two together.

It was a remarkable story, and Mallory knew she should feel very lucky. They were being rescued, for God's sake—saved. Ruth and the baby would get the medical attention they needed, Marissa would get her ankle set, and little Sarah would get the first decent meal she'd had in over a week. Mallory knew she should be feeling on top of the world—everyone was all right, she had her sister back, and they were returning to their lives again. She should be ecstatic, grateful, excited, happy. She should be...but she wasn't.

The huge turbine on the top of the helicopter began to spin, its high-pitched whine waking the baby in Ruth's arms. He started to cry, but his tiny wails were soon drowned out by the noise. Mallory looked out the open side door to Graywolf, who stood crouched beside the craft, his long black hair secured in a braid down his back. He was shaking hands with Sam Begay, the white man's gesture looking spontaneous and genuine between the two Navajo. He wouldn't be coming with them, but instead would hike back to the Jeep. Mallory had offered to stay with him, had very nearly begged to stay with him, but he wouldn't hear of it. It was time they parted ways.

She glanced down at the strap that held her in her seat. She didn't feel secured in the helicopter, but trapped. She knew he didn't welcome the attraction he felt for her, knew there could never be a future for them, that he would never love her, but it didn't seem to matter. *She* was in love with *him,* and nothing was going to change the way she felt—not time, not distance, and not even his absolute rejection.

Officer Sam Begay hopped inside the helicopter just as it started to lift off the ground, taking a seat beside the pilot. Mallory leaned toward the door, the seat belt cutting into the flesh at her sides. She stared out the open door at Graywolf, her eyes filling with tears. It was time to go, time to say goodbye, time to move on, but her heart was breaking.

I love you.

She wanted to scream the words at the top of her lungs, she wanted to stand in the open doorway of the helicopter and shout it across the desert. She wanted him to hear it over the wail of the baby, over the roar of the engines. But it wasn't necessary.

She looked into his eyes as the aircraft slowly drew higher and higher.

I love you.

He knew. He understood. Yet still he let her go. There was no place in his life for her, no place in his heart for her love.

She watched him until the helicopter turned, and he disappeared among the rocks and brush of the foothills. Sinking back into her seat, she squeezed her eyes tight, feeling the sting of tears burn. But when she felt a hand on hers, she opened them again.

"It hurts," Marissa murmured, leaning close and giving her hand a squeeze. "I know it hurts."

"Oh, Marissa," Mallory moaned, feeling tears spill down her cheek. Yes, her sister did know. Their special "twins" radar made it possible for them to feel each other's pain, and Mallory remembered how she had felt Marissa's when Josh's father had walked out on her. "What am I going to do?"

Marissa patted her hand lovingly. "You'll get by. Trust me, you'll get by."

"I'll never forget him."

"No, I don't expect you will."

"But the pain," Mallory sobbed, the feeling of loss so tremendous she thought she wouldn't survive. "Will it ever go away?"

Marissa slipped her arms around her sister, and pulled her close. "No," she admitted, sighing deeply. "But somehow you learn to live with it."

Live with it, Mallory thought, long after the tears had dried. She stared blindly out across the huge expanse that was the Big Res. Is that what Marissa has been doing all these years—living? Or had she simply been losing herself in the lives of others so she didn't have to think about the huge, empty void in her own life?

Living. For her there would be no living without Graywolf. Oh, she'd go on all right. She'd go back to D.C. She'd get up every morning, brush her teeth and comb her hair. She'd put on her makeup, go to work and do her job, but there'd be no real "life" in any of it. She'd be simply going through the motions.

She turned and looked at Marissa, who was now lost in her own thoughts, and felt as though she were seeing her sister for the first time. She realized then this was what it had been like for Marissa all these years. For sixteen years she'd been going through the motions, living life without really living it at all.

Mallory turned and glanced down at the landscape passing quickly below them. She'd been alive down there, out in the desert, in the wilderness with a man as mystic and mysterious as the land itself.

Absently, she reached for the pendant around her neck, only to discover that it wasn't there. "Oh, my God."

"What is it?" Marissa jumped, startled. "What's wrong?"

"My necklace." She turned to her sister, the feeling of loss almost overwhelming. "It's . . . gone."

Marissa tried to comfort her, but it did no good. Mallory was miserable. First Graywolf, and now this. She'd lost again. Another treasure gone.

Mallory closed her eyes, feeling a swell of emotion form in her throat. Benjamin Graywolf had given her more than the moon and the stars, he'd given her life—*real* life—and she would never forget.

I love you.

Graywolf heard the words in his head. They echoed through his brain, making the ache inside his chest feel suffocating and lethal. He had to stop thinking about it—had to stop thinking about her. Whether it felt like it or not, he'd done the right thing. Like the cavalry, Sam Begay had shown up just in the nick of time, sparing him a fate that would surely be worse than death. He hadn't realized until he'd watched that helicopter fly away that he'd been in over his head. Another day, another hour with the woman, and he'd have been lost forever.

Graywolf shoved the bedroll into the back of the Jeep and slammed the hatch closed. He squinted up at the sun, its searing rays burning his skin and causing the perspiration to pour off his naked chest. It would be a long, hot drive back, and even pushing it, he wouldn't reach his hogan before nightfall.

He thought of Mallory, of their drive through the desert together. Even though he'd tortured her with silence, he'd been aware of her presence every mile of the way. Then all he could think about was getting away from her, getting her out of his life. But now she was gone, and the empty feeling inside him was like a void that could never be filled.

He reached into his back pocket, into his wallet, and pulled out the picture he'd taken from Marissa Wakefield's bedroom. Smiling up at him were Mallory and Marissa Wakefield's two impish faces, except they looked different to him now. They didn't seem to be identical any longer, not quite so much the same.

When he'd looked at the picture before, he'd had trouble telling the two children apart—which was Mallory, and which was Marissa. But no longer. Now there was no confusion, no moment of doubt. He'd had time to study them, to know their differences. He'd looked into their eyes, had peeked into their souls. The picture hadn't changed, but he had. He saw them now as the women they were, two completely separate and unique individuals.

He wanted the woman—as much as he'd tried to fight it, he wanted her. He wanted her on that shining white iron bed, with the pretty pink comforter and frilly pink pillows. He wanted her white body beneath his, her white hair spread out across the mattress. He wanted to touch her and kiss her and bury himself so deep inside her that he'd forget about red skins and white prejudices, until native intolerance and modern bigotry didn't matter anymore.

I love you.

He heard the words in his head again, felt them stirring in his heart, and he closed his eyes to a wave of longing that rendered him momentarily helpless. He shouldn't be thinking about this, shouldn't think about her. It was over, and he'd escaped just in time. He would go back to his people, back to his hogan, and start the long journey to oblivion. He'd ask Hosteen Johnny to perform a sing—a curing ceremony, or an enemy way—to help purge the memories, to help make him forget.

He slipped the picture back into his wallet, then yanked open the door of the Jeep and slid behind the wheel. He twisted the key in the ignition, coaxing the engine with several impatient depressions on the gas pedal. The motor reluctantly roared to life, and he let it idle for a moment, coughing and sputtering.

They'd be in Flagstaff by now—back in the white man's world. They'd be at a hospital somewhere, getting poked and prodded, scrubbed and cleaned. She'd get back to normal, back into routine, back to work. She was a reporter, and this would make one hell of a story. She had promised him it was all "off the record," but he would prepare himself for the worst. He knew all too well that promises to a savage in the desert were easily forgotten in the white man's world.

He shoved his foot down hard onto the clutch, and reached for the gearshift knob. He told himself he would deal with that when the time came, deal with the betrayal and the disappointment, but it wouldn't be easy. Mallory Wakefield wasn't like Susan. There had been something perversely . . . *honest* in Susan's betrayal. He'd known from the first that she was a spoiled little rich girl. He didn't like it that she'd sold him out, but it hadn't surprised him, either. He'd sensed an honor in Mallory, a decency, that would make a betrayal all the more hurtful.

He yanked the car into first, grinding the gears noisily, but as he started to pull forward, something caught his eye. A shaft of sunlight glinted off something on the floor mat, momentarily blinding him. Reaching down, he fumbled around until he felt something. Catching it up in his fist, he straightened up.

Even before he opened his hand, he saw the picture in his head. Curled against the roughened texture of his skin was Mallory's necklace—the delicate chain holding a crescent moon.

Mallory stood braced against the cool tile, letting the water cascade over her aching body. She'd long ago scrubbed the desert grime from her skin and hair, but the tepid spray felt soothing, and the drone of the water broke the sullen silence that seemed to surround her. It was late, and she was exhausted, but she couldn't bring herself to move. Marissa's little house was deathly still, and the quiet was driving her crazy.

It had been a hectic day, to say the least. It seemed like a lifetime ago that she'd woken up beside Graywolf to see that helicopter hovering above them, and yet it was only this morning. One day, and her whole life had changed.

The break to Marissa's ankle had been serious. They'd been airlifted to a hospital in Flagstaff where she'd been examined and X-rayed. She'd been fitted with a temporary cast, but the doctors had insisted that she stay the night for observation, and so they could fit her with a permanent walking cast in the morning. Ruth and the baby had been examined and released—her anxious husband was at the hospital waiting for his family with open arms.

Mallory smiled, remembering the look on the young man's face when he saw his son for the first time. There hadn't been a dry eye in the house. He then bundled his family into his aging station wagon and headed back to the reservation. Mallory pictured them in her mind, sitting before a warm fire in their tiny hogan. True wealth had nothing to do with bank accounts and creature comforts, she mused as the water flooding over her slowly began to grow cold, but rather the quality of the love that was shared.

Which, she thought as she reached for the faucet and shut off the spray, just left her. Despite her protests, the medical staff at the hospital had insisted on giving her a thorough examination. As she'd predicted, they'd found nothing wrong, and she was released with a clean bill of health. With Sam Begay's help, she'd made her report to the Arizona State Police, then accepted the offer from their office to drive her to Marissa's house.

She opened the shower door and reached for a towel, patting herself dry. She slipped into Marissa's short cotton nightshirt, and combed out her long, wet hair.

She regarded herself in the mirror, looking at the spot around her neck where the pendant once hung. Oddly enough, the fact that it was gone didn't bother her so much any longer. She had her sister back, that's what was important. The necklace had been a pretty keepsake, a memento left over from a time when she thought anything was possible.

She knew better now. There would be no moon and stars for her, no happily-ever-after. She was a thirty-three-year-old divorcée in love with a Navajo shaman who didn't even like her. Hardly the fairy-tale ending she'd expected when she'd graduated from Jackson High School fifteen years ago. For the girl voted most likely to become a millionaire, she'd failed miserably.

With her hair dry now, she flipped off the light and headed back into the bedroom, feeling the fatigue of the long day in every move she made. The moonlight was bright, streaming through the narrow slits of the mini-blinds and creating a precise pattern of white light across the bedspread.

She glanced at the clock-radio beside the bed. Nearly midnight. She'd told Marissa she'd be back at the hospital in Flagstaff before noon to pick her up. That wouldn't leave much time for sleeping in.

Still, standing just above the bed, she hesitated. The house was so silent, so still, it unnerved her a little. She stood in the darkness, listening for a moment. The neat, tidy house on the cozy, little street had its own curious sounds, and she couldn't help thinking how refined and decidedly urban they were in comparison to the wild, uncivilized music of the desert at night.

She thought of Graywolf, of their makeshift campsites and roaring open fires. In the darkness they had sat and listened to the cries of coyote, the hooting of owls, even the howl of a wolf. Graywolf had teased her with stories of skinwalkers—demons and evil spirits—and the Navajo

Wolf. He had cautioned her about the *chindi,* spirits of the dead who searched out and preyed upon the living. And in the vastness of the desert, in the darkness of night, beneath a blanket of a thousand stars, she had found herself almost believing. She almost believed he was magic, that he could change shape, become the Wolf.

She thought of him, picturing his tall frame in her mind. It had almost been real. She could almost believe that she'd been bewitched, captivated by the shaman's magic, charmed by the ways of the Old Ones.

The sound of tapping on the window of the front door had her mind snapping back to reality. She glanced at the clock beside the bed again and felt an icy chill run the length of her spine. It was after midnight. Who would be coming to the door at this hour?

Feeling suddenly more alone and more vulnerable than she had when she was in the middle of the desert, she tiptoed out of the bedroom. Moving soundlessly through the living room, she peeked around the corner, through the little foyer to the beveled glass front door.

The moonlight through the window painted a familiar silhouette on the glass, and Mallory's heart leapt to her throat. She hesitated for a second, dizzily wondering if this was real, or if it was a dream. Was this actually happening, or was it just a result of some mystic incarnation?

But the hesitation was only momentary. Why should she care what was fantasy and what was fact? Was an illusion any less real if it gave her what she wanted?

Without further hesitation, she ran to the door, flinging it open and hurling herself into Graywolf's waiting arms.

Chapter 12

Graywolf stood at the door, staring into the dark house and asking himself what the hell he was doing there. His heart beat like thunder in his chest, and his lungs seemed starved for oxygen. It was late—too late to be knocking, too late to be chasing around the countryside for dreams that were impossible to have. She was going to think he was crazy, out of his mind, mad—and she would be right.

In his hand he clutched the gold necklace, that tiny bit of precious metal that had caused him so many sleepless nights. He could have just mailed it to her, dropped it into an envelope, slapped a stamp on it and been done with it. Instead, he'd come after her as if he were carrying an organ for a life-saving transplant. Without even being aware of it, he'd been looking for an excuse, and he'd grabbed at the first one he could find.

What was the matter with him? Fate had handed him a perfect opportunity. He could have walked away from her, unscathed and unharmed—no battle scars, no injuries. He would have been let off scot-free.

And yet there he stood, like a beggar in the night.

There was still time, he told himself. Still time to turn around, climb back into the Jeep and get the hell out of there, and no one need ever be the wiser. She'd never have to know how close he'd come, how much he'd needed her, and how very desperate he was.

He looked at the necklace in his hand. He remembered how it had shone against her smooth, creamy skin. He remembered the feel of her against him, the soft texture of her lips, the taste of her in his mouth.

With a muffled curse, he squeezed closed his fist and tapped gently on the window. He waited, holding his breath. The silence around him was alive with sounds, and yet he heard nothing from inside the house. There was no response, no stirring around, no voice or inquiry.

They'd told him at the hospital in Flagstaff that Mallory Wakefield had been released, and the war-weary nurse at the emergency desk remembered hearing her accept a ride back to Sedona from a state policeman.

He glanced at her rental car parked in the same spot in the drive where it had been on the morning he'd picked her up to start their search. So the fact that it was here now meant nothing. There were other cars for her to rent. He turned and peered through the window into the dark house. Maybe she'd changed her mind. Maybe she wasn't here at all, but in a motel somewhere in Flagstaff, instead.

He pushed the breath out of his lungs in one long, uninterrupted sigh. He'd been saved again. Fate seemed to have handed him one more opportunity, had managed to prevent him from making a big mistake—and even in a shaman's world, that kind of deliverance twice in a life-time was rare. He did what he could to put the disappoint-

ment aside by telling himself it had all worked out for the
best, that he'd saved himself a lot of heartache and embar-
rassment. He realized as he stood there now that he'd had
no idea what he'd planned to say to her, no idea why he
came or what he'd intended to do.

Then he heard the noise—feet on carpet, the sound of
running. But before he had time to think, before he could
compute and conclude, the door had been flung open and
Mallory was in his arms.

The shock was electric, sending feelings and sensations
racing through like brilliant bolts of lightning. Her mouth
on his was frantic—wild and demanding—and for a moment all he could do was stand there and accept.

"Oh, God, Graywolf," she groaned against his lips. "I
prayed you would come, I prayed you would come."

She kissed him again, fervid and reckless. Her tongue
dove deep, bold and uninhibited. Her arms were like ivy
twisting around his neck, and her slim body pressed into him
so tight he staggered back a step with the impact.

Graywolf's head was spinning, and his mind seemed to
have forgotten how to think. But at that moment, with this
woman in his arms, her mouth doing unbelievable things to
his, thinking wasn't something he was interested in doing.
He reached for her, his hands moving over soft curves and
her womanly form.

The thin nightshirt felt as diaphanous and sheer to his
hungry hands as fine silk against her skin, hiding nothing
but inciting his senses to an almost unbearable degree. He
wasn't thinking of white or red, of taboo or tradition. There
was only the woman in his arms, and the knowledge that she
wanted him with a desperation and desire he'd never known.

"I love you," she whispered, sinking her hands into his
long, straight hair. "Graywolf, I love you."

Yes, she did. He felt her love, felt the power and the force, felt the frankness and the commitment ... and the hopelessness of it. The words were like arrows through his heart—piercing and painful.

"No," he murmured, pulling his mouth from hers. He set her away from him, seeing the need in her eyes and feeling himself die just a little. "No love. There can be nothing more—no strings, no commitment, no future. Just this. Just tonight."

She looked into his dark eyes. There was no need for special gifts or second sight to read what was in them—the raw vulnerability, the distrust, the suspicion. She couldn't force him to trust her any more than she could force him to love her, and all the begging and pleading would do nothing to change his mind. If this was it—if this one night was all he could give her, all he had to offer, she would take it with no question. There would be time later to worry about why and how, to cope with the loss, and to grieve.

"Just tonight," she agreed, stepping close and encircling his neck with her arms. She pulled his lips close. Negotiations had ended, policy had been set, and ground rules established. This night would be theirs, and she was determined to take from it all that she could. She ran her hands up his back, over his broad shoulders, and let them tangle in his long hair. Maybe there would be only one night, but there would be no holding back.

Something in Graywolf freed itself, something that had been holding him back, keeping his feelings at bay. He'd been honest with her, and he was free now to take from her what he could. Steal away as much of her love as he could in the time they had left, and hope it was enough to last him the rest of his life. She understood what he could give her, and she'd been willing to accept. For them there would be no tomorrow, and yet, she had pulled him into her arms and kissed him as though tomorrow would never come.

Graywolf felt the world tilt off its axis, felt the ground beneath his feet quake and tremble. Dizzily he thought of the First People beneath the surface of the earth, spirits of his ancestors clamoring for the outside. But no ancient epic was responsible for the pitch and sway. It was the wild, erratic beating of his heart, and the desperate desire for the woman in his arms.

He pulled her close, his hand moving over her in a silent, reverent worship. She was the embodiment of everything he'd ever dreamed of, he'd ever hoped to have. She was *his* woman—he'd laid claim to her long before she'd ever walked into his hogan. She'd been a part of him from the beginning, part of the life he'd lived, part of the air he'd breathed, part of the dreams he'd dreamed, and she would stay with him long after the giant bird had carried her back to the land of the Round Eyes.

His hands traveled down, over the gentle swell of her bottom. He pressed her into him, his body so hungry for hers he thought he might die on the spot.

"Mallory," he murmured against her lips. He picked her up in his arms, carrying her through the dark house to the small bedroom. Marissa Wakefield's conservative furnishings were nothing like those of her youth. There might not have been a white iron bed, no fancy pink comforter or frilly pillows, but fantasy had become reality nonetheless. Mallory was in his arms—hungry for him—and it was more than he'd ever hoped for.

Mallory felt the mattress against her back, felt his hands moving over her, restless and urgent. He caressed her legs, her lips, her breasts, his hands leaving a trail of fire in their wake. Need arose in her like a swell moving through a calm sea, building potency and force, searching for the shoreline where it could erupt chaotic and strong. She'd never felt like this before, had never thought herself capable. This was more than passion, more than desire. The strange, exotic potion coursing through her veins bordered on obsession. She'd become a stranger to herself—an alien creature, desperate and hungry for the man who'd become the center of her life, the gate to her soul.

She reached for him, wanting to feel the massive body against her, wanting to assuage the terrible ache inside her, but he stepped just out of reach. She stared up at him, his white T-shirt glowing translucent in the moonlight. In one smooth motion, it was gone, leaving his mahogany chest open to her hungry gaze. Sitting up, she reached for her nightshirt, slipping it from her body with no thought to modesty or reserve. She was beyond that now—beyond the point of no return.

Graywolf stared at the sight of her before him. His mouth had gone dry, the gnawing in his gut changing the hunger in him to near craving. He murmured a prayer, an ancient chant, in silent plea that the vision of her was real.

Her body was perfect—more perfect than he remembered, more perfect than he could have imagined. In the moonlight she was almost dreamlike—her skin as white as snow, as perfect and as flawless as the finest rendering of an artist's brush or sculpture's hand. She was a goddess, his ideal of perfection and excellence. He was awed by such beauty, humbled that she offered it to him.

"Graywolf," she whispered, rising to her knees. She lifted her arms to him, beckoning him to come.

"So beautiful," he murmured almost absently. He was hesitant, half afraid that if he were to reach out, she would disappear. But then her hands were on him, pulling him close, moving over him and driving him mad. "I want you so much."

"I want you, too," Mallory sighed as his arms snaked around her and crushed her to him. "I always will."

Graywolf savaged her mouth, pushing her soft lips apart and plunging deep with his tongue. The taste of her incited him, heating his blood, invading his system like some kind of exotic drug. He was propelled by forces beyond himself, beyond tangible thought and reasonable demands. He felt empowered, imbued with superhuman strength, supernatural sight, as though he'd chewed the forbidden peyote bean and entered a magical realm of altered awareness and mystic perception. She was his destiny, his fate, and he surrendered completely.

Mallory accepted the almost brutal kiss, reveling in the raw, wild nature of it, and the man in her arms. His hands moved over her—bold and seeking, causing the ache in her to become a delicious agony. She slid her hands down his powerful torso, finding the buttoned fly of his jeans and yanking it open. Inside, she surrounded him with her hands and felt a tremor rumble through his body.

The feel of her hands on him had the breath catching in Graywolf's throat. Something snapped in him, some slender thread of restraint, some thin strand of control. He pressed her onto the bed, her hair spreading out against the mattress like a halo of white light around her. He kissed her neck, her shoulder, the line of her chin. With hands and mouth he honored her breasts, reveling in their fullness and masterfully bringing their soft, pink centers to firm tautness.

He wanted to know all of her, he wanted to touch and taste every texture, every characteristic. He wanted to worship and revere, to revel and enjoy, but the longing in him was becoming unbearable. Forces were building in him—primal and basic—and even his iron strength couldn't keep them at bay. She made him feel like a god, but he was, after all, merely a man, and the need for her threatened his soul, his sanity, his senses.

He pushed against her, moving her legs apart and settling himself between them. He heard her groan softly, a plaintive, needy sound that ricocheted through him. Rising up, he looked down at her lying beneath him. Her eyes had been closed, but she opened them now and fixed her gaze on him. Her beautiful face was streaked with need, and her lips silently repeated his name—a sensuous, carnal chant. *Graywolf, Graywolf.*

He slipped his jeans to the floor, taking a small packet from the pocket before letting them slide onto the carpet.

"There can be no mistakes," he murmured, in a coarse voice. They had agreed on one night, and the thin latex shield that he used to protect them both would ensure there would be no regrets.

In one powerful move, he entered her. For a moment, he could do nothing—not even move. Everything had fallen along the wayside, discarded and forgotten. Conscious thought ceased, involuntary movements were ignored, and ambient noise was quelled. It was all he could do to brace himself against the violent assault to his system, to the frenzy of emotion and sensation that coursed savagely through his body.

"Mallory," he murmured dizzily, the ringing in his ears making his own voice sound muffled and faraway. "Oh, Mallory."

Her body moved beneath him, sending delicious slivers of sensation jolting through him and starting a chain reaction in him. Life returned in one blinding flash as air began circulating through his lungs, blood started pumping hot through his veins, and muscle found form and motion again. He pushed into her deeply, hearing the sound of her soft groan in his ear and feeling himself go a little mad.

See me, now that I am one with another.

The chant flowed through his brain, like the song from an ancient medicine man—haunting and powerful. It was as though he'd finally discovered what it was to belong, to feel at one with nature and the earth, to be a part of the stars, and to touch the heavens.

See me...

The words screamed silently in his ears, reverberating hotly through his system like molten lava down the side of a cliff.

He was one—with himself, with the earth, with those who had come before. He was part of the grand scheme, part of that blissful harmony of the ancients, that timeless and eternal unity of souls. Each brush of skin to skin, of man to woman, made him feel more alive, more connected. And even as the storm raged inside him, he felt at peace. He was one with his woman.

Mallory felt the air leave her lungs in one, long gasp as her body slowly transformed to mold intimately with his. The night, the moment, the man, had become everything, and she could think of nothing else. Her world had become Benjamin Graywolf, and the act of love they shared.

And for her it was love. Never in her life had she felt like this, had she cared so much, or so deeply. He was everything she'd ever wanted, more than she'd ever hoped to have. It didn't matter that there were no promises, no guarantees. His honesty had bordered on brutal—one night, and nothing more. But as she felt his body move inside her, as she felt herself come alive with new life and new passion, she knew that one night with him would be worth a lifetime in the arms of any other man.

She was hungry—so hungry for him, and the motion of his body inside hers made the hunger almost unbearable.

She felt herself falling, falling, tumbling out into space—reaching, wanting, hoping.

She felt him tremble, felt desire quaking through his system, and it made her desperate for more. She twisted beneath him, the needs in her quickly becoming cravings. Her hands moved over him, wild and ravenous—over his shoulders, down his hard torso, over the rounded swell of his bottom. He was magnificent—firm and perfect, and she couldn't seem to get enough.

"I love you," she whispered, slipping her legs around his waist as his huge body drove into her over and over again. "I love you. I love you."

Graywolf heard her words over and over again—felt them in his heart and in his head. He knew he should stop them, knew he should tell her to stop, tell her no, but he couldn't. They were such beautiful words, like magic in his ears—a soothing balm that healed and protected. After a lifetime of hard breaks and harsh realities, he wanted the gentle comfort of her love, he wanted to wrap himself in it, to be consoled and shielded by its purity and its strength.

He was the shaman, he knew the ancient ceremonies and aged chants. But her medicine was much more powerful. She had cast her spell on him, had worked her wizardry and performed her art. He could think of nothing but her—of touching her, holding her, being inside her. Her love was a warm, wonderful place—a place where skin color didn't matter, and Indian wasn't a dirty word, and for just this once—just tonight—he could forget.

Mallory felt something in her snap, something powerful and profound. It was as if the world had slipped away, leaving only the man and the moment—and she was quickly losing control over both. Each powerful thrust of his body, each caress of his lips or touch of his hand, caused a flood of fire to ravage through her. She felt herself propelled upward, traveling at the speed of light to a place she'd never been before. She was moving faster and farther than ever before. New worlds were opening up to her with every breath, new horizons were being conquered with every touch.

Never had it been like this before, never had *she* been like this before. It was all so new, so different, and yet he gave her no time to be cautious or afraid. When the zenith came, it came for her in one blinding moment of sight and sound, of body and soul. She was hurled out into space, her body convulsing wild and erratic. She had no thoughts of control, no idea of escape. She just held on to him, and let him guide her beyond.

Graywolf felt her body tense, heard the sharp intake of breath into her lungs and the strangled gasp in her throat. He pulled his mouth from hers, looking into her face and feeling the hold on his own control begin to slip.

In the moonlight she was magnificent. Her beautiful face was a portrait of ecstasy, distorted only by the sweet agony of rapture.

He pulled her close, his body moving instinctively as she made her way through the tortured labyrinth of delirium. But the effort was quickly becoming too much. His body shook, crying out for solace and completion, and his mind was feverish with the soft, carnal sounds that she made.

Hunger gnawed at him, urgent and critical, and his breath came in huge, heaving gasps. Shivers of excitement darted through him, like tiny sparks of lightning along a wire. She was like a finely crafted instrument tuned to perfection, and in her arms he'd become a master musician.

"I love you," she groaned, her voice raw and made all but mute by the turbulence of the moment.

But Graywolf heard—with his heart rather than his ear, and felt the last fragile hold on his sanity give way. With an anguished growl, he surged into her.

. . . one with another . . .

The words chanted through his brain like an ancient sing, revered and respected. They were one—joined by an emotion so profound he dared not give it voice.

His body trembled, convulsing with sight, sound and sensation. She was his, they belonged together. One. In that moment he gave her all he had, all he possessed—his love, his life, his soul.

With his lips to her ear, he whispered to her his secret Navajo name.

"You're very beautiful."

Mallory turned her head and looked at him, finding his comment as astonishing as it was unexpected. "You think so?"

They lay together, their bodies still locked in an intimate embrace. Graywolf's head rested against her shoulder, and his mouth brushed the tender skin of her neck. Her blond hair looked like white silk in the moonlight, and he picked up a long strand and lazily twisted it through his fingers. "You sound surprised."

Mallory shrugged, his compliment making her feel oddly embarrassed. She'd always assumed that she was attractive enough, that she held a certain attraction for the opposite sex. After all, other men had told her she was beautiful. It was just that until now, until this man, she'd never really *felt* it. "I guess I am—a little."

He twisted onto his side, bending his arm at the elbow and resting his head on his hand. He gazed down into her crystal blue eyes, which were dark and murky now. "Oh, come on. You're not going to try to tell me no one's ever said that to you before."

She smiled. "No, that's not it. I just didn't..." She stopped, letting her words drift.

"Just didn't what?" he prompted. His fingers dropped the long strand of hair and began to trace the delicate swell of her breast.

"I guess I didn't think you thought so," she murmured after a while.

"I'm Navajo," he said, bending down to place his lips where his finger had been. "Not made of stone."

"I know," she whispered, her breath catching in her throat. "But you never acted as though...I didn't even think you liked me."

He lifted his head. "I didn't. But those nights in the desert were awfully long. I would lie there and think of you." His rigid mouth softened with a smile. "You sort of grew on me."

"You fought it."

"Maybe," he shrugged. "Indians aren't suppose to want white women. That's been...*discouraged* in the past."

"Well, this isn't the Wild West any longer," she pointed out. "It isn't exactly like my pappy is going to be roundin' up the posse to come after you, or anything like that."

"You're white, and I'm Indian, that's never going to change," he pointed out. "And it's obvious you've never had a mob of reporters after you."

She pulled back a little. "You still think I'm going to write about all of this?"

He shrugged, his nonchalance betraying his real feelings. "Maybe you will, maybe you won't. It doesn't matter anymore."

She regarded him for a long time, his handsome face shadowed by the darkness. "You still don't trust me at all, do you?"

"Don't take it so personally," he said lightly, pulling her back into his arms despite her feeble attempts to stop him. "There aren't a lot of people I do trust."

"But I do take it personally," she said, absorbing the words and his bitter tone like a blow to the chest. "How could I not? I told you I loved you. Doesn't that mean anything?"

Graywolf's body tensed, and he pulled away. He stood, oblivious to his nakedness, walked to the window and stared out into the night. "Love...was your choice."

Mallory suddenly felt naked, vulnerable and exposed. She reached for the sheet, pulling it up around her even as the tears spilled down her cheeks. "You're such a coward."

"Not a coward," he said quietly. "Just a realist."

"You're running scared."

He turned around slowly. "Don't make this into something more than it is. It's one night—nothing more, nothing less. It's that simple."

"There's nothing simple about any of this," she said, her voice cracking. She scooted up to lean back against the headboard. "Whether you want to accept it or not, I love you—and there's nothing you can do to stop the way I feel." She paused, her chest rising and falling with angry breaths. "And you're a fool to think I had a choice at all."

He walked back to the bed, lowering himself down beside her. "Do you want me to leave?"

"I want you to be honest with me, and with yourself."

He reached for her, yanking the sheet away and pulling her beneath him. "I want you, how's that for honesty?"

He moved his body into hers, pressing his mouth against her lips and kissing her even as the fire in his loins built to an inferno. He didn't want to talk it out, didn't want to explain or define what he felt or why. He wanted her, that was all that was important.

Mallory surrendered to his lovemaking—she could do nothing else. In the end it didn't matter if he trusted her or not, if he liked her or loved her or would be there forever. He was the man she loved, and she would take from him what she could, for as long as he'd let her.

"You want me," she murmured in a thick voice.

"I do, very much."

"That's never going to change."

As he gave in to the passion, gave in to the desire pounding through him, he knew her words would stay with him for a long, long time. She'd gotten under his skin, gotten to him in a way no other woman had—not even Susan. He'd hoped that this night would be his cure, would purge him of all need, of all vulnerability, but now, he wasn't so sure.

He wanted her with a desperation he'd never known before, with a recklessness that could only end in disaster. He'd allowed himself one night to get her out of his system, to rid himself of the craving once and for all. But now, with her in his arms, with her touching him and surrounding him with her love, he wasn't so sure.

His life stretched out before him, empty and barren, with the light of a special love nowhere to be found.

Chapter 13

"I thought Indians call their men braves."

"We do."

"Hmm," she murmured thoughtfully, giving him a skeptical glance.

Graywolf turned to her, the predawn sky through the window looking pale and bleak. "Are we going to start this again?"

"Start what?" Mallory asked innocently.

"This coward thing," he said. They were both propped up against the headboard, the pastel sheet tossed haphazardly across them. "We weren't going to talk about that, I thought we'd agreed."

"Well, I'm breaking the agreement," Mallory said, turning her head and looking up at him. "It's a woman's prerogative to change her mine, you know."

"You're not changing your mind, you're changing the rules."

She shrugged carelessly, giving him a small smile. "You're the lawyer, so sue me, then."

"Mallory," he said with a sigh, sliding down onto the mattress and taking her with him. "This is serious. I don't want to hurt you. Don't make this into something more than it is."

"It's too late for that," she whispered, looking up into his dark eyes. "I already have."

"But I told you from the beginning," he said with a frustrated breath. "This was it—just tonight. That's all there can be."

"I know what you told me," she admitted willingly, reaching up and sliding her hand along his cheek. "But I still want more."

Frustrated, he stared up at the ceiling. "It's impossible and you know it."

"Do I?" she asked, turning onto her side and looking down at him. "What's so impossible about it? Explain it to me."

He gave her a dubious glance. "You know very well what I'm talking about."

"You mean that red-and-white thing—that 'you're a big bad Injun and I'm the frail white woman' thing?" She rolled her eyes. "Don't you think that argument wears just a little thin in this day and age? I mean, for God's sake, this isn't 1860, I'm not one of the women from the wagon train. We're two reasonably intelligent, well-educated people. Are we suppose to let some ridiculous customs and prejudices get in our way?"

"It's more than that and you know it!"

"No," she insisted. "I don't. Maybe you should enlighten me."

He glared up at her. "Don't make me hurt you."

"Too late, you've already done that," she told him, hiding the pain with a matter-of-fact voice.

He felt a cold chill spread through him. "Look, let's just drop it. It's nearly daylight. I should go."

"Oh, no, you don't," she said, grabbing his arm as he started to get up. "Not until you answer my question."

"I already have," he said, angry that it was ending so badly. "It just wouldn't, that's all there is to it."

"Because you're being stubborn."

"No."

"Because you're a coward."

"No!"

"Because you don't want to try?"

"No, damn it, because . . ." His voice thundered in frustration, and he pounded his fist down hard on the bed. "Because *I don't love you.*"

His harsh words reverberated through the quiet house, and Graywolf cursed violently under his breath. He hadn't wanted to say it, hadn't wanted to hurt her in that way. The night with her had been like no other. Why couldn't she have just left well enough alone? Why couldn't they have ended it without the hard feelings and ugly scenes? But she'd pushed and prodded him, had interrogated him with that reporter's mind of hers.

"I don't believe you."

He stared up at her, rendered speechless with surprise. He wasn't sure what he'd expected—tears, maybe, angry recriminations, hurling insults. But not this. "What did you say?"

"I said that's bull," she told him, moving her body over his. "I don't believe any of it."

"I'm just trying to be honest—"

"You're just trying to make excuses," she said, cutting him off. She leaned close, brushing her lips against his.

"You love me—you don't have to say it. I know. I know it just like I knew that Marissa was in trouble. I...just... *know*." She kissed him, slipping the sheet out from between their bodies.

"Mallory, please, listen—" he said, wanting to protest, wanting to explain, but already his arms were moving to embrace her.

"No, you listen," she said, interrupting him with another kiss. "I love you, and you love me, too. We could make it work—I know we could, but not if you don't give us a chance." Moving with slow, deliberate motions, she joined their bodies together. "I'll wait until you're ready. I'll wait even if you never will be ready." Her lips moved against his, her voice barely above a whisper. "I'll wait for you, Graywolf—forever, if I have to."

Graywolf closed his eyes, succumbing to what he was helpless to resist—her. She was right, of course. He did love her—wholly, desperately, absolutely. But one of them had to be practical, one of them had to think of the consequences. She had no concept of what their life would be. She hadn't known prejudice, didn't understand it the way he did. She'd never dealt with the pressures of an intolerant society and didn't know what it would do to their love.

He rose up, turning and reversing their positions on the bed. She stared up at him, her lips moving as she whispered his secret name over and over again. For now, while she was in his arms, while her beautiful body caressed his, love was not only enough, it was everything. He wanted to touch and explore, to study and memorize, all that there was of her. He loved her, with all of his heart, with all of his soul. And for what time they had left, for however many hours or minutes that was allotted, he would give himself to her completely.

* * *

"I don't understand," Marissa said, shaking her head. "I'm the one who spent the night in the hospital. So how come you're the one who looks like hell?"

Mallory shifted her eyes from the road just long enough to shoot her sister a tired smile. She didn't doubt she looked like hell—she certainly *felt* like it. "Is it that bad?"

Marissa nodded, making a face. "I'm afraid so." She watched as Mallory turned her attention back to the highway. "Bad night?"

"Actually, it was a wonderful night," Mallory said with a sad smile, thinking back to the long hours of love. But then the morning had come, and she remembered how it had felt to watch Graywolf walk away. She felt the sting of tears and tried her best to blink them back. "It was the morning I had a tough time getting through."

"This has to do with him, doesn't it," Marissa said. "Benjamin Graywolf."

Mallory shrugged, not trusting her voice. The highway blurred as tears filled her eyes, and she batted them away with an impatient hand. "It's . . . it's over now."

"It doesn't sound over for you," Marissa observed.

Mallory looked at her sister, the expression on her face saying so much more than her words ever could. "He's got this thing—about him being Indian, me being white," she said, a tear sliding unnoticed down her cheek. "He doesn't trust me, I know that. But I know he loves me, I *know* it damn it, I *feel* it. But he won't even listen, won't even give us a chance."

Marissa reached across the seat and placed a comforting hand on her sister's arm. "You must love him very much."

"I do," Mallory whispered. "Oh, I do. But he says I just don't understand."

"Maybe you should listen to him."

Mallory reared back, pulling her arm away. "What do you mean? How can you say that?"

"Mallory, listen," Marissa said earnestly. "I've worked on the reservation, lived there, made friends there—and it has opened my eyes to a lot. People like you and me, Mallory, we don't know about hardship and prejudice—not really, not like people on the reservation do. My God, it's a different world out there. Our lives are fairy tales compared to what these people face every day. I mean, can you imagine what it is to go to bed hungry each night, or not have enough clothes to keep you warm in the winter, no shoes that fit?

"That kind of poverty is appalling to us, but it's just par for the course to the Navajo. We can't even begin to understand how difficult, how hopeless, that can become." She leaned over and took her sister's arm again. "I know you love him, and I've seen the way he looks at you. But he comes from a very different world, he's led a very different kind of life. Growing up on the reservation isn't easy, and I can only guess at what he's had to face—bigotry, indifference, privation. You can't blame him for being a little cynical when it comes to white society." She hesitated for a moment, giving Mallory's arm a squeeze. "And you can't blame him for wanting to protect you from all of that."

Mallory wanted to rage at her sister, wanted to yell and scream and argue with her, tell her she had it all wrong, that none of that applied to her and Graywolf. That they were different, their love was special, and all the intolerance and difficulty didn't apply to them. But the fact was everything Marissa had said was true—all of it.

Her head ached, the pounding at her temples making her feel sick. She didn't want to think about all of this now, didn't want to think about the differences between them and the obstacles that stood in their way. She loved Graywolf. Why wasn't that love enough?

Just then a pickup loaded with howling teenagers barreled down on them from a freeway on-ramp, making it necessary for Mallory to swerve quickly in order to avoid a collision. Marissa grabbed for her leg, wincing painfully as the sudden motion caused the unwieldy cast on her ankle to fall heavily against the dash.

"Damn," Mallory swore, shooting the reckless young driver a dirty look. Her head still pounding, she wiped away the moisture from her eyes and sighed heavily. "There's a coffee shop just ahead. What do you say to some coffee, maybe some lunch?"

"Sure," Marissa said in as light a voice as she could muster while shifting her foot back into a more comfortable position. Her ankle throbbed, but she was grateful for the distraction. The mood between them had gotten very somber, and it didn't take her "twin radar" to see that her sister was miserable. She swatted at the cumbersome cast. "I don't know how I'm ever going to make it through six weeks with this thing. I swear it has a mind of its own."

The coffee shop was identical to the thousands just like it that lined the highways of the nation, with its stock design and gaudy interiors. Mallory helped her sister out of the car and into the familiar-looking foyer. A tired-looking hostess greeted them inside and led them through the restaurant to a booth near a window that offered an unrestricted view of the cars zipping past noisily along the freeway outside.

The sisters had long ago become oblivious to the stares their appearance always attracted, and they ignored the curious glances of the other patrons as they passed. Mallory helped Marissa into the booth, gingerly guiding the clumsy cast into a comfortable position, then slid into the seat opposite her. Once settled, they perused the oversize menus.

"He said he didn't love me."

Marissa glanced up from the menu, surprised. It was obvious Mallory hadn't appreciated her comments earlier, so she'd been prepared to drop the subject. "Is that what you think?"

"I think he'd like to convince himself of that."

"But..." Marissa prompted when Mallory fell silent.

Mallory shrugged, smiling a little. "But I don't think when it comes to love we always have a choice in the matter." She put down her menu and looked across the table to her sister. "I know I didn't."

Marissa reached across the table and took her twin's hand. "I hate to see you hurting."

Tears glittered in Mallory's eyes. "Well, you know how the song goes—love hurts." She shrugged carelessly. "I told him if he ever changed his mind, I'd be waiting."

Marissa gave her a doubtful look. "And you meant that? You'd really wait?"

Mallory shook her head, forcing out a sad laugh. "Pretty pathetic, isn't it." The smile faded quickly and she grew serious. "But this isn't the way it was with Randy. I mean, I felt bad when it ended between us, but we both moved on. With Graywolf..." She closed her eyes and dragged a hand through her long hair. Opening her eyes, she searched her sister's face helplessly. "Oh, Marissa, I'll never get over him." She glanced down at the menu again, the flashy photos of the restaurant's entrées making her feel queasy. "You think I'm a fool, don't you."

Marissa coughed out an inelegant laugh. "You're worried *I'm* going to think you're a fool?" Marissa gasped, her mouth breaking into a wide smile. She tossed the menus down on to the table in front of her. "Does the name Dylan James mean anything to you?"

Mallory remembered the father of Marissa's child all too well. "That was a long time ago."

"It was a lifetime ago," she admitted with a sigh. She turned and stared out the window. "But as pathetic as it sounds, I still think of him. I still remember."

Mallory followed her sister's gaze out the window to the cars speeding past. "The Wakefield twins," she sighed sadly. "We're a pair, all right."

Marissa gave her head a shake, scattering the memories that had haunted her for fifteen years. "You know," she said, looking across the table to her sister. "You never did tell me about him—Graywolf, I mean, about how you met, how this whole thing got started. It all happened pretty fast. That's not exactly like you."

Mallory nodded her head in agreement. It wasn't like her. Since her marriage had ended, she'd had little interest in romantic entanglements. Her failure to make it work with Randy had left her reluctant to begin another relationship, hesitant to try again. And yet she'd hardly been hesitant with Graywolf. In fact, she'd gone out on a limb—confessing her feelings and pleading with him to stay. But there had been something different about Benjamin Graywolf from the beginning.

She thought back to that first day, to that long, hot drive out to Graywolf's hogan. He'd been so abrupt with her then, so curt and rude. He hadn't wanted her there, had wanted no part of her at all. But even then, even with his hostility and his rudeness, there had been something about him, something that had gotten to her, something she had never forgotten. Was it possible she had sensed something? Had she known at that first meeting just how important he'd become to her?

So much had happened since that first encounter, so much had changed, and so many feelings had been revealed. It seemed hard to believe so much could change in such a short period of time.

"I first heard about him from Detective Begay," Mallory began, thinking back to those frightening days when Marissa was missing and she could get no one to listen. All during their lunch, and for the rest of the drive back to Sedona, Mallory recounted everything to her sister, a complete chronology from her first encounter with Graywolf, through the episode at Barney's Tavern, to the discovery of the crescent moon and stars. Relating the details of the story was almost cathartic for her, and by the time she pulled the car to a stop in the driveway of Marissa's little house, she was exhausted and emotionally drained. Graywolf was still gone, but sharing her feelings with Marissa had helped.

Inside, there were two messages waiting on the answering machine. For a moment Mallory allowed a glimmer of hope to rise, fantasizing they were from Graywolf, saying he'd changed his mind and he wanted her with him, but that faint hope soon died. One message was from her editor, reminding her the powwow was scheduled to begin next week and to give him a call, and the other was from Wayne Clair at the *Register* in Flagstaff, who'd picked up the story of her sister's rescue and wanted to know if she had "anything" for his paper.

She didn't.

Falling onto the bed beside Marissa—the bed she'd shared with Graywolf only hours before, she closed her eyes. She didn't have the energy to answer the messages, or the interest. She knew she had to start thinking of work again, knew she had to put her feelings aside and get on with her life—but not now, not tonight. Maybe tomorrow it would be better, maybe tomorrow it wouldn't hurt quite so much.

She opened her eyes and stared up at the ceiling. Who was she kidding? It wasn't going to get any better—not today, not tomorrow, and not the day after that. She'd just have to try and get used to it—learn to live with it. One way or another she was going to have to find a way to live without Graywolf, just the way Marissa had learned to live without Dylan James.

"For you. A gift."

"Oh, no," Mallory said, shaking her head. "No, I couldn't." She tried to hand the delicately carved, turquoise-studded silver bracelet back to the aging Navajo woman who sat behind the makeshift counter in the small booth.

"It's yours," the woman said simply, smiling broadly. She gestured to the necklace around Mallory's neck. "Silver stars to match a golden moon."

Mallory's hand went to the necklace around her neck, remembering the night Graywolf had put it there. "Well, I'll take it," she said, after a moment, looking with affection into the woman's worn, weathered face. It was a kind face, a wise face, a face that spoke volumes, that told stories and relayed emotions that no words could ever tell. "But I insist on paying for it."

The woman shook her head stubbornly. "A gift," she insisted. "Friend to friend."

Mallory almost felt like crying. In the course of the last five days, Ida Tso had become her friend. They'd met on the opening day of the powwow as Ida and her family had prepared their small, hastily constructed stall for business. There were scores of small booths lining the tribal marketplace, representing hundreds of tribes and their native handicrafts from around the country, but Mallory had been drawn to Ida's by the brightly colored Navajo rugs that covered the crude, clapboard walls, and by the beautifully crafted silver jewelry displayed in her shiny glass cabinets.

Something had happened on that first afternoon, something in her conversation with the Navajo woman had stuck with Mallory, causing an idea to start forming in her head. She'd begun to see the approach for her articles on the powwow, the angle she wanted to take, and what her focus would be.

Ida Tso was a fascinating woman—an *ahnii*, matriarch of her clan, who was both revered for her wisdom and respected for her age and her knowledge. Mallory wanted to make Ida and her family the basis for her articles, highlighting what the powwow meant to them, what hopes it represented, what struggles they'd overcome to get there, and what sacrifices they'd had to make.

She'd talked her idea over with Ida and, with the older woman's consent, had begun spending much of her time with the Tso family—both at their booth in the marketplace and in the small camper and tent in the temporary campsite outside the festival grounds. In the five days since, Mallory had met many of Ida's clan as they'd stopped to help out at the booth. She'd interviewed Ida's daughter Esther and son-in-law Charlie on concerns they had for their children at the reservation schools, and had played with their new baby daughter. They were warm, loving people, and Mallory had come to have enormous respect for both Ida and her whole clan.

Mallory looked down at the bracelet Ida had thrust into her hand. It was narrow and elegant, and the craftsmanship was exquisite. A row of delicate stars had been painstakingly etched into the silver, each star with a turquoise center. The jewelry that lined Ida's display case had made Mallory think of Graywolf, and of the beautiful pieces that had filled his studio.

Graywolf. Just thinking of him had a rush of longing traveling through her. It had been twelve days since she'd last seen him, since she'd held him in her arms and told him how she felt. Twelve days—not even two weeks, and yet already it felt like a lifetime.

Five days ago, Mallory had arrived at the Navajo National Fairgrounds with mixed emotions. While she was anxious to get back to work, anxious to absorb herself in a story and a cause, she was painfully aware that this was Graywolf's country, these were his people, his world. Everyone she saw, everything she did, reminded her of him.

He would be attending the powwow, she knew that for a fact. But with hundreds of tribes represented at the conference, and thousands of tourists attending from across the nation, the chances of her running into him did seem remote. But she had managed to run into Hosteen Johnny, who had greeted her with a smile, calling her Hair of Sunshine again. So, remote or not, the possibility of meeting up with Graywolf was there, and she couldn't help but be edgy. What would she do if she saw him? How would she act? What would she say?

She slipped the bracelet over her hand and onto her wrist. The shiny silver glinted brightly in the sunlight. While the thought of seeing Graywolf again terrified her, the chance that she might not frightened her even more.

"Perfect," Ida said, assessing the bracelet as it dangled from Mallory's wrist. "As though it was made for your hand alone." She chuckled, obviously pleased, and made a sweeping gesture with her hands. "Like the People had written it in the stars."

"Okay, okay," Mallory conceded, slipping an arm around Ida's broad, squat shoulders. She'd come to appreciate Ida's dry wit and sense of humor over the last few days. "But enough with the mysticism. You've convinced me. I'll take it, I'll take it." She tightened her hold, giving Ida a gentle squeeze. "I'll treasure it always. Thank you."

"Hosteen Johnny named you Hair of Sunshine," Ida said thoughtfully. "But I will call you Pretty Friend."

Mallory blinked, surprised. "You know Hosteen Johnny?"

Ida nodded. "He is a wise man, a great healer, *yataalii*. He says you have a generous heart." Ida smiled up at her. "And I think he is right."

Mallory felt emotion thick in her throat, and looked down at the bracelet on her wrist. "You're the generous one."

"You are a kind lady," Ida said, beaming up at Mallory and patting her hand affectionately. "*Biligaana* aren't always kind to Navajo."

Mallory felt a sinking feeling in the pit of her stomach. Her eyes had been opened in the last several days to the poverty and the hardships of reservation life, and her heart went out to the people and their suffering. Looking down into Ida's wise, weathered face, she was suddenly aware and resentful of the history of suffering and abuses visited upon the native nations at the hands of the White Eyes.

"Let's hope someday all that will change," Mallory said quietly with a sad smile. She remembered Graywolf's harsh words about her assignment to report on the powwow, how he'd ridiculed and belittled her desire to inform and educate her readership on Native American cultures. He'd been wrong to prejudge her motives and scorn her efforts, yet she could understand his anger and mistrust.

Trust. It was the one thing she knew she could never have from him. He could spend the night in her bed—maybe even love her just a little—but trust? It was out of the question. She was white, she was *biligaana,* she was part of the world of the White Eyes, and she wasn't to be trusted.

Mallory closed her eyes to the frustration—a feeling that was becoming all too familiar. It wasn't fair. He was holding her responsible for the sins of others, for things she had no part of. He wasn't giving her a chance.

She took a deep breath, forcing the feelings aside. Fair or not, it didn't matter. He would never trust her, and she would be wise just to accept it. Like living without him, it was something she'd have to get used to.

"Hey, you two," Charlie Nez called as he walked up to the booth with his young daughter in his arms. "The Council of Tribal Elders is about to convene. We've got seats saved, but you'd better hurry. The tent's filling up fast."

Ida smiled up at her son-in-law and gave her little granddaughter a peck on the cheek. "Help me lock up."

Handing the child to Ida, Charlie pulled the plywood cover down over the stall and secured it with a heavy padlock. "All set."

The general meeting of the Council of Tribal Elders was the hallmark of the convention—not an event for the tourists. Delegates from each lodge represented at the powwow would meet to address issues and concerns they each had determined to be the most urgent in their communities. These issues would then be discussed and examined, and the floor would be open for dialogue. It was the aim of this general meeting that through discussion and exchange, possible solutions and conclusions could be found and considered for not only the most immediate, pressing concerns of each of the individual communities represented, but also long-range goals could be set and implemented. Whether the issues were government intervention into tribal business, or health and educational concerns on the reservation, the hope of the council was that by banding together and better understanding the problems each individual lodge faced, they could reach out to one another and form a network of assistance.

The green-and-white-striped tent was enormous, and by the time Mallory and her friends arrived, it looked as though all of the more than five hundred seats had been taken. The raised dais at the front of the tent held three long tables, set in a semicircle. Microphones lined each table, and placards in front of each announced the particular tribe or lodge represented, and the name of the individual delegate.

Charlie pointed to a row midway down the center aisle where Esther had saved them seats, and while he and Ida made their way to them, Mallory headed for the press box near the front of the stage.

The crowd was noisy with excitement, everyone anxious to have their own particular agendas and needs open to discussion and analysis. Mallory stepped past the microphone that had been placed in the center aisle for questions from the floor, and slid into the press box—which was merely a section of folding chairs that had been roped off from the rest of the crowd. But most of the seats in the press box were vacant. The small crowd of reporters and cameramen stood at the front of the box, jockeying for position and optimum camera angles.

Mallory recognized a couple of AP reporters, and one from the *Flagstaff Register* whom she'd met when she'd stopped by Wayne's office to pick up her fax. She gave them each a brief nod as she elbowed past, making her way through the crowd. No novice to the news pack, she wasn't intimidated, and she jostled herself into a position near the stage where she could hear and have an unrestricted view. She had just pulled her hand-held tape recorder from her bag and was fumbling around for her tablet and pen when the delegates began entering the tent from a side opening. Climbing the steps to the dais, the solemn-faced assembly began making their way to their seats.

Of the hundred or so tribes and lodges represented on the council, Mallory noted that only a few were represented by women—less than ten. Making a face, she pulled her tablet from her bag and made a note of that on the page. Maybe their cultures shared more than they thought.

With the appearance of the delegates on stage, the crowd began to quiet down. Council president Joseph Brightraven stepped to the center podium, clearing his throat loudly, and called the meeting to order. The crowd stilled almost immediately, with only the sounds of the desert wind gusting through the tent flaps breaking the sudden silence.

Brightraven, a Cherokee from New Mexico, made a few brief opening remarks, then introduced the other delegates and the nations they represented. Mallory had just flipped on her tape recorder and was about to make a notation on her tablet about the delegate of the Navajo being a woman, when she stopped suddenly. She had caught a movement from the corner of her eye, something that caused the blood to drain slowly from her face. Turning her head, she looked up just in time to see Benjamin Graywolf step into the tent from a side entrance.

Chapter 14

Mallory felt light-headed, and the ground beneath her feet seemed suddenly to have a subtle tilt. She staggered to one side, colliding with the man standing next to her.

"Hey, watch it," he snapped angrily, lifting the clumsy video camera from his shoulder and rubbing the inky spot where her pen had jabbed his arm.

"I'm sorry," she apologized, feeling startled and disoriented. She reared away, overcorrecting in her haste and bringing her foot down hard on the toe of the *Register* reporter. "Sorry," she said again, spinning around, cringing. "I'm very sorry."

Clumsily she managed to nudge away from the stage to a quiet spot near a folding chair at a far side of the press box. For five days she'd wondered how she would react to seeing Graywolf again—and now she knew. She was a wreck. Her palms were sweating and her heart raced like crazy in her chest. It was ridiculous, and one way or another she was going to have to find a way to pull herself together.

With a hand on the chair to steady her, she took several long, deep breaths, forcing her heart rate to slow by sheer willpower alone. When she felt better, she turned again to the direction of the side entrance. Her body and her emotions still reacted strongly to the sight of him, but the shock had diminished, and her legs felt much sturdier beneath her.

He looked so handsome standing there, so endearingly familiar that it almost hurt her to watch. Yet as distressing as it seemed to be, she found it impossible to tear her gaze away.

Seeing him after so many days, and so many long nights alone, was like finding an oasis in the desert. She drank in the sight of him, her thirst insatiable. His powerful shoulders and impressive build were no less imposing in the casual dress clothes he wore now than they'd been in the Levi's and work shirts he'd worn in the desert. It was all she could do to stop herself from tearing through the crowd and running to him.

She'd seen him as a native craftsman at work in his studio, as a tracker on the trail of his prey, even as a shaman with second sight. But in the dress shirt and expensive slacks, he looked every bit the lawyer now. The pale blue oxford shirt made his skin look as smooth and rich as mahogany, and the fine wool slacks draped his legs with tailored perfection. Even with his long hair falling loose around his shoulders, he wore his grace and profession well.

But as she stood watching him, an icy chill made her shiver. An odd, uneasy feeling began to spread through her body—an uneasiness not unlike she'd felt when Marissa was in trouble. Something was wrong—but it wasn't her twin sister this time. It was something else, something she couldn't quite put her finger on. But it had to do with the tautness of Graywolf's expression, and the tension in his stance.

It was only then that she realized Graywolf looked... scared.

A gust of wind blew lazily through the tent, sending the walls billowing outward and sawdust swirling around her ankles. She was being silly, she told herself as she glanced up to the podium and at Joseph Brightraven, who still addressed the crowd in his slow, deep monotone. She was feeling uneasy because of Graywolf, because of seeing him again. Still, as the crowd erupted into applause at something Brightraven had said in his opening remarks, she couldn't quite shake the feeling.

Mallory's interest grew when Sam Begay joined Graywolf beside the stage. As the two men began to talk, her feeling of uneasiness increased. It became obvious they were arguing, and their animated conversation was growing more and more heated.

Mallory slipped her tape recorder and tablet back into her bag and ducked under the tape that roped off the press box. Making her way through the crowded seats and narrow aisles, she headed for them. Something was going on, and one way or another she was going to find out what it was.

"You're sure?"

Graywolf turned and looked into Sam's coal black eyes. "I'm sure."

"What if... " Sam let his words drift.

"What if what?" Graywolf demanded. "I'm wrong? It's okay to say it."

"Okay, I will," Sam said, emotion making his voice rise. "What if you're wrong? It's a possibility, you know."

Graywolf closed his eyes, drawing in a frustrated breath. "Are you willing to take that chance?"

"But—"

"There are no buts," Graywolf insisted, angry now. "Look, Sam, you wait much longer, you might as well forget it. This will all be moot, anyway. It's on your head now. I've done what I can."

Sam regarded Graywolf for a moment, his dark eyes narrowing with thought. Slowly his hand moved to the walkie-talkie on his patrol belt. "I sure as hell hope you know what you're doing," he said to Graywolf, bringing the walkie-talkie to his mouth. After several static-filled messages passed back and forth, he returned it to his belt and looked up at Graywolf. "You going to make the announcement or do you want me to?"

"I have no authority here," Graywolf said simply. "You're the one with the badge."

"Yeah, I've got the badge," Begay muttered, nodding his head. He glanced back at Graywolf as he started for the stage. "But it's your ass on the line this time."

Graywolf's eyes narrowed. "Better my ass than a lot of dead Indians."

Another gust of wind blew through the tent, sending a dust cloud roaring down the aisle, and Graywolf's fists clenched tightly at his side. He watched as Sam and the other officers made their way into position, and felt an uneasy prickling of nerves along the base of his neck.

"What was all that about?"

"Mallory," Graywolf whispered, turning at the sound of her voice. She looked like a vision standing there, her blond hair falling loose and free, her lips full and pink. He staggered back a step, wondering for a moment if she were another divination, an apparition from a dream, or if she was real. The sight of her had the breath catching in his throat, and for a moment all he could do was stare.

"Hello, Graywolf," she said, hoping he wouldn't notice the catch of emotion in her voice.

"How . . . how are you?"

Mallory looked up at him, feeling a little foolish now. What could she have been thinking rushing over like she had? There was no apprehension in his face now, no sign of fear or concern. Surely she must have imagined all that. What did she do now?

"Fine," she said, a stiff smile cracking her lips. "I'm fine." She gestured to Sam, who was now making his way up the stage to the podium. "What's all this about?"

Graywolf looked up at Sam on the stage, and then back to Mallory. "Damn it, Mallory," he groaned, almost beneath his breath. His feelings came back to him in a rush, as did the fear. "What are you doing here?"

"What do you mean, what am I doing here? I'm covering the powwow. You knew that."

Yes, he did. And he'd prayed she'd gotten her story on the first day and would have been long gone by now. "Look," he said, taking a step toward her. "You've got to get out of here."

"What?" Mallory stared up at him, confused. In the matter of a heartbeat, his expression had changed, and all her apprehensions came flooding back. "Graywolf, what are you talking about? What's going on?"

He grabbed her by the hand. "I don't have time to explain. Just leave—now." He pulled her toward the exit. "Wait for me outside, I'll explain everything then."

"No—you'll explain it now," she insisted, pulling her hand free. "What's gotten into you? I want to know what's going on."

"Damn it, Mallory, don't argue," he swore, reaching for her again. "There isn't time. You've got to—"

But the rest of his words were drowned out by Sam's voice booming over the loudspeaker. "Ladies and gentlemen, may I have your attention."

"There's something's wrong, isn't there," she demanded, her eyes moving from him to the stage and back again. *"Isn't there."*

His dark eyes narrowed, and he slowly let go of her hand. "Smell a story?"

His cold words pierced her heart like an arrow. There it was again—the doubt, the distrust. She wanted to tell him he wasn't being fair, that he was hitting below the belt and she didn't deserve it, but the loud screech over the PA system as Sam began to speak had them both looking toward the stage.

"May I have your attention, *please?*" he asked again. "There has been a small fire in the electrical cables at the rear of the tent." There was an audible gasp from the audience, and Sam quickly added, "There is no cause for alarm. I repeat—there is absolutely no cause for alarm. The fire has been extinguished—it's out. Again—*the fire is out!* But for safety reasons the fire marshall has asked that we clear the tent so a thorough inspection can be made. There are officers in the aisles and at the exits to assist you, so I ask you at this time to evacuate the tent—there is no need to rush—but please exit the tent at this time. The meeting will be rescheduled. Please leave the tent now."

"A fire?" Mallory gasped as a small uproar exploded in the crowd. She turned to Graywolf, her mind moving immediately to Ida and her family lost somewhere in the mob of people streaming toward the aisles. "My God, Graywolf, I've got friends in here."

"We've all got friends in here," he pointed out. He grabbed her by the shoulders, pushing her toward the exit. "You have to go now."

She struggled against his hold, but his strength was too great. "You have to tell me," she pleaded. "I have to know. Is it out? Is it really out?"

What was he supposed to say? Was a lie really a lie if it saved someone's life? He looked down into her sea blue eyes and felt something stir deep inside him. She was terrified, and he knew she asked out of concern, not as a reporter. He reached out and took her hand, feeling every muscle in his body grow tense. "It's really out."

"Honest?" she asked, searching his face.

Graywolf looked away, knowing what was at stake. "Honest."

She offered little resistance then, letting him lead her through the exit and out onto the hot, dry blacktop. She nodded her agreement when he asked for her promise to stay, and watched in dazed silence as he returned to the tent to help others out.

The wind outside was arid, and dry, and it gusted about, sending huge clouds of dust billowing up from the ground. She glanced down at her bag, and for a moment she thought of the tape recorder and notepad inside. But she had no time to think about reporting on a story or lining up interviews. She had to find Ida and the rest of her family and make sure they made it out of the tent all right.

"Is that all of them?"

Sam glared up at Graywolf, sweat soaking through the felt of his cowboy hat. "I said I'd get them all. That's all."

Graywolf let Sam's irritability pass. Officer Sam Begay had gone out on a limb for him this afternoon, and he was grateful. As it was, poor Sam was going to have enough explaining to do. Still, Graywolf couldn't regret the decision. He'd rather risk getting egg on his face than see a lot of good people get hurt—or worse.

"Less than fifteen minutes," Graywolf said, looking down at his watch. He glanced out the side exit of the empty tent to the spot where he'd left Mallory. She was nowhere in sight now, but that suited him just fine. The farther away she was from here, the better.

"You tell me to clear a tent, I clear a tent," Sam said, some of his humor returning. He removed his hat and swiped his wet forehead with the sleeve of his khaki shirt. "But I tell you, I thought we were going to lose it there for a while."

"I know," Graywolf murmured as the wind howled through the cavernous tent. He didn't want to think about how close the crowd had come to panicking. "The work crews?"

"Just finishing up," Sam assured him. "They've cut the power to the cables and secured what they could. The fire department and paramedics are on standby, and my people are keeping the press at bay." He stopped and looked up at Graywolf. "You satisfied?"

Graywolf smiled, offering Sam his hand. "You know Begay, you're not a half-bad cop."

"Would you mind coming back to Tuba City with me and telling that to my captain? He's going to just love this when he hears."

"We're fine, the baby's fine," Ida assured Mallory, reaching out an assuring hand. "No need to worry."

Ida did her best, but Mallory had seen the worry in her eyes. With the exception of spotting Marissa hobbling out of that cave on the reservation a couple of weeks ago, she couldn't remember being as glad to see anyone in her life as she was to spot Ida, Charlie, Esther and the baby in the crowd streaming out of the huge tent.

Even with Sam's pleas for order and the presence of uniformed officers to oversee the flow of the crowd, the exodus out of the tent had been difficult. Some people had ignored the appeals to exit in an orderly fashion and had begun pushing, causing a momentary panic. Several people were knocked to the ground, a few fell over folding chairs, but luckily officers were quick to respond and took swift action to defuse the situation.

"Well, I'm just glad you're all out safely," Mallory said, taking Ida's arm and leading her toward a row of picnic tables across from the convention tent.

"You and me both," Charlie agreed, helping his wife to a shady spot out of the sun. "A big crowd like that—it's easy for people to panic. Then somebody really could get hurt."

Mallory nodded as she helped Ida to a seat, then turned and glanced back at the tent. "It looks as though everyone got out okay, though. Thank God for that."

"What happened, anyway," Esther demanded, lowering herself down onto the hard ground and cradling her infant son in her arms. "Was there a fire?"

"Some kind of electrical one," Mallory explained.

"But they'd already put it out," Charlie observed. "I don't know why they had to interrupt the meeting."

"Better safe than sorry."

They all turned around at the sound of the voice behind them. Mallory looked up into Graywolf's eyes and felt her entire body go weak with relief.

"Try to explain that to my screaming baby," Charlie Nez joked, smiling and extending a hand. "*Yaa eh t'eeh,* Graywolf."

"*Yaa eh t'eeh,* Charlie," Graywolf said, returning Charlie's traditional Navajo greeting and the untraditional white man's handshake. He moved then to give Ida a hug. "Everyone all right here?"

"We're fine," Ida assured him, smiling up at him. "Just a little shook up."

Graywolf greeted Esther, taking time to give the crying baby a gentle pat on the head, then turned to Mallory. "You okay?" he asked quietly.

"F-fine," Mallory stammered, still shocked by his familiarity with her friends. "I'm fine. You know Ida, her family?"

Graywolf glanced down, spotting the silver bracelet on Mallory's wrist. "The reservation can be a lot like a small town," he said, reaching down and taking her hand in his. He pulled her wrist close and studied the bracelet. "And sometimes it seems that everyone is related to everyone else."

"You mean..." Mallory gave her head a shake. "You mean you and Ida? You're related?"

"This is nice," he said, turning to Ida and gesturing to the bracelet. As he looked back to Mallory, his hold on her wrist tightened. Could it be possible that she'd grown even more beautiful? That he could want her more now than he had out on the desert? "Moon and stars," he murmured, moving the silver band around her wrist with his finger. "Ida is Hosteen Johnny's niece, my mother's cousin."

Mallory couldn't hear much after that. The ringing in her ears was much too loud. Ida was saying something, and Graywolf answered. Esther joined in the conversation, and then they all seemed to be laughing. But as far as Mallory was concerned, it all could have been happening on another planet. It seemed impossible that of all the thousands of people at the powwow, she would have stumbled upon relatives of his. Do coincidences like that really happen, or was there some kind of cosmic conspiracy going on in her life?

But it wasn't the quirky happenstance that had her mind spinning, it wasn't the pandemonium of the crowd or the excitement with the evacuation. It was Graywolf—it was seeing him, it was his presence, his nearness, the sound of his voice.

She felt so awkward, so ill at ease. She'd never been in a situation like this before. How was she supposed to act? What did she say? They were far from strangers, yet did their time together really qualify them as lovers? They'd shared a moment, a passion, an adventure in time, but that time had ended twelve days ago. Where did they go from here?

But even as her mind reflected on the unusual predicament she found herself in, there was a more immediate concern that seized her attention. *He still held her hand.* He was still touching her, and that thought alone consumed what rational thought she had left.

His attention was with the others, with the conversation he shared with Ida and her family. But as he spoke, as he laughed and joked with the others, his thumb absently stroked the palm of her hand. It was an innocent gesture, unplanned and unintentional, but like an ancient method of torture, the small, subtle motion was slowly driving her insane.

She could think of nothing but him—of him holding her, touching her. She remembered the feel of him, the taste of him, and how she longed for him again. She thought of how his skin had looked in the moonlight, heard the sound of his soft groans in her ear, and felt the weight of his body against hers.

I love you.

She had said those words to him. She had opened her heart and offered it to him, and yet he'd refused her gift and walked away. So where did that leave them now? Did that give him the right to hold her hand, to make her crazy with longing? Who was Benjamin Graywolf now—friend, lover, stranger or enemy?

"What are you thinking?"

Mallory jumped, realizing he was watching her with dark, mysterious eyes. She looked quickly away, afraid of what he might see in her eyes. "Uh, nothing. Nothing at all."

An explosion of wind and dust blasted across the desert, sending canopies flying, ripping paper signs from their posts along the marketplace, and picking up debris from the blacktop walkways and tossing it around in all directions. Charlie's wide-brimmed felt cowboy hat was snatched from his head, and he took off through the stalls after it.

Mallory protected her eyes from the dust, shielding her face with her free hand. "This wind, it's getting worse."

The knot in Graywolf's stomach tightened. "Mallory," he said above the din of the wind. Squeezing her hand tight, he pulled her close. "Mallory, listen to me. There's something I have to tell you."

Mallory opened her eyes. There had been something in the tone of his voice, something that had the hair on the back of her neck standing on edge. Looking up at him, she felt a tremor rumble through her. "What it is? What's the matter?"

He stared down at her, trying to decide what to say, trying to find the right words. But then it was too late. Another blast of hot wind charged out from across the desert, stronger this time, and a terrible groan sounded from behind them.

Mallory turned, her hair flying wildly around her face. She watched in disbelief as the wind tore through the massive tent, ripping up stakes, tearing at moorings, and sending the tremendous canvas toppling to the ground.

"Oh, my God," she cried in a strangled gasp, her voice blending with the screams of others as they all watched, horrified. She staggered back a step, her legs weak and uncertain, and felt Graywolf's hands at her waist, steadying her.

Within a matter of seconds, the giant tent lay in shambles, its huge anchor posts snapped and broken like matchsticks in a fire, bits and pieces of what had once been the dais lying scattered and broken amid the tangled debris on the ground.

The crowd that had scattered after the evacuation slowly began to gather again. Police and fire officials were quick to move in, cordoning off the area and keeping the crowd at bay. The wind was all but gone now, almost as though it had never existed at all, and an eerie stillness seemed to settle over the area.

Oddly quiet, people milled around, as though lulled by the suddenness of the incident, and the horror. Most could only stand and stare, gazing down at the demolished structure inside which only short minutes before hundreds had been gathered.

Cameras clicked frantically, and reporters seemed to appear out of nowhere. Mobile units crowded the parking lots, raising their satellite dishes skyward and transmitting live feeds to their mother stations across the country. They all wanted to be first with pictures, first with the story. Amazingly, miraculously, a tragedy had been averted, and the news spread fast.

Feeling was slow in coming back. Mallory stared down at the ravaged remains of the tent, feeling stunned and numb. But her mind reeled, thoughts flying fast and furiously in her head. She couldn't stop thinking about the people who had been jammed inside that tent only moments before the collapse. It would have been such a terrible disaster, such a tragedy, had the crowd remained inside.

Mallory turned and looked up at Graywolf. She remembered him at the side entrance of the tent—the look on his face, the tense set of his shoulders. She'd known then there was something the matter.

"You knew, didn't you?" she said amid the confusion going on around them.

He looked away, freeing her of his hold, and said nothing. He didn't have to see her face to know what was there. He'd seen it before—in other faces, at other times—the shock, the amazement, the...fear. Mallory was aware of his special gifts, knew it could enable him to help people from time to time. But would she understand that it sometimes was more than simple hunches and intuition, that sometimes it tormented him and made his life torture?

"That's what you were trying to tell me, wasn't it?" she continued, following him. "There was no fire—there never was. You knew. You wanted those people out of there because you knew this was going to happen."

Graywolf closed his eyes, trying not to think of the horrible vision that had come to him in the night. He didn't want to remember what it was he had seen—the broken bodies, the bleeding children, the cries of the people. He just wanted to forget, to pretend it never happened and pray that it never would again.

"That's not important now," he said in a flat, unemotional voice. "Everyone got out in time, that's all that's important."

"Graywolf," she whispered, reaching out and resting a hand along his back. "You saved those people's lives. You saved my life."

Graywolf felt the warmth of her palm against the material of his shirt, and it radiated through his body like a warm ray of sun. It had been twelve days since he'd left her standing on the porch of her sister's tiny bungalow in Sedona—twelve long, grueling days.

But as long and torturous as the days had been, the nights had been worse. It would have been better if he'd never gone to her, if he'd never shown up on her doorstep that night. It would have been easier then—easier to forget, easier to go on. He never should have touched her, never should have allowed himself one night in her bed.

But as it was, he had touched—he'd touched, and he'd shared, and he'd loved. It had been a mistake, a big mistake. One he would spend the rest of his life trying to get over. He knew now what it was to taste heaven. He longed to hold her again, to feel her against him and taste her in his mouth. He knew exactly what he was missing, and that made it impossible for him to forget.

"Look," he said, taking a deep breath and doing what he could to push all those feeling aside. "I don't want to talk about this. Just forget it, okay?"

Mallory stared up at him in disbelief. "What do you mean, forget it? How do I do that?" She searched his face. "Graywolf, what happened today is extraordinary. It's an incredible story."

The cold spread through his system like a blast of arctic air. "Oh, wait, I get it now," he said in a harsh voice. "It's an exclusive."

"Exclusive?" she asked, giving her head a shake. "What are you talking about?"

"The story," he said simply. "I mean, how lucky can you get? It all but dropped into your lap." He laughed, a grating sound that had little to do with humor, and gestured to the newspeople gathered around the collapsed tent shooting video, snapping pictures and conducting interviews. "Look at them out there, climbing and crawling all over one another. But I guess you don't have to worry about them scooping you, do you? You've got the inside angle."

"You think I want to report this?" Realization hit her like a sock on the jaw, and she staggered back a step.

"Well, don't you?" he asked flippantly. "I mean, you are a reporter, aren't you? And a story like this doesn't just come along every day." He raised his hand up, reading an imaginary headline. "Shaman's Vision Averts Disaster. Yeah, I like it." He leaned close, giving her a cynical smile. "Just make sure you spell my name right, okay?"

"Stop it," she demanded, feeling the sting of tears in her eyes.

"But just a little advice," he said with feigned enthusiasm. "I'd maybe leave out the part about sleeping with the medicine man. It doesn't really look good for your credibility, you know what I mean? Besides, pretty little rich girls with long blond hair really shouldn't be going to bed with redskins, anyway."

"How dare you," Mallory challenged, her anger making her start to shake. "How *dare* you say that to me."

"How dare I?" he repeated. "You expect me to believe a reporter would walk away from a story like this? I know a little something about you media types, or have you forgotten?"

Mallory marched up to him, aware of how their argument had caught the attention of Ida and the others. But she was too hurt, and too furious to care. How could he accuse her so unjustly? She thought he knew her better than that, thought he'd come to care. But now she understood just how wrong she had been. Nothing she did or said would make any difference. He didn't trust her—not because she'd betrayed him, but because of who she was, and what she did.

"I haven't forgotten anything," she said in a low, carefully contained voice. "Including what a prejudiced, closed-minded, intolerant son of a bitch you really are." She turned and stalked off toward the parking lot.

Graywolf stared after her. She'd called him prejudiced— *him.* That was the most ridiculous thing he'd ever heard. He wasn't prejudiced. Jaded, maybe, embattled, certainly, but prejudiced?

Graywolf shook his head, clenching his fists at his side. What would someone like her know about prejudice, anyway? What did she know about hardship and injustice and the kind of anger that can seize your soul?

"Was it my imagination, or was that lady just a little angry with you?" Charlie asked dryly, gazing over Graywolf's shoulder as Mallory stormed toward the parking lot.

"Reporters," Graywolf scoffed, but watching her push through the crowd and disappear within the maze of cameramen, reporters and mobile remote units left a cold, empty feeling in the pit of his stomach. He turned around slowly, gazing into Charlie's watchful eyes. "You can't trust any of them."

"Think so?" Charlie asked, arching a brow.

"I know so," Graywolf said. "Take it from me, a reporter is always on the lookout for a story—don't ever forget that."

"Oh, I won't, I won't," Charlie assured him. "I guess we just sort of stopped thinking of Mallory as a reporter when she drove Esther and the baby to the clinic when my truck broke down the other night. She just seemed more like a friend after that."

Graywolf's eyes widened in surprise. "She drove to the clinic?"

"Yeah, but thanks to you I'm onto her now," Charlie assured him. "And I can see now that her coming by the trailer last night and sitting with the baby so Esther and I could go out for a while—well, hell, that must have just been her cagey way of worming her way into our confidence.''

Graywolf stared at Charlie, imagining Mallory in Charlie's tiny camp trailer, and felt himself begin to cringe. ''She baby-sat?''

''Yeah,'' Charlie said, the smile slowly fading from his lips. ''She did. Funny thing, though, none of that's in the articles she wrote about us.'' He shot Graywolf a sidelong glance. ''They're done. She let us read them, you see.''

Graywolf glanced back across the parking lot, feeling small and pathetic. He tried to picture Mallory out there somewhere, lost and alone in that sea of cars and chaos. He of all people knew how warm and how caring she could be, how generous and good-natured. So why then had he turned on her so? Why was he being so hard, so willing to think the worst?

''Don't take it so hard,'' Charlie said, as if in answer to Graywolf's unspoken questions. ''Everyone's allowed to act like a jerk sometimes.'' He smiled and gave Graywolf a friendly slap on the back. ''Even a shaman.''

Chapter 15

Graywolf leaned into the flames, letting the heat sear his bare skin. The air inside the small lean-to was stifling, burning his lungs with each breath, and the perspiration streamed from his pores in a thousand tiny rivulets. He was woozy from the heat, yet he forced himself to stay within the meager enclosure.

He welcomed the cleansing burn of the fire, wanted its flames to purge him of the poisons in his system, wanted it to leave him purified, healed. But closing his eyes, he knew it would take more than a sweat bath to cleanse him of the sickness that plagued his soul.

In the darkness he could see Mallory's face, hear her voice in the quiet rustle of the night. There was no curing ritual, no powerful medicine or appropriate sing, that could make him forget her, that would make her vanish from his thoughts. She was a part of him now, like his arms or his legs. Her image was firmly imprinted on his brain, etched indelibly in his heart. Yet, there he sat—before a scalding fire, looking for absolution and wanting nothing more than to forget.

The sound of his own words played unmercifully in his head—over and over again. If he could just make them stop. He didn't want to remember how much he'd hurt her, didn't want to think about the stupid things he had said. If he could just find the right ceremony, recite the proper chant, exercise the correct magic, that would let him go back, that would give him a second chance, prevent it from ever having to happen at all.

But even the strongest medicine would never make her smile at him again.

He searched that secret part of his consciousness, that hidden point of awareness where the visions flowed and insight swirled like the waters of the river. But with frustrating awareness he was forced to accept that secret spot held nothing for him now—no foresight as to where she was, no prediction as to what she was feeling, no prophecy as to what would come.

He forced the familiar swell of anger down in his heart, concentrating instead on the cleansing flow of the sweat as it washed away the poisons. He'd grappled with the question too many times in the past, too many times he had searched for an answer that wasn't there. Why didn't he just accept the fact that he would probably never know why his visions were so often filled with the faces of strangers—with people and places that had little to do with him and his life. He would never know why they revealed so little for him. Why was what he could give so freely to others denied to him? He yearned to know something about her, craved for that special insight, that undaunting awareness, and yet he sensed nothing.

It had been five days since the collapse of the tent, since the television and newspapers had reported on the freak event, and since Graywolf had barricaded himself in his hogan. Five days ago he'd wanted to prepare himself for the onslaught of publicity and unwanted attention he'd been so convinced would follow.

But there had been no onslaught, no mob of reporters, no pursuit. He'd had five long days in the desert alone—five days to realize what a fool he was.

The story was an old one now. The reporters were gone, the cameras had moved on to other places, the powwow was over, the crowds had vanished and the tribes had gone home.

He remembered the accusations he'd made, the reproach he'd felt. Besides Sam Begay, she was the only other person who knew the truth of what had really happened in that tent, who knew that the evacuation had been no coincidence, no fluke of circumstance. And because she knew, he'd allowed his doubts and insecurities to gain the upper hand.

He'd accused her of wanting a story, of using what had happened and what she knew to get a jump on the competition. He'd imagined it all happening again—the lurid headlines, the unwanted spotlight, the journalists and the crackpots—everyone after him for a piece of the action. All the unpleasantness, all the news hype and media blitz that he'd finally been able to put behind him would start all over again.

He'd thought of Susan, believing the situations to be so similar, so much alike. He remembered how Susan had reacted—jumping into the spotlight and selling him down the river. He'd just assumed Mallory would do the same thing.

His mind shifted to the series of articles in the *Washington Chronicle* that Hosteen Johnny had dutifully delivered to him each day. He'd read all three of the beautifully written pieces that had chronicled the lives of Ida and her family—their struggles, their sacrifices, and what they'd hoped they would gain for themselves and their nation by coming to the powwow. Nowhere in the articles had Mallory mentioned the tent collapse or a shaman's vision that had averted disaster.

He'd made a mistake—a big one. Mallory wasn't Susan—wasn't anything like her. She hadn't betrayed him, hadn't let him down and hurt him, and yet he'd treated her as though he'd expected her to do just that. He'd believed she would react the same way Susan had because . . .

He opened his eyes, feeling cold inside despite the sweltering embers and feverish air. Why had he made that assumption? Why did he find it so difficult to give her his trust, his faith? Mallory and Susan were two different people, they led different lives, wanted different things out of life, and yet he'd been comparing the two almost from the beginning. Why? They had nothing in common except that they both were—

He heard her words echoing in his head. *Prejudiced.* It was an ugly word—and it brought with it a history of bitterness and suffering. But could it possibly be that she had been right? Had he become so wrapped up in his own efforts to rectify the injustices his people had suffered at the hands of the White Eyes that he was blind to his own bias, his own intolerance?

Staring into the fire, he imagined her face—the golden hair, the blue-green eyes, the flawless skin. Physically she was as far from Navajo as you could get, yet never had he met anyone more at harmony, more in tune, with the world around her.

See me, now that I am one with another.

At one. She was at one—she knew what it was to be in harmony, to be at peace with herself and with nature. She sensed her sister's danger because it had thrown her world out of harmony. She hadn't mocked and ridiculed his gifts, hadn't used or exploited them, because she understood them. She understood they were a part of him, part of what kept him centered, what kept him in harmony. Never had he met a white person so attuned, so balanced, so Navajo in thought and expression.

She had called Ida, Charlie and Esther her friends, and after having read the articles she'd written about them, he didn't doubt her feelings were sincere. She had written about her friends with genuine love and respect, taking time to get to know them and understand something about their lives, and their dreams. He thought of her strength and determination during their long search through the desert, remembered her warmth and compassion with Ruth during those long hours of labor. She was a woman who held nothing back, who gave of herself to those who needed her, to those she loved.

Love. She had told him she loved him. She had whispered those words to him over and over again. Would he ever hear those words again? Was her heart still open to him, or had his cruel words closed it to him for good?

A sense of longing swept through him, and the tiny enclosure suddenly seemed sweltering and cramped. He thought of their night together, of the feel of her in his arms, of the passion they had shared. She'd opened her heart to him, given him her love, her compassion, and it hurt him now to think how little he'd given her in return.

A coyote howled in the distance. The baleful cry sent a wave of loneliness through him. Despite the fact that he'd tried very hard to convince himself otherwise, their night together had been more than just a night of mutual attraction, more than just two people reaching out in the darkness. She had touched him that night, had found her way through all the barriers and the barricades, through the preconceived presumptions and veiled prejudices, to that carefully guarded place where he kept his love.

In one fierce motion, Graywolf pushed out of the lean-to. Beneath the huge desert moon, he filled his lungs with the cool night air. The fresh oxygen moved through his system, clearing his head and causing his body temperature to drop. Sweat streamed down his body as his arms reached out for the stars. He called out to the cosmos—a piercing warrior's cry to answer the lonely wail of the coyote.

He wanted to be healed, wanted all the impurities out of his system, out of his soul. He wanted harmony again, wanted to know the peace and security of his place among man and nature. He shouted out again, calling for restoration, for rejuvenation, for recognition.

See me. See me Changing Woman. See me Lord of the White Eyes. See me Yellow Hair. See me Love.

He turned and ran to the small stream that ran behind the sweat house. He collapsed into the cool flow, letting the clear water rush over him, letting it take the poison of his foolishness, the toxin of his stupidity, along with it.

"Look, Wayne," Mallory said, trying without much success to keep the exasperation out of her voice. "How many times do I have to tell you? There's nothing else. You know everything."

"My reporter was there," the editor from the *Flagstaff Register* argued. "She saw Sam Begay, saw Ben Graywolf." He leaned forward and set his coffee mug down on the small table in Marissa's breakfast nook. "She saw the look on your face."

"Then she saw something that wasn't there."

"You sure about that?" Wayne asked, giving her a deliberate look. "You're not holding out on me, are you? I mean, if you're saving this for Glen, I can tell you this isn't something the *Chronicle*'s going to be interested in. But the *Register,* it's got great local appeal for us."

"Give it up, Wayne. This is old news," Mallory said with a laugh. She stood up and reached for the empty coffee mug, thinking she would never again interview anyone without remembering this morning. Being on the hot seat was no fun, especially when you didn't feel like talking. "Now, look, I've got a plane to catch this afternoon. You're going to have to get out of here."

"All right, all right, I'm leaving," he said with a good-natured smile and a resigned sigh. He stood up, lifting his suit coat off the back of the chair. "You know, we're always looking for new people at the *Register.* I could make you an interesting offer."

Mallory smiled. "Thanks, Wayne, but I'm happy where I am."

"You sure?" Wayne asked, stopping at the door and turning back around to look at her. "Think about it. Arizona's a great place—a lot of single men, clean air, good weather—and hey, your sister even lives here."

Mallory laughed and shook her head. "I appreciate the offer, I really do, but I'm not looking for a man, and my sister is moving to California in a few weeks at the end of the school term."

Wayne shook his head. "Some days it just doesn't pay to get up."

They both laughed then. After exchanging a friendly goodbye, Mallory stood at the door and watched as Wayne's sporty foreign import sped down the street and disappeared around a corner.

"Is this blue bag ready to go?"

Mallory turned and walked back inside the house when she heard Marissa's voice. "All ready," she said, heading for the bedroom.

"I'm going to need help zipping it closed," Marissa said when Mallory walked into the room.

Mallory surveyed the overstuffed soft-sided suitcase Marissa struggled with on the bed, and the two others that stood zipped and ready to go on the carpet. "Where did all this stuff come from? Are you sure all this is mine?"

"Every skirt, shirt, sandal and sweater," Marissa said with a grunt. "Now, get over here and sit on this thing so I can zip it up."

It actually took both of them sitting on the sturdy canvas bag before they could coax the zipper closed.

"There," Mallory said with a sigh, lifting the bag from the bed and setting it with the others. "That's everything."

"Well, just to be sure," Marissa said, dragging her heavy cast leg to the closet and sliding open the doors. "Let's do a final check."

"Don't you dare," Mallory warned, stopping her sister. "I don't have room for another thing. If I've forgotten anything, you keep it."

"Okay," Marissa conceded with a laugh. "I just hope it's something I can use." She slid the doors closed and turned to her sister. "How did it go with Wayne?"

Mallory sighed heavily. "About as you'd expected—awkward and unpleasant."

"That good, huh?" Marissa said, nodding her head. "What did you tell him?"

"The same thing I told him the first time he came over, *and* the second—nothing."

"What makes him so sure there's more to all this?"

Mallory shrugged. "He knows Graywolf, knows about his...well, he knows about him. Unfortunately, he's a good reporter and has put two and two together."

"I take it he hasn't talked to Graywolf."

"No," Mallory said, shaking her head. "He knows he'd get nowhere with him. He figured I'd be his best bet. If anyone was going to spill the beans, it would be me." She gave a sad, cheerless laugh. "Apparently he wasn't the only one."

"Graywolf didn't believe it, either," Marissa said. "Not really."

"You weren't there," Mallory reminded her. "You didn't see him, didn't hear the things he said."

"I didn't have to be," Marissa insisted. "Think about it, Mallory. He's been plastered across the headlines in the past, and all he could see was it happening all over again. He was scared, and he struck out. How do you think he must have felt when he read your articles in the *Chronicle?* You don't think he's regretted what he said?"

"Don't tell me you think he read them," Mallory said, tossing her hands in the air. "And I can't believe you're defending him."

"I'm not," Marissa insisted, her voice softening. "Not exactly, anyway. I know you were hurt, and I know it wasn't fair, but I'm not sure you're seeing things clearly."

"Oh, he made it very clear," Mallory said, adamant. "He doesn't trust me—he never has and he never will."

"You told me yourself there had been someone else, a woman—a white woman in the past—who had hurt him, betrayed him."

"And so that automatically means I would betray him?" Mallory demanded emotionally.

"No," Marissa said calmly. "But it just means that he's human, that he's afraid of being hurt just like everyone else."

Mallory slumped down heavily onto the edge of the bed. "I told him I loved him. Didn't that mean anything to him?"

Marissa sat down next to her sister. "I'm sure it meant a lot."

Mallory looked at her sister, her eyes filling with tears. "I'm not her—I'm not that other woman. Doesn't he know I'd never do anything to hurt him?"

Marissa slipped a comforting arm around her sister's shoulders. "I'm sure he understands that now."

The telephone rang, and Marissa reached toward the nightstand by her bed to answer it. As she talked, Mallory stood up and walked into the bathroom. She'd gone over all this a million times in her head since that day at the pow-wow, and it was driving her crazy. She heard his words over and over again in her head, saw the cold, angry look in his eyes.

She had to stop thinking about it, had to stop thinking about *him*. Her flight back to D.C. would be leaving in a few hours. She didn't want to spend what little time she had left with her sister rethinking all those painful memories. There would be time later for all of that—a whole lifetime.

Washing her face with cool water, she did her best to shove all those painful feelings aside. She marched back into the bedroom, feeling determined and renewed, just as Marissa was hanging up the phone.

"It's a good thing I brought that carry-on bag," she said with a forced cheeriness. "Or I never would have gotten all this stuff to fit inside...." But her words trailed off when she looked up and saw her sister's expression. "Marissa, what is it? What's the matter?"

"It's Josh," Marissa whispered, her lips starting to quiver. "Oh, Mallory, he's been arrested."

Graywolf listened to the even, monotonous tone and felt his blood pressure rise. No answer—*again*. There had been no answer at Marissa Wakefield's house all afternoon. Where the hell was she? More to the point, where the hell was Mallory?

He slammed the telephone down hard, causing two of the officers sitting at a nearby desk to look up and stare.

"Hey, easy on the equipment," George Robins pleaded. "Taxpayers in this country frown on crazy Indians who come in here and break up the joint."

Graywolf ignored George's mocking barb and pushed himself away from the desk. He walked to the window, staring out the plate glass to the street below. He'd driven straight to Sedona from his hogan, but he'd only confirmed what the unanswered telephone had already told him—neither Mallory nor her sister were there. He'd driven on to Flagstaff more out of frustration than anything else. If George couldn't help him find her, he had no choice but to fly to D.C. and plant himself in her office until she showed up.

He thought of the disembodied voice he'd talked to at the *Washington Chronicle*. It had told him only that Mallory Wakefield wasn't expected back at the newspaper until Monday morning. The only suggestion the saccharine sweet voice could offer was that he try back then.

Monday. Graywolf rubbed at his scratchy eyes. Today— or what was left of it—was Saturday. What was he supposed to do until then? This was driving him crazy.

"Aren't there some strings you could pull? Phone calls you could make?" Graywolf asked wearily, walking back to the desk and collapsing in the chair.

"Another missing person?" George asked slyly.

Graywolf gave him a dark look. "You could at least find out if she has a reservation on a flight out of here."

"The airlines aren't supposed to give out that sort of information," George reminded him.

"They wouldn't for me, but they would for you," Graywolf insisted. "Look, George, flash them your badge, tell them it's official police business or something."

George set down the file he was reading and peered at Graywolf over the top of his horn-rimmed glasses. "But it isn't official police business. It's a love-crazed Indian on the warpath."

Graywolf drew in a deep breath, feeling himself growing one step closer to desperation. He would admit to being in love, but not love-crazed—not yet anyway. "George... please."

George Robins reached a hand up slowly and pulled his glasses off. Until that moment, he hadn't realized just how important this was to Graywolf, or how serious. Looking up at his friend, he reached for the phone.

It didn't take long to get the information he was after. Hanging up the telephone, George scribbled something on a Post-it and handed it to Graywolf. "She's got a shuttle out of Flagstaff to Dallas at 7:30, then makes a connecting flight to National." Stretching out his wrist, he checked his watch. "If you leave right now, you just might make it."

Graywolf kicked his feet to the floor and stood up, snatching the Post-it from George. "I owe you one, buddy."

"You bet you do—a big one," George said as Graywolf turned and started for the door. "And take it easy," he called after him. "Don't expect me to be fixing any speeding tickets."

But Graywolf didn't hear George's warning, or anything else. He was already past the squad room and running for the elevator, his mind mapping the fastest route to the airport. He had to get to Mallory, had to stop her from getting on that plane, had to stop her from leaving. He wasn't sure yet what he'd do when he found her, what he'd say. The important thing was that he find her, that he see her, that he hold her again.

Chapter 16

"Here, let me help you with that."

"Thank you," Mallory said, smiling gratefully at the gray-haired man behind her. She let him take the clumsy carry-on bag she'd been struggling with, and helped him guide it into the overhead luggage compartment. She stepped to one side then, out of the aisle to let him pass. "Thanks again."

She slid into her window seat, hoping that by some miracle the two seats beside her would remain vacant. She wasn't in the mood for conversation—frankly, she wasn't in the mood for much of anything. The drive to the airport had been long and hot. She was exhausted, and just wanted to sit back and do nothing—especially not think. Unfortunately, that wasn't easy to do.

She turned and gazed out the small window, watching as a baggage cart loaded with suitcases circled close to the plane. This wasn't an easy trip to go home from—so much had happened in her life, so much had changed. She thought of D.C., thought of the muggy weather the summer would bring, thought of the traffic, and the people, and her crowded, cramped apartment.

She'd always loved the bustle and excitement of living in a big city, loved the people and the places and the noise. But that had been before she'd seen the desert sky at night, before she'd lain beneath a huge expanse of stars and before she'd come to understand just what wide open spaces really were. That had been before Graywolf. Her attitude about a lot of things had changed since he'd walked into her life, and now nothing would ever be the same again.

She thought of him, picturing him at different places, different times—in his hogan, behind the wheel of his Jeep, at night before an open fire. Would he ever go back to D.C., back to the land of the White Eyes? Would he ever look her up if he did?

A swell of emotion rose in her throat, and she quickly closed her eyes. It seemed unlikely that would ever happen, even less likely that he would look her up if it did. They both knew where the other stood, they'd said pretty much all there was to say. She should probably just accept the fact that she would never see him again.

Reality sucked, she thought bitterly as she opened her eyes and watched the luggage as it made its way up the conveyor belt and into the belly of the plane. And reality for her was that it didn't matter if they *ever* met again or not. She was going to see him, anyway, every day for the rest of her life—in memories, in dreams, and in that awful aching in her heart.

She took a deep breath, pushing back the memories with a little shake of the head. She didn't want to think about it now— she couldn't. Not now, not when leaving was difficult enough, not when going home meant giving up what little hope she'd had, not when she felt so alone, so empty.

She took a deep breath, shifting her weight restlessly. The two seats beside her remained empty, and she almost wished now that someone would occupy them. Not that she really felt like talking, but at least it might keep her from thinking.

Mallory picked up a magazine from the pouch in front of her. Thumbing through it, her thoughts turned to Marissa, and the telephone call that had brought her to tears.

It had been hard to leave Marissa—for a lot of reasons, but especially with her so upset about Josh. Mallory was happy that her sister was finally going to get what she always wanted—her own son back. But it wasn't going to be easy for either of them. Josh had a lot of problems, especially now that he'd been arrested and was facing a charge of arson. And Marissa was going to have to face Dylan James again—the man she had once loved, the man who had walked out on her and their unborn child, and the man who had arrested Josh.

"You just wait until we get home, Harold."

Mallory glanced up at the couple making their way down the aisle toward her, and knew she should have been careful what she wished for. The sinking feeling in the pit of her stomach told her the sparring couple were her seatmates.

"Just find the seats, Harriet, will you?" her husband grumbled from behind her. "We're late enough as it is."

The woman moved laboriously down the narrow aisle, the fragrance of her perfume billowing around her like a dense cloud. "I'm giving that travel agent a piece of my mind."

"Oh, stop your complaining, Harriet," her husband groaned. "All you do is yammer, yammer, yammer."

"Well, you tell someone you want a motel near the airport, you expect a motel near the airport. Is that too much to ask?" she asked as she checked the seat numbers posted along the aisle. "And this is the last time I let you talk me into flying coach—being herded in like so much cattle just so you can save a few lousy dollars."

"Just find the seats," Harold pleaded, shoving a paper shopping bag into the overhead compartment.

"You never know who you're going to get stuck next to," she groused in a whisper that wasn't really a whisper at all.

Mallory had wanted a little distraction, a little meaningless chitchat to help pass the time, to help get her mind off her troubles. But somehow, looking at Harold and Harriet, she didn't think that was going to happen. This commuter hop from Tucson to Denver was suddenly looking very long, and very boring.

"Hello," the woman said with a plastic smile, eyeing both Mallory and the empty seats beside her with equal distaste. She clutched her purse tightly to her side as she slipped into the row.

Mallory nodded and did her best to smile. "Hello."

"Oh, I wonder," Harriet asked, pointing to Mallory's purse on the floor beneath the seat in front of her. "I wonder if you'd mind moving that. The handle is hitting me in the ankle."

Mallory looked down at her purse and flipped the handle to one side. "Is that better?"

"Well," Harriet said with a false smile. "I guess it will have to do, won't it."

Mallory rolled her eyes and turned back to the window. She almost laughed at the absurdity of it all. Why should anything about this trip be easy?

"Going far?"

"Hmm?" Mallory asked, turning back to her seatmate. "I'm sorry. What did you say?"

"I asked if you were going far?" Harriet repeated again. Apparently she'd determined her personal safety was intact, and that it would be all right to be civil.

"Oh," Mallory nodded. "Washington."

"State? Or the other one?"

"The other one," Mallory said with a little laugh. She'd have to remember that one for her friends in the newsroom.

"Well, now," Harriet said, her smile warming. "Isn't that exciting. Do you know anyone interesting there? I hear Teddy Kennedy..."

But Mallory heard little else after that. She smiled and nodded as Harriet chattered on, but her mind drifted off—thinking about desert nights, and a sky as dark as a shaman's eyes. And she probably could have drifted quite some time, but a commotion at the front of the plane shook her from her reverie and had her sitting up in her seat.

Several flight attendants rushed to the front of the plane, and there was loud talking and a flurry of activity. But with the tall seats and the crowd of other passengers, she could make out little else.

"What in the world is going on up there?" Harriet demanded, turning to her husband. "This is what happens when you fly coach, Harold." She rose up out of her seat, craning over the heads of the passengers in front of her. "Just look at that, will you. Some Indian up there, making a fuss—acting crazy if you ask me." She settled back into her seat. "I told you, Harold, you never know what kind of riffraff you'll run into."

But it wasn't Harriet's crass comments that had Mallory taking another peek over the rows. It was something familiar—the sound of a voice, a glimpse of a face.

"Sir, I cannot let you on the plane without a boarding pass," the flight attendant insisted, her voice rising. "Sir, *please*. The plane is about to take off."

Mallory had just shifted her head to one side to peer around the large hat of the woman in front of her when she saw Graywolf break past the attendants and come barreling down the center aisle toward her.

"Oh, my God," she whispered, as a thunderous ringing sounded in her ears. She fell back against her seat, stunned.

Graywolf's eyes searched the rows, ignoring the curious looks of the passengers and the cluster of fretting flight attendants he'd left in his wake. He spotted her almost immediately, his dark eyes zeroing in like a hunter on the scent of his prey.

"My God, Harold," Harriet screeched, grabbing her husband's arm. "He's coming this way."

"Mallory," he said, stopping at her row.

"Graywolf," she managed to gasp in a strangled whisper. "W-what are you doing here? What do you want?"

"I have to talk to you," he said, leaning close and ignoring the cowering couple between them.

"Now? I can't now," she protested, feebly gesturing about. "The plane. There's no time."

"Come with me."

"Sir," an official-looking woman in an airline uniform said, tapping him on the shoulder. "Either you leave this plane immediately, or I'll call security and have you removed. Do you understand?"

Graywolf looked at the woman, then back to Mallory. "Please."

"*Sir,*" the woman said firmly, her arms crossed over her chest.

He reached out his hand, extending it toward her. "Mallory, *please.*"

She looked up into his dark eyes and a feeling of alarm spread through her. He was frightened, she realized. She knew it, could *feel* it, just like she could feel her sister's fears. Benjamin Graywolf was frightened—scared to death, in fact. Had something happened—to Hosteen Johnny, to Ida, to him?

She felt confused and disoriented, and needed time to think. But there was no time—no time for careful consideration, no time for weighing of issues or arguments pro and con. There were too many people talking, too many people shouting and issuing orders. Yet despite the confusion and chaos, one voice rose above the others, one voice she responded to. Reaching up, she took Graywolf's hand.

"Well, have you ever!" Harriet mumbled indignantly as Mallory squeezed past.

"We're leaving in less than five minutes," the flight attendant told her as she started down the aisle. "I can't hold the plane."

"I understand," Mallory said, feeling Graywolf's hand at her arm. "I'll be back."

They made their way out of the plane, past the curious stares and impatient scowls of the other passengers. The loading gate area was all but empty now, with only the airline staff behind the counter. Mallory walked to a deserted spot by a huge picture window that looked out over the docked plane, and turned to Graywolf.

"What's happened?" she demanded. "What's the matter?"

Graywolf looked into her eyes, trying to gauge what she might be thinking, trying to find some insight into what might be in her heart. But it did no good. He garnered nothing from her cool, blue gaze—no intuitions, no hunches. Where were all his special abilities? Where were his visions and his perceptions when he really needed them? He felt deserted and alone. How did he start? How did he explain to her that he'd finally come to his senses, that he couldn't live without her and wanted her with him? What if she wouldn't listen? What if it was too late?

"About the powwow," he started, feeling more vulnerable and alone than he ever had in his life. "I acted like a jerk. I hurt you, and I'm...sorry."

"That's it?" she charged, unconsciously taking a step forward. "You wanted to apologize?" Her hands went into fists. "You pulled me off that plane to tell me you're sorry?"

"Yes."

"You didn't think of calling me? Or writing? You had to yank me off an airplane?"

"I had to see you, I had to tell you face-to-face."

Mallory shot a nervous glance out the window. "Look," she said, moving back towards the loading gate. "Forget about the powwow. We both said things...we were both upset."

"No," Graywolf insisted, following her as she moved and growing more desperate. "It was more than that. You were right."

"About what?" she asked, rounding the row of empty chairs leading to the loading gate.

"About me," he said finally, catching her by the arm and bringing her to a stop.

"About you?" she repeated. She looked up at him, struck again by an overwhelming feeling of panic and fear. "What is it Graywolf? Why are you really here?"

"You were right about me. I didn't trust you because—"

"Because?" she prompted when his words drifted off. "Because I'm *biligaana,* and you don't trust *biligaana.* Well I am *biligaana,* Graywolf. I am white, and that's never going to change—and neither are you."

"No," he said, shaking his head. "It's not that, it's not that at all. I didn't trust you, I...couldn't."

"You couldn't?" she said, her voice full of doubt. "What does that mean?"

He looked down at her, feeling her anger and wanting to die inside. "I couldn't because I was scared." He gave a sad, lonely sounding laugh. "Don't you get it? I'm the shaman, the lawyer—the one everyone comes to for answers. I'm suppose to have the cure for what ails everybody, the solution for all their problems, but when it came to you..." He shook his head. "You scared the hell out of me, Mallory. I'm *still* scared. I cared too much, wanted you too much, I— I wasn't ready." He reached for her again, pulling her into his arms when she offered no resistance. "You said you knew I loved you, that you'd wait for me until I was ready." He pulled her close. "Mallory, I'm ready. I'm ready now."

"Graywolf, I—"

"The only thing that frightens me now is losing you. That scares me to death," he said, cutting her off and lowering his mouth to hers.

Mallory surrendered to his kiss, emotion swelling in her heart. The earth had shifted on its axis, had righted its orbit, and everything was back in place again. She was in the arms of the man she loved, where she belonged, where she wanted to be.

"Tell me it isn't too late, tell me you'll stay with me," he whispered, brushing a hundred tiny kisses against her lips. "Tell me you'll marry me. I love you."

"Graywolf, I don't know what to say, I don't—"

"Don't say anything," he murmured, pulling her close for another kiss. "Just feel."

Mallory did feel—all the love, all the emotion flowing out of him. She felt breathless and light-headed, like a kid at Christmas who'd gotten everything they'd ever wanted.

"I do feel, Graywolf," she murmured against his lips. "I feel it all."

"You'll stay then?" he asked, pulling away just far enough to look down at her. "You'll marry me?"

"Yes," she whispered as the plane outside began slowly to back away from the terminal. "Oh yes."

There was a hurried walk to his Jeep after that, a short drive to the airport hotel, and then a long evening of touching, healing and making love.

"Are you sure you don't mind about the move?" Graywolf asked, running a hand along the gentle curve of her waist. "I feel a little guilty—you're the one having to make all the sacrifices."

"Small concession," she said, looking up at him. "What's for me in D.C.—a job? An apartment?" She snuggled closer. "My life is here now. With you."

"Yeah, it is," he said, smiling wide. "We'll have to decide where we'll want to live, you know. You liked Sedona, or maybe we should think about Flagstaff. I'm sure Wayne would want you at the *Register.*"

She sat up a little. "What's wrong with the reservation?"

He glanced down at her, surprised. "You mean . . . you'd be willing to live there?"

"Why not?" she asked, leaning up and pressing a kiss along his lips. "But as long as I'm with you, it doesn't matter where we live—house, hogan, I don't care."

Graywolf felt a swell of emotion in his chest like a physical blow. Gathering her in his arms, he pulled her close, feeling happier than any one man had a right to be. "I love you," he said, kissing her long and deep. "And I'm going to build a house on the reservation big enough to fit a tribe in."

"The Graywolf tribe," she whispered with a smile.

"It won't always be easy you know," Graywolf said in the darkness, his smile fading just a little. He lazily wove a lock of her hair through his fingers, the moonlight glinting white through the strands. "You saw the stares from the people on the plane."

Mallory raised her head up from where it rested on his shoulder and looked down into his shadowed face. "People were staring because they thought you were a terrorist or something, not because you're an Indian and I'm not."

Graywolf shrugged causally, but his face remained serious. "But there will be stares and comments."

"So let them stare, let them say whatever they want, what do we care?" she said, running her hand along the smooth plane of his chest. "Besides, people have stared at Marissa and me our whole lives. Trust me, you get used to it."

"I do trust you," he whispered, reaching down to grab her hand and lifting it to his lips. "Life on the reservation can be rough—I don't think you realize what you're getting yourself into."

"Maybe not," she admitted. "But I'll get used to it." She cocked her head to one side, giving him a skeptical look. "You know, if you're trying to talk me out of this, it won't work. You asked me to marry you and I accepted—I'm holding you to it."

He kissed the palm of her hand, and then pulled her close. "Are you sure? I just don't want you to be disappointed."

"You're being too serious," she complained, leaning down and pressing a kiss against his lips. "The only thing I'll be disappointed about is if you can't get my luggage back from D.C." She leaned her body close, her voice turning to a whisper. "Do you realize, I've got nothing to wear?"

He had to smile then. She was right, he was being too serious, looking for problems that weren't even there. He rolled onto his back, pulling her on top of him and let his hands slide over her body. "Talk about vision."

"Come on, medicine man," she murmured against his lips. "Show me your magic."

* * * * *

COMING NEXT MONTH

#655 MacDOUGALL'S DARLING—Emilie Richards
The Men of Midnight/Heartbreakers
Andrew MacDougall believed in his two best friends, a misty loch creature...and little else. Love and marriage were certainly not meant for him. But Fiona Sinclair's homecoming stirred up memories of their long-ago bond, one he knew still existed from its hold on his heart.

#656 THE BACHELOR PARTY—Paula Detmer Riggs
Always A Bridesmaid!
Something wasn't right about newcomer Sophie Reynolds, and Sheriff Ford Maguire needed to know her story. Because Sophie and her precious baby made him want to feel again—trust again. Until he learned she was a woman on the run....

#657 THE COWBOY AND THE COSSACK—Merline Lovelace
Code Name: Danger
OMEGA agent Nate Sloan was deep under cover—and deep in trouble. His orders had been simple: infiltrate the state of Karistan and locate a missing nuclear arming device. But this Wyoming cowboy hadn't factored beauty Alexandra Jordan into his game plan. For if he had, he would have known the stakes included his heart.

#658 AT THE MIDNIGHT HOUR—Alicia Scott
Liz Guiness knew what had drawn her to the isolated manor home: six-year-old Andrew. Yet she couldn't imagine what held her there. Certainly not Richard Keaton, Andrew's darkly fascinating father—a man accused of murder. Still, Liz couldn't help but stay—and succumb to her dangerous desire.

#659 HUNTED—Jo Leigh
He had to save his family. FBI agent Mike McCollough refused to let a crazed killer hurt his ex-wife, Becky, or their son, Sam. But in the secluded retreat he'd secured as their haven, Mike discovered that his still-passionate feelings for Becky posed the greatest danger....

#660 TRUE LIES—Ingrid Weaver
Undercover phenom...master of disguise...Bruce Prentice *always* got his man. So nothing had prepared him for lovely Emma Cassidy, sole suspect in a drug-smuggling operation—and every inch a woman. Bruce knew her secrets cut deep and that he alone could unlock the truth—but at what price?

MILLION DOLLAR SWEEPSTAKES (III)

No purchase necessary. To enter, follow the directions published. Method of entry may vary. For eligibility, entries must be received no later than March 31, 1996. No liability is assumed for printing errors, lost, late or misdirected entries. Odds of winning are determined by the number of eligible entries distributed and received. Prizewinners will be determined no later than June 30, 1996.

Sweepstakes open to residents of the U.S. (except Puerto Rico), Canada, Europe and Taiwan who are 18 years of age or older. All applicable laws and regulations apply. Sweepstakes offer void wherever prohibited by law. Values of all prizes are in U.S. currency. This sweepstakes is presented by Torstar Corp., its subsidiaries and affiliates, in conjunction with book, merchandise and/or product offerings. For a copy of the Official Rules send a self-addressed, stamped envelope (WA residents need not affix return postage) to: MILLION DOLLAR SWEEPSTAKES (III) Rules, P.O. Box 4573, Blair, NE 68009, USA.

EXTRA BONUS PRIZE DRAWING

No purchase necessary. The Extra Bonus Prize will be awarded in a random drawing to be conducted no later than 5/30/96 from among all entries received. To qualify, entries must be received by 3/31/96 and comply with published directions. Drawing open to residents of the U.S. (except Puerto Rico), Canada, Europe and Taiwan who are 18 years of age or older. All applicable laws and regulations apply; offer void wherever prohibited by law. Odds of winning are dependent upon number of eligibile entries received. Prize is valued in U.S. currency. The offer is presented by Torstar Corp., its subsidiaries and affiliates in conjunction with book, merchandise and/or product offering. For a copy of the Official Rules governing this sweepstakes, send a self-addressed, stamped envelope (WA residents need not affix return postage) to: Extra Bonus Prize Drawing Rules, P.O. Box 4590, Blair, NE 68009, USA.

SWP-S795

He's Too Hot To Handle...but she can take a little heat.

SILHOUETTE
Summer Sizzlers

This summer don't be left in the cold, join Silhouette for the hottest Summer Sizzlers collection. The perfect summer read, on the beach or while vacationing, Summer Sizzlers features sexy heroes who are "Too Hot To Handle." This collection of three new stories is written by bestselling authors Mary Lynn Baxter, Ann Major and Laura Parker.

Available this July wherever Silhouette books are sold.

As a *Privileged Woman,* you'll be entitled to all these *Free Benefits.* And *Free Gifts,* too.

To thank you for buying our books, we've designed an exclusive FREE program called *PAGES & PRIVILEGES™.* You can enroll with just one Proof of Purchase, and get the kind of luxuries that, until now, you could only read about.

BIG HOTEL DISCOUNTS

A privileged woman stays in the finest hotels. And so can you—at up to 60% off! Imagine standing in a hotel check-in line and watching as the guest in front of you pays $150 for the same room that's only costing you $60. Your *Pages & Privileges* discounts are good at Sheraton, Marriott, Best Western, Hyatt and thousands of other fine hotels all over the U.S., Canada and Europe.

FREE DISCOUNT TRAVEL SERVICE

A privileged woman is always jetting to romantic places. When you fly, just make one phone call for the lowest published airfare at time of booking—or double the difference back! PLUS—

you'll get a $25 voucher to use the first time you book a flight AND 5% cash back on every ticket you buy thereafter through the travel service!

SIM-PP3A

FREE GIFTS!

A privileged woman is always getting wonderful gifts.
Luxuriate in rich fragrances that will stir your senses (and his). This gift-boxed assortment of fine perfumes includes three popular scents, each in a beautiful designer bottle. <u>Truly Lace</u>...This luxurious fragrance unveils your sensuous side. <u>L'Effleur</u>...discover the romance of the Victorian era with this soft floral. <u>Muguet des bois</u>...a single note floral of singular beauty.

YOURS FREE!

$50 VALUE

FREE INSIDER TIPS LETTER

A privileged woman is always informed. And you'll be, too, with our free letter full of fascinating information and sneak previews of upcoming books.

MORE GREAT GIFTS & BENEFITS TO COME

A privileged woman always has a lot to look forward to. And so will you. You get all these wonderful FREE gifts and benefits now with only one purchase...and there are no additional purchases required. However, each additional retail purchase of Harlequin and Silhouette books brings you a step closer to even more great FREE benefits like half-price movie tickets... and even more FREE gifts.

L'Effleur...This basketful of romance lets you discover L'Effleur from head to toe, heart to home.

Truly Lace...
A basket spun with the sensuous luxuries of Truly Lace, including Dusting Powder in a reusable satin and lace covered box.

Complete the Enrollment Form in the front of this book and mail it with this Proof of Purchase.

PROOF OF PURCHASE
Offer expires October 31, 1996

SIM-PP3